THE FIREWEED MOON

BY BARBARA J. DZIKOWSKI

The Fireweed Moon (Moon Trilogy, #3)

The Last Moon Before Home (Moon Trilogy, #2)

The Moonstoners (Moon Trilogy, #1)

Searching for Lincoln's Ghost

THE FIREWEED MOON

BARBARA J. DZIKOWSKI

WIARA BOOKS

2023 Wiara Books Trade Paperback Edition

Printed in the United States of America by Wiara Books

Library of Congress Control Number : 2023905682
ISBN - Paperback: 978-0-9840305-8-3
ISBN - Ebook : 978-0-9840305-9-0

For more information, or to book an event, contact :
https://www.barbarajdzikowski.net

Book design : Vince Pannullo

Cover image credit : iStock.com/panaramka, "Milky Weed Fireweed Field at Night"

First Edition : July, 2023

For my party of four—
with my whole heart and thankfulness
for all you are to me.

And for Love—
Who holds everyone,
and makes *what is good and true and right*
last forever.

PART ONE

PART ONE

ONE

THE MISSING BIBLE, 1953: HYSSOP, LOUISIANA

IT wasn't just a Bible. It was a Bible where verses were underlined, then annotated in the margins by an impassioned, nearly indecipherable scrawl, as if hastily transcribed by one who had actually walked beside Christ—a Matthew, a Mark, a Luke, or a John. It was a Bible that confirmed disciples still lived among us.

Anyone who knew him knew it was he who had written all over this Bible—the one with the beat-up front cover, torn completely in half under the words *Holy Bible*. They knew it was he who had used those scribbled, marginal contemplations (and extended notes stuffed inside) to formulate his sermons, sermons that, if heard by the right ear at the right time, had been known to transform hearts and minds, save broken souls—even broken bodies—right on the spot. Why, they'd even saved that crazy woman, that Lily Trudeau, from her own noxious melancholy.

They knew that Bible had power.

But when he was murdered, his Bible disappeared. In the aftermath, whether they deemed it sacred or dangerous, it was the first thing for which followers and foes alike ransacked his home. They rifled through his drawers, his closets, his attic, every crevice of his house—even pried apart the floorboards.

But it was never found.

TWO

A STRANGER, 2017: WEEPING WILLOW, OHIO

A S Leon Ziemny made his early-morning trek to the Garden of Resurrection Cemetery, a strange inkling gripped him: His life was about to take a detour. Not a man of intuitions, he let the feeling pass and kept on walking, distracted by the sight of three of his weeping willow trees up ahead, their graceful, pliant limbs in full bloom. No wonder Noël had been so enchanted by these trees. No wonder she'd once described the wind blowing through their low-hung branches as "the hand of God in motion".

Leon referred to them as *his* trees because, after all, he was the one who had replanted them throughout the town after Noël and the trees she would remember had long since died. He was the one who had given their roots a good soaking in buckets beforehand, the one who had dug their holes deep enough, fertilized them with cow manure from old Joe Harrison's farm, and watered them every week during that first year. A lot of effort, to be sure, but that was fifteen years ago. As soon as the willows started sprouting up to maturity, the residents got so fired-up by the restoration that they appealed to the town council to revise the name—from nondescript *Willow, Ohio* (since willows came in umpteen varieties) to more exact *Weeping Willow, Ohio*. Now most of the trees had reached their full, glorious height, some as tall as fifty feet. Weeping Willow, Ohio, so renamed, had been restored to its uniqueness, and Leon's work was done.

But the town's gratitude wasn't why he'd gone through all that trouble. Though replanting those trees was his reason for moving here in the first place, he did it as his way of atoning for his absence during Noël's pregnancy and subsequent death. As his way of honoring the daughter who had been born, *their* daughter, whom Noël had named Willow after the trees, the daughter he didn't know existed until she appeared in his life nearly twenty-five years later and became his salvation. He did it for the two who had taught him what love really meant.

Today was the first of August, a Tuesday, the humidity already sticky behind his neck at eight a.m. Though the cemetery was on the outskirts of town where the sidewalks ended and the open fields began, almost two miles away from his home, Leon walked there every Tuesday, if the weather was favorable. The long hike first thing in the morning gave him plenty of time to think things over, unclog his brain from the "gunk" that accumulated, as his late father Walt might have put it.

The annoying ringtones of *Louie Louie* jarred his ruminations—'sixties rock and roll was the balm for whatever ailed him, but cell phones had a way of ruining a perfectly good song. Digging the phone from his pants pocket, he stopped in place. In his estimation, you walked or you talked, not both, if you wanted to do either justice.

On the other end of the line was Jeff Miller, owner of the only motel in Weeping Willow. Leon couldn't imagine why on earth he'd be calling. Jeff and his wife Linda had operated the tidy, stone-faced inn for more than fifty years; their boarders mostly including the Millers' own gigantic brood when they were back in town, a brotherhood of semi truckers who could smell a good deal when they found one, and travelers passing through on their way to somewhere more important, lured into lingering by the sight of so many weeping willows in one place. Jeff and Linda ran the inn like a mission more than a business, and they filled it with wooden plaques about treating travelers like cherished friends.

And so it seemed unusual that Jeff was calling to tell him that he'd just turned away his newest customer, though there were plenty of available rooms. He did so, Jeff explained, because this was an unusual stranger: No semi-truck, no companions, a Louisiana license plate—and he went on to describe the man to Leon. "But here's why I called you," he said. "He's looking for your daughter. He asked me for directions to her house."

Leon had to stop and think a second. His daughter had been living in New York City for years, yet the house Leon lived in legally belonged to her and was still listed in her name. "What does he want with Willow?"

"Beats me," Jeff said. "But I thought you should know."

†††

Leon always took his own sweet time in the Garden of Resurrection where he meticulously tended Noël's grave and those of her relatives. It had been quite a while since he'd visited the graves of his own family, consisting only of his parents and one sibling, Ricky, all buried in the sprawling Polish cemetery back in Langston, Indiana, over a hundred miles away. Langston was the place Leon had been born, raised, and lived, until he moved to Weeping Willow at the age of fifty-eight after the last of them, his father, had passed away from Alzheimer's. Sometimes he felt guilty about neglecting their graves. But Weeping Willow, Ohio— peaceful Weeping Willow—was where he lived now, and he supposed that made it okay to come to this cemetery regularly and there not so much. After all, he was now seventy-four years old, his once dark hair gone silver gray, and his desire to jump into the car for extended road trips had faded away, along with so much else.

Across his shoulders he carried a leather bag, his "man purse" he liked to joke, packed with the Tuesday supplies he needed— clipping shears, a trowel, rags, and anything else it took to keep the graves looking neat. He used to make the weekly walk with his black lab, Spike, but his faithful companion was gone now too. Leon still missed the sight of Spike's wiggling nose sniffing the air in ecstasy as they traveled the Tuesday route together, side by side.

Once arrived at his destination, Leon bent to scrub the granite with a rag he'd already wetted at the nearby pump. Thankfully, the walks had kept his body flexible, with a slim torso of a man half his age. Dolly, the divorcee at the tavern, had a yen for him, hoping for a repeat of the one night they'd spent together a few years back after Leon had drunk way too much gin. When he woke up in the morning, there he was in Dolly's big, soft, sagging bed, with big, soft, sagging Dolly right next to him. The horror of it made him swear off hard liquor for good.

All in all, Leon felt as fit as when he was thirty, though he realized his luck could run out any minute. Look at what happened to the neighbor down the street, just a year older; he'd slipped in his shower last month, broken his hip, and they carted him off to a nursing home in Bedlington. At this stage of life, Leon knew things could flip on a nickel.

It was mid-morning by the time he was finished with the graves. When he looked up, a man was getting out of a shiny sedan several yards away and Leon immediately figured him to be the one Jeff Miller had warned him about. The well-dressed stranger moved slowly from tombstone to tombstone, leaning on a slim black cane and stumbling occasionally on the uneven ground, his head bowed the entire time as if searching for a specific name. Leon guessed he was about his own age, maybe slightly older, maybe slightly younger—who could tell nowadays? But his appearance was enough to capture Leon's full attention. Not his physical appearance, which was ordinary enough; he was slender, with a black goatee and curly white hair cut close to his scalp, dressed in an olive polo shirt and khaki trousers. Despite his unsteady gait, the man carried himself with purposefulness.

No, the stranger was an anomaly in this graveyard (and in this town) for one reason and one reason alone: He was Black. Not only that, but he was a Black man searching for a grave among a sea of white dead.

After shoving his garden gloves into his man purse, Leon slowly approached him. "My name is Leon Ziemny ... can I help you find someone in particular?"

The stranger looked down at Leon's extended hand and shook it, though cautiously, Leon observed, before nodding his head once in further greeting. It was then that Leon caught sight of the man's eyes, a hazel color, nestled into russet skin deeply lined in the usual places of a long life, but in some unexpected ones too—like the wrinkles beneath his cheekbones and on either side of his chin. Every inch of his face seemed overused by emotion.

"Do you know where I might find the grave of Lily Trudeau?" the man asked.

Leon removed his White Sox cap, wiped his sweaty brow before replacing it on top of his head. Honesty always seemed the best policy. "Yup, I know exactly where. She happens to be my mother-in-law."

The man's chin dropped, as if he was astonished. Leon

motioned for him to follow, and he did. "Can I ask how you knew her?"

"I didn't." The stranger's eyes fixed on the large, gray granite stone now in front of him. "But my brother did."

His *brother*? Ah, yes—the light switched on in Leon's brain. He hesitated a second before he dared ask. "Any chance your brother's name was ... Raymond Roberts?"

The stranger looked up. "How'd you know that?"

"Why don't we go grab a cup of coffee in town and have a talk? Since I walked here, do you mind driving?"

The man paused as if debating whether or not the arrangement was a safe one. "Yeah, sure," he said. "In fact, I'd appreciate it very much." Looking down again at the stone, he read Lily's inscription out loud, a couple lines from some famous poem that Noël had chosen, about the union of beginnings and endings and the fire and the rose being one, then looked at Leon. "What's that supposed to mean?"

"Hell if I know." Leon shrugged. "I don't write 'em, I just clean 'em."

The man's face broke into a grin. "By the way, my name is Booker."

✝✝✝

Leon was greeted by a hail of good mornings as he entered the Turning Point Tavern. Weeping Willow had a population of less than a thousand, and he was, by now, a familiar fixture among them. Though the tavern kept the booze flowing all day long, Leon came there for the tasty meals. It was the only source of honest-to-God home cooking in town, a break from the row of fast-food chains lining the outer limits of the main road, forcing The Seashell

Supper House, the only other local eatery, to close its doors a few years back. What a blow that had been.

When he and Booker entered, Dolly Schmidt rose from a stool at the counter and tugged her tight pink uniform over her belly. Though the sight of her always pinched Leon with a jolt of guilt, he didn't let it show, priding himself on being a pretty good poker player. A one-night stand with a desperate woman was a dangerous thing, a cruel one too, yet he couldn't deny the pitifulness on both their parts for allowing their loneliness to get the better of them that night. Afterward, Leon had made it perfectly clear he wasn't interested, but to this day, Dolly seemed fixated on the notion that the two of them had some kind of future. The only future Leon envisioned was his own grave beside Noël's in the Garden of Resurrection.

"Hiya, handsome." She put down two coasters, the long fingernails on her age-spotted hands painted up like a young girl's—bright red with little embedded rhinestones. "What's your pleasure this morning?"

"A cup of coffee." Leon said it without looking at her, surveying the menu instead, written in chalk on a blackboard near the counter. The Sunrise Special sounded just about right—one egg, toast, hash browns.

Dolly disappeared for a few seconds before bringing a silver pitcher to the table and pouring him a mug of steaming coffee. "You want coffee too?" she asked Booker, almost like an afterthought.

"That would be nice," he said.

"Black ... I'm assuming."

The stranger ignored her tone, lowered his eyes. "I'd like a little cream too, if you please."

After filling Booker's mug, Dolly set the pitcher down, tossed a handful of creamers on the table in front of him before refocusing her gaze on Leon. "You want to order something, sweet thing?"

"I'll have the Sunrise Special."

"Make that two," Booker said.

She didn't take her eyes off of Leon. "I know *you* don't take any cream. Do you, sugar?"

"Nope." Leon said. "And I've sworn off sugar too—in my coffee and everywhere else." He sealed the comment with a cold stare.

Dolly's eyes dimmed in a way that made it clear he'd hurt her feelings, but hell, if he didn't set boundaries with her every once in a while, she'd keep making a command performance, and he and Booker had private business to conduct. Besides, her rudeness toward Booker was offensive.

After she walked away, Leon spoke in hushed tones. "I was wondering about your age." Sitting beside Booker on the drive over, he'd tried to figure the math, but gave up. He had no idea, really, how old Raymond Roberts would be by now, had he still been alive, but he assumed he'd be around Lily's age. That information was etched right there in the granite he cleaned off every Tuesday: Lily was born in 1926, her husband Jack in 1918.

"I was thirteen years younger than Ray." Booker stirred a creamer into his mug. "I'll be seventy-eight years old this month."

Leon nodded. "Where you from?"

"New Orleans."

New Orleans was an awfully long way off for an old man to be traveling from, all alone. "So what brings you to Weeping Willow?"

Booker glanced around, shifted his body. "Look, I don't know how much you know about any of this."

"I know enough." Leon followed Booker's uncomfortable scan of the room, the eyes of the other diners darting away. People in this town didn't need fancy electronic gadgets to do their snooping. As long as their ears could hear, and most still could, no one's conversation was safe, especially when there was a stranger in town. "Would you be okay with coming to my house to talk about this? No Sunrise Specials, but I've got plenty of coffee."

-THREE-

SECRETS AND REVELATIONS

AFTER leaving the tavern, Leon directed Booker toward his white-shingled home. They entered through the patio doors off the back deck, Leon's usual entrance rather than the front door. "Make yourself comfortable," he said, pulling out a chair at the table in the quasi-dining room open to the adjacent kitchen.

Booker took a seat, while Leon set out to find his coffee brewing machine, opening the higher cabinets one by one until he found it. He seldom used the old contraption, preferring instant coffee from a jar, but this seemed a meeting befitting something fussier. Besides that, he could already tell from the things Booker said and the way he'd said them, that he was well-educated, a notch above Leon. Several notches.

As the coffeemaker slowly belched out the dark liquid, he set a small pitcher of milk on the table and sat down across from Booker. "Where should we start?"

"How about telling me what you know," Booker said.

What he knew ... easier than it sounded. What Leon knew was a long, winding, pretty horrific story. One shocking inciting incident that led to another and another. "Well, for starters, I know your brother was a pastor back in Hyssop, Louisiana, in the 'fifties. Am I right?"

Booker nodded.

"And I know that's where he and my mother-in-law became … friendly."

"*Friendly*? That's an interesting way to put it."

"Okay then, they had an affair. I was trying to be polite."

Booker's expression remained unchanged, not the least bit surprised or fazed by the news. "Look, Leon, I came here for truth, not politeness. Just give it to me straight, man."

Already, he liked Booker. His directness, anyway; no game playing. Leon valued straightforwardness, even to the point of bluntness. What use was beating around the edges? "And I know your brother was murdered because of it."

Booker's eyes narrowed. "You *do* know a lot. How'd you come to know it?"

The coffee machine stopped gurgling. Rising from the table, Leon filled two china cups and brought them back to the table. "My wife told me."

"Your wife? You don't mean Noël, do you?"

"Yeah, Noël." Now it was Leon's turn for scrutiny. "How do you about Noël?"

"Yes siree, Leon … I'll tell you how I know about her." Booker glanced around the room. "I've been searching all over hell's half acre to find that mysterious woman named Noël Trudeau. Finally, I hit the jackpot. Think I might be able to talk with her?"

Leon took a quick sip. (Shit, it was strong; he had miscalculated the scoops.) "I'm afraid not," he replied. "She's dead."

Booker's lips flattened, his face glazing over with sadness. "I'm sorry."

"She died a long time ago. In childbirth." Even after all these years, it still stung whenever Leon had to inform someone of Noël's death, which was never nowadays. Right now would have

been a good time to pull out a cigarette but, like hard liquor, he'd
given up smoking too, and moments like this had him wondering
why. "You still haven't told me what brings you here to Weeping
Willow."

"In case you haven't noticed, I'm an old man." Booker held his
hands out flat in front of him, a tangle of veins protruding through
his thin skin. "And when you're old, you want to finish up your
unfinished business. You know what I mean?"

Leon fingered the china cup as it sat in its saucer, part of a
blue, flowered-pattern set that belonged to his mother. She used to
bring it out only one time a year, at Thanksgiving. "I know exactly
what you mean. I'm no spring chicken either."

Booker smiled, but his eyes remained somber, distracted.
He looked over toward the living room. Leon's home was open
concept: he'd knocked down some walls when he moved in, so you
could see it all at a glance. "I worshipped my brother when I was a
kid growing up in Birmingham," Booker said. "Ray was brilliant,
and it opened doors for him. Got him into a good Black college
for starters, then on to a master's in Divinity. Even after all that, he
ended up in a hell-hole like Hyssop ... Did you know he was only
twenty-seven when they murdered him?"

"That's too goddamned young to die, isn't it?"

"I was fourteen years old when it happened." Booker's face
hardened. Leon recognized the expression—the way a face steels
itself before revisiting the unbearable. "You know, my brother
doesn't even have a grave. He died the worst kind of death imaginable, and they didn't even bother to give him a proper grave." He
looked Leon square in the eyes. "Did you hear *that* story, too? Do
you know the way he died?"

Leon knew the story all right, every last gory detail. He
remained silent.

"Did you know that my brother was chained to the back of a pick-up truck?" Booker continued, his eyes flashing with emotion. "Did you know he was dragged through the streets of Hyssop, howling and screaming like a dying animal, until he was shredded into pieces, dismembered, unrecognizable as a human being? Did you know they hung what was left of him on a tree, in front of his own church?"

Leon nodded, yet still kept his mouth shut. What could anybody say about a barbaric death like that one?

"Plenty of people saw it, heard it, but no one dared say a word," Booker said. The rage in his eyes muted to a look of haunted reflection. "We were still living in Birmingham at that time. The police called and told us some crazy story about Ray going off in some millwork plant, picking a fight with some white guy, and accidentally falling into one of their wood chipper machines. The local paper corroborated the story, but it smelled to high heaven. My daddy went to Hyssop right away, trying to find some answers, but that wasn't so smart. He made the mistake of talking to the wrong people, ruffled some feathers, and was lucky to get out of there alive. So Mama went there next. She had a gentler way with people, and she did it right. The Black folks trusted her enough to confess the story was a big lie. It was no wood chipper, they told her, though the men who killed him did work at the millwork plant."

Booker's eyes locked on something outside the patio doors, though Leon doubted he was seeing anything other than the images in his mind as he resumed his story. "Ray was violently murdered during the night, they told my Mama, by a guy named Hal Walston, the plant foreman, and a group of his buddies after word had gotten out that Ray had been meeting alone in his church with a married white woman. That's how we found

out Ray was involved with … with your mother-in-law." Booker
scanned the kitchen. "Walston had connections to the Klan, but it
never went to trial, not even close. The local Blacks were too afraid
to say a word, let alone testify—they knew justice didn't stand a
chance if Ray's involvement with a white woman became common
knowledge. But I was never convinced it was true, since it was
all second-hand. My brother was totally dedicated to his ministry,
not to skirt-chasing. And he certainly wasn't stupid enough to get
into a relationship with a married white woman. Ray was a charismatic religious leader with a social conscience and a bright future,
dangerous to them for those reasons, and I always suspected those
white men made up the whole story as an excuse to kill him."

Leon debated whether or not he should tell him the rest of
the story. He'd first learned the truth on the very day he and Noël
were on their way to get married—she'd confessed her family
secrets that day because she thought he might change his mind
after hearing them. Once, only once, he'd blurted out those secrets
and paid the ultimate price—the end of their marriage—so he
never repeated them again, not even to their daughter. Why inflict
those old wounds on Willow? But it was more than that. Willow
had inherited that stinkin' depression from the Trudeau side of
the family and he couldn't bring himself to dump their history—
two suicides, to be precise—on top of it, and risk magnifying her
depression, especially when he'd learned that suicide tended to run
in families. Leon shook his head. "Nope, it wasn't made up. Their
affair was a hundred-percent real."

Booker paused. "Before I ask you how you know that for sure,"
he said, "I'll answer your question. I came to Weeping Willow
because my brother had papers, lots of them. He was a prolific
writer, and he had a gift—how should I say this?—he was a gifted
theologian who understood the Bible better than a lifelong scholar.

It came natural to him—in here." He patted his palm against his heart. "Once he got the schooling, there was no stopping him. After he was murdered, his writing disappeared into thin air."

Leon shrugged. "Sorry to hear it, but what's that got to do with Lily?"

Booker heaved a deep sigh, stretched out his long legs. "As a last resort, I guess I was hoping that maybe Lily's family knew something about Ray that I could use. Maybe give me a name of someone he might've given the papers to, you know, that kind of thing. Or maybe he'd even given them to her, to Lily … But it seems the trail's gone cold."

Leon nodded. "I don't know a thing about any papers."

"I thought it was a long shot, but I had to try." His face sagged. "I've been searching for a trace of my brother for years. Then I gave up. Now I'm old, and time's running out." He finally took his first, slow sip of coffee, before clinking it back into its blue-flowered saucer. "Ray had an old family Bible that once belonged to our great-great-grandfather—he was born into slavery and died in it. As the story went, one day, in a drunken rage, his slave owner tore the cover half off of his Bible and tossed it into the trash. My great-great-granddaddy managed to retrieve it. Even though he didn't know how to read, he cherished laying his hands on a real Bible. Do you know what I mean when I say that? I mean, it wasn't a slave Bible where large portions were left out so that slave owners could justify slavery. That beat-up old Bible was passed down from generation to generation, until my father gave it to Ray for his fifteenth birthday. It was sacred to us. Not just because of its history to our family. Not just because that uncensored Bible led our people to spiritual liberation. But because of its effect on Raymond. It was like finding the missing piece of his life. He wrote all kinds of God-given insights into the margins. After he died, that Bible went missing."

At the mention of the Bible gone missing, Leon felt a jolt surge through him, like an electric current. A forgotten memory was resurfacing.

"I did my research," Booker continued. "I found out Lily died a long while back. And two of her sons too, Beauregard and Adam. I was able to find old records, obituaries, newspaper clippings. I found out Beauregard, Lily's oldest son, was a big war hero who gave the ultimate sacrifice in Vietnam. And I found out Adam, her youngest, was a Vietnam vet who committed suicide." Booker went over to the duffel bag he'd slung against the wall and pulled out a piece of paper. "I even made a genealogical chart for the Trudeaus to help me keep them straight. But I never could find the other son, Stephen, or the daughter named Noël. The only viable address I could find was for a Willow Trudeau in this town, and I thought she might be some relation. You know her?"

"What?" Still struggling to bring the long-lost memory into focus, Leon had been only half-listening.

"I asked you if you know someone named Willow Trudeau."

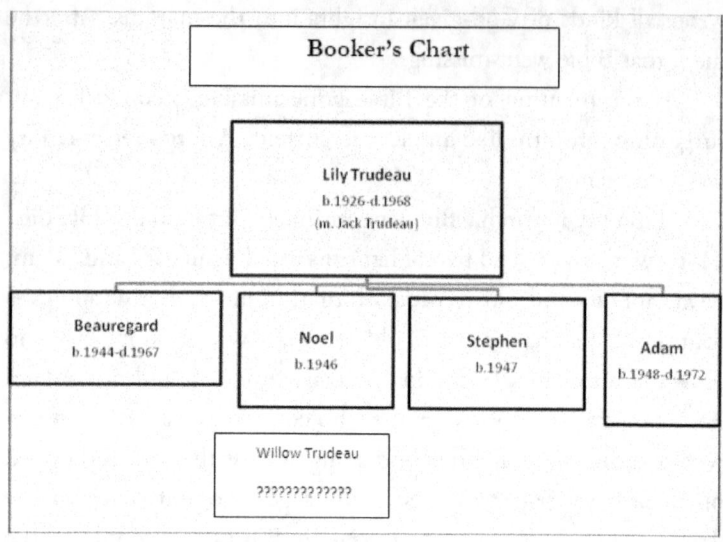

"Willow? Sure I do. She's my daughter."

"Your daughter!" Booker lifted his eyes toward the ceiling. "Yes, indeed. Finding you was the end of a long search, fruitless as it's starting to seem. Finding you was my last hope."

He eyed Booker sadly. If he was this guy's last hope, he suspected he owed him the whole bitter truth. But *how* should he say it? He couldn't just blurt it out, could he? "Let me see that chart," Leon said. After grabbing a pen off the kitchen counter, he took several minutes to fill-in the rest, the complete lineage, but he wasn't ready to hand it back to Booker quite yet. Not until he explained things. "After the Trudeaus ran away from Hyssop," he began, "in the middle of the night, no less—they ended up settling here in Weeping Willow. The kids came of age in this house and eventually went off on their own."

He watched Booker give the surroundings another inspection,

razor-sharp this time, as if taking in every nook and cranny. "You mean Lily used to live here?"

"They all did. Lily and her husband Jack both died here. Steve, the last remaining sibling, had moved to California by then, and he never bothered to sell the house. He rented it out a couple times over the years before giving it to my daughter Willow when she came of age, but she never lived here. So after my own family in Indiana died, I relocated to this town and moved in."

Booker seemed astonished. "They actually moved into *this* very house?"

"Yup. Straight from Hyssop, Louisiana. Back in 1953."

"I'll be damned."

"Like I said, they left Hyssop in the dead of night—the night your brother was murdered. Jack piled their stuff in the car and got the hell out of Dodge. It was a big trauma for the kids. Noël was only seven, and she never got over it."

His elbow on the table, Booker rested his cheek against his palm. "I'll be damned," he repeated. "So… what was Lily like?"

Leon lifted a shoulder. "Who the hell knows? She went—insane, I guess you'd call it—the night they left Hyssop. She didn't speak a word after that. She barely blinked. She was like a dead woman, except she kept on breathing." Leon's brows furrowed as he prepared himself for what he had to say next—the first revelation. Here goes, he thought. "Jack Trudeau was the one who arranged your brother's murder."

"And it served his killer well." Booker nodded, taking in the news as if it were no revelation at all. "Walston became the owner of the business after that. I heard that Jack Trudeau finalized the sale of the millwork plant just a few hours before Ray was murdered."

"Yeah, Jack was a mean son of a bitch. I don't think I ever disliked anyone as much as him." As Leon continued to struggle to find the right words to tell Booker the rest of what he knew, he watched him take another sip from his mother's old china cup. It seemed out of place, incongruous, to be sharing such a savage story in such a civilized way. The old memory was now congealed in his brain: Noël's brother, Adam, sitting beside him in the limousine behind Lily's hearse before they left for her funeral service; Noël's father standing outside, talking to a group of mourners; and Noël?, nowhere in sight—and Leon had asked Adam, why in the world was it taking her so long to leave that funeral home? What in the world was she doing in there?

"How come you're so certain Lily and Ray really had an affair?" Booker asked.

"Well, because ..." He stopped.

Booker stared at him, unblinking.

"I know it to be a fact because ..." Here came revelation number two. "Lily had your brother's child. A son."

"What?" Booker's eyes widened to a look of near terror. "Holy Moses, Leon! How do you know that? Do you know anything about him? Where he is?"

"He's lying next to Lily. He was stillborn." Sliding the updated genealogical chart in front of Booker, Leon watched the way his shoulders went slack, slowly collapsing as if the life were draining out of him. "His name was Monroe."

"That's Ray's middle name." A single tear streamed down Booker's cheek. He swiped it away, but as soon as he did, fresh tears took its place. "A baby. I had no idea. Oh, my ... oh, my ... oh, my."

Leon had always thought of Lily's shocking affair and the resulting murder mostly in terms of the way those events had disrupted, indirectly ruined, Noël's life, and even more indirectly, his own because of the lasting trauma they had caused her. Now, as evidenced by the utter despair on Booker's face, their story was taking on a new shape and dimension, flesh and bones, a bitter cost, to more than just them. A much more bitter cost.

"Be careful what you wish for, I guess," Booker said. "I'm the one who came here for some answers, but I never thought that—"

"I know one more thing too." Leon interrupted. He had to get this final thing, the last of the big secrets, off his chest, and he was anxious to get it over with. "I know where that Bible went."

Booker sat upright in his chair, his attention riveted. As Leon opened his mouth to form the words, that crazy bird clock over the table began chirping out the time. Twelve unstoppable tweets from the cardinal on top. Damn that clock! Leon knew he should have disabled it long before now, except that it was Rocket who had given it to him, last Grandparents Day.

Finally, silence filled the room. "The Bible went with her," he said.

Booker's eyes remained glued on him. "What are you trying to say, man?"

"In the hearse, on the day of Lily's funeral, Noël's brother told me he saw Noël putting your brother's Bible inside of Lily's coffin as he left the funeral home—he recognized it because of the torn cover. I'm telling you that Lily was buried with it."

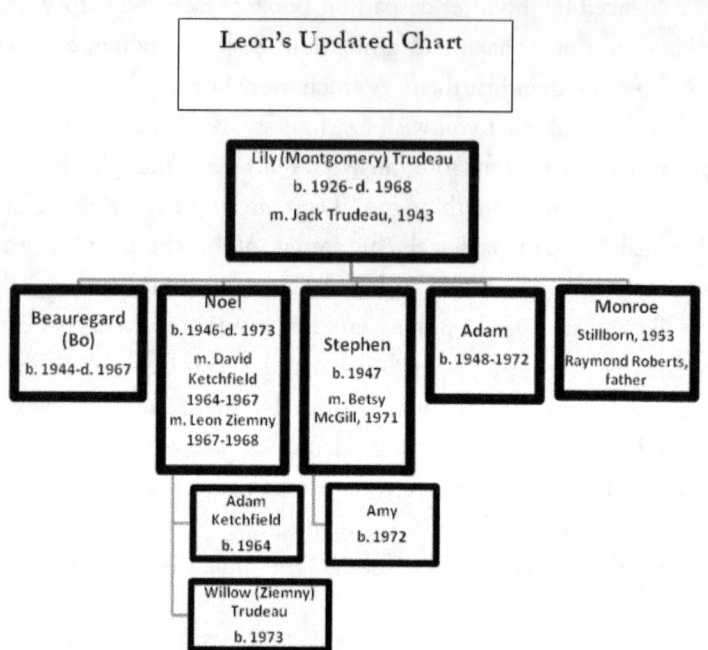

Leon's Updated Chart

Lily (Montgomery) Trudeau
b. 1926- d. 1968
m. Jack Trudeau, 1943

Beauregard (Bo)
b. 1944-d. 1967

Noel
b. 1946-d. 1973
m. David Ketchfield
1964-1967
m. Leon Ziemny
1967-1968

Stephen
b. 1947
m. Betsy McGill, 1971

Adam
b. 1948-1972

Monroe
Stillborn, 1953
Raymond Roberts, father

Adam Ketchfield
b. 1964

Amy
b. 1972

Willow (Ziemny) Trudeau
b. 1973

-FOUR-

BEGINNINGS AND ENDINGS

THE lights from the tall building across the street shining into her eyes, Willow Trudeau tossed and turned in her bed. It wasn't the lights that were keeping her awake; she was used to those. It was the clunking, banging sounds of the plumbing in the wall. *Ba-bang, ba-bang, ba-bang.* The incessant noise forced her to surrender any chance of sleeping, and she sat upright against the headboard.

Old, bad pipes were part of a bigger problem, and so was her whole situation. She was forty-four years old, unmarried, childless and another scorching, lonely summer was passing her by. Another of her paintings remained unsold. Yesterday, the apartment super had simply thrown up his hands over the knocking noises in the pipes and left. Just given up. *Really?* The metaphor was now hitting her like a migraine. It was time for her to give up too, not on life, but on New York City and her dreams of being an artist.

Willow lived on the fifth floor, the highest level in the "historic" (as in, antiquated) brick building, and the tiny bedroom was ungodly hot. She had a window air conditioner, but it didn't help much. Her thoughts racing, she gulped from a plastic bottle of water on the nightstand. In the beginning, New York had made her quiver with excitement—its raw, visceral sense of adventure, its invitation to endless possibilities. In those days, she could be standing at an intersection amid a mass of people waiting for the walk signal, when she'd feel a sudden thrill for having integrated herself into this gigantic, throbbing heartbeat of humanity. Everything was fast-paced, oversized here, in a constant state of flux; change the only permanence. Its allure shimmered on the surface; nothing went deep. Friends came easily, went easily. Opportunities drifted in and out. As did the men, interested in her for a "New York minute", until the cost got too high and she felt plundered by them. In time, she learned to give nothing of herself away in the relationship turnstile.

The empty plastic bottle crackling in her grip, Willow knew she had to face it: She was in the backwind of New York's favor.

Now what?

She got out of bed, padded into the miniscule galley kitchen—every surface reachable from the spot where she stood—and prepared a cup of tea.

It wasn't like she couldn't do her "day job" remotely from anywhere—Willow was a freelance writer for an international art magazine (her specialty areas, Post-Impressionism, Modern Art, and Neo-Impressionism). Up until the week before, she'd also been an agent for her late Uncle Ricky's paintings, but the final two of them from his Brown Series had just been sold to a wealthy couple in Denver for their sprawling cabin home. Willow was as cautious about who received Uncle Ricky's artwork as a social worker was for adoptive parents, and the paintings would look perfect there, rich and evocative in their earth tones. Uncle Ricky had been an amazing, versatile artist, before his sudden death from alcohol poisoning—posthumously, his paintings had been in even greater demand. Though Willow learned to know him through his art, the older she got, the more she grieved the lost chance to have known *him*, the actual man—her father's only brother—for longer than just four months.

Full mug in hand, she sat down in front of the Art Deco fireplace (the feature she most loved in this old apartment), carefully taking a sip of the steaming mug of tea. Selling the last of Ricky's paintings was another sign. There was no reason, none whatsoever, to remain in New York.

†††

Willow spent the next few weeks putting her plan in motion. She cancelled the lease for her art shop in Soho, crated her own paintings and arranged to have them shipped to her. The furniture in her apartment was rented; the truck had come promptly to reclaim it. The rest of the stuff she stacked by the dumpster out back. After that, she packed her personal things—as much as she could fit inside her old Subaru.

It was done. There was no turning back.

At the crack of dawn on the first day of August, her late grandfather Walt's small, lacquered icon of the Black Madonna of Częstochowa snug in her pocket, she began the journey to the only place that reasonably resembled home. Her father and brother lived in Weeping Willow ... that would make it home enough. Besides the permanence of family, she needed to be in a place where she could see a thousand stars at night.

†††

She could easily make the trip in one day, in eight hours or so, give or take, but Willow decided to take her time, make a few stops along the way. No one would worry—she hadn't told them she was coming. The longer she drove, the more she found herself drifting into a state of autopilot, a pleasurable blend of absorbing the scenery and allowing her tangled thoughts to unknot, free-flow. As she neared the Allegheny Mountains in Pennsylvania, the scenery became breathtaking. Having grown up in San Diego, she felt most secure when surrounded by mountains.

She switched on the radio. Mozart was playing. Between the music and the mountains, she began slipping into a deeper state of mind, as if watching herself from a distance. The odd feeling surfaced in rare moments—an awareness of a deeper self that she called her *Internal Observer*, peering out through her own eyes, evoking a sense of tranquility, and giving her glimpses of the recurring themes and patterns of her life. Willow wondered if this Internal Observer could be her soul, studying her from afar as if she were an actor on stage.

Maybe all of our lives could be thought of that way; as a performance. It only depended on where the director chose to cut. End it at a happy moment—like when she first connected with her long-lost father and his family back in her twenties—and it became a Hallmark movie. End it at a moment like this one, and … well, life went on, didn't it? The actor and scenery changed; the Eternal Observer did not.

Willow switched the dial to another radio station. No more Mozart. Now it was Journey with a hard drumbeat singing about people in love going their separate ways, and a fleeting thought of Nick Hardy jumped into her brain. Where did *that* come from? She and Nick had parted over a decade ago.

Willow was a born thinker, a born wanderer. In her opinion, the two went hand in hand. Like most of her choices, her travel destinations were off the beaten path. She'd been captivated by the glowworm caves in New Zealand, the Hagia Sophia in Istanbul, the rainbow mountains in Peru.

Traveling woke her up. When she was in a brand-new place, she *saw* it. After it became familiar, she didn't see it anymore, the same way she had stopped seeing New York City. Was it like that with people too, and that's why they ended up going their separate ways? Leave them, or they leave you, and you always see them; the deep, aching hole from their absence keeps them forever alive.

She stopped at a toll plaza, the parking lot jam-packed at the height of vacation season including rows of RVs on the far end. Sounds reverberated in the expansive, open interior as she stepped up to the counter to order a Big Mac and fries. Mostly families were seated in the hard, shiny red seats attached to the tables, and she sat down next to one of them. She would have preferred to sit farther away, but the place, like the parking lot, was filled to capacity.

Willow sometimes played a game where she assigned emoji's to strangers, to the one predominant mood she thought defined them. The baby in the stroller, Happiness, was dribbling chocolate malt all over his chin while his mother, Lovingly Weary, moistened a napkin with her saliva and dabbed at it. The older child, a toddler with floppy red hair, Mischief, was making faces at the baby, while the father, Bored Stiff, kept chewing his burger with an expression that said he wished he were back on the open road. Even as uninterested as the father appeared, here was a real family, the case to be made for not going separate ways, for allowing people and places to become too familiar. Catching her own reflection in the oversized mirror on the wall, sitting alone while the world bustled around her, she felt ... Invisible.

Nibbling a French fry, she washed it down with a sip of cola, a twinge of sadness pulling at her. Truthfully, sadness was a relief. All that pretending—to fit in, to be perky, to stay strong—it took so much energy that it was a relief to let it go. Sad was the middle gear, the most authentic place she knew, in between the never-ending trying that preceded it and the depression that followed. Sadness was when the heart was most vulnerable, the most wide open, when the Eternal Observer was most likely to make itself known. Sadness was everyone's most authentic place, wasn't it?

By the time she was back in her car, clicking her seatbelt around her, the melancholy was creeping back, the first familiar pangs of a depression that collapsed her from time to time. She tried to push it away, the way she always tried, but the Atlas-sized rock was rolling straight toward her. It wasn't just her failed art career—(if no one hung your paintings, sang your songs, recited your poetry, were you *really* an artist? Or just a deluded imposter?)—it was more like a weight she had carried from the very beginning.

The simple truth was, her birth into this world was what had killed her mother. Even after learning that the full-term pregnancy would take her own life, her mother chose Willow. What purpose could she ever fill to repay the cost of her mother's life?

Try as they might, no psychiatrist could quite take that torment away. Our inner child can be our worst abuser. "We have to go back to our original wound if we are to heal," they told her. Heal it? She was all for it, but how? By joining a club? By reciting positive affirmations? By jogging? By eating gobs of fruits and veggies? She had done them all, ad nauseam. Now she was fit as a fiddle … *and* depressed.

The thought made her chuckle, a good sign. She brushed the pocket with her grandfather Walt's icon tucked inside. It helped to know it was there, that *he* was there. His Polish mother had given him the icon when he was still a child, just before she put him on a steamer bound for America. Hoping to join him later, she never could, as it turned out. Willow's father, the man she still called Leon, was her anchor, but his father Walt was her North Star. Like her, Walt knew firsthand how the wound of a lost mother never quite healed. Yet, sometimes, like finding Leon and Walt, flowers grew over it.

While she was vacationing in Alaska, there had been a devastating fire. Afterward, a field of wildflowers—she learned they were called *fireweeds*—appeared out of nowhere over the scorched, black earth. Fireweeds were the first flowers to bloom—and thrive—in places of trauma and devastation. They told her that those same pink and purple flowers had even grown over the ashes where the bombs had dropped on London during WWII. Up close, their translucent petals seemed far too fragile. Where did they come from? How did they grow?

Willow had been fascinated by them, and she attempted to capture their mystique on canvas. Oh, how she tried, but she wasn't able to get their color and texture quite right. She settled for the best she could do, a painting she called *The Fireweed Moon*, depicting a field of fireweeds growing over the charred earth in the moonlight.

That painting now thumped in the back seat, along with a couple of other canvasses.

✝✝✝

As the sun was setting around eight-thirty that evening, Willow passed the green highway sign that informed her she was five miles away from the town of Weeping Willow. She was struck by the quiet beauty of this part of the country. It wasn't callous or indifferent, the way New York could be. It was simpler, gentler, as if the clock were winding backward into decades before she was born—back to the 1950s, maybe—an era she knew only from the black-and-white TV reruns of *Leave it to Beaver* she sometimes watched as a child, starved for the loving parents that tucked Beaver into a safe bed every night.

Entering the city limits, she passed the large white sign that read, "WELCOME TO THE HOME OF THE WEEPING WILLOWS" and soon she saw a cluster of them lining the road— the trees! *Her* trees!—the lush weeping willows that Leon had replanted for her and her mother.

A gush of warmth enveloped her. The sight of them felt welcoming, personal. She was right to come here, yet she couldn't help but wonder, what was the draw that had lured them all back to this place?—first her mother who came here to die, then her father who came to build a new life, then her brother after retirement, and now her.

Though dusk was falling, she didn't head to Leon's house quite yet. Instead, she drove a little farther, through the open, wrought-iron gates of the Garden of Resurrection to visit her mother's grave. According to Leon, Noël had been captivated by the inscriptions here, so it puzzled Willow that he had never added one to her tombstone. On second thought, pretty words weren't Leon's thing—actions were—and as usual, he had tended Noël's grave as meticulously as a miniature French garden, flanked by a bush on either side bearing dozens of ruby-red roses, Noël's favorite flower, in full bloom.

No, Leon wasn't one to reveal his love on the surface, as words etched into granite. The father Willow had come to know held it much deeper than that; the way a tree stores sap.

FIVE

OF DIXIE CUPS AND RECORD PLAYERS

AFTER discussing the Trudeaus' history until well past sundown, Leon suggested to Booker that they resettle on the back deck, where his coffee refills were replaced by a bottle of sherry that Leon had brought out from the house, along with a couple of Dixie Cups. While he retrieved his sweatshirt from the hook on the inside of the patio doors, Booker slipped his own jacket around his shoulders. "Look at us," Leon said. "A couple of old farts, shivering out here on a summer night. Getting old is a bitch."

"You got that right." Booker eagerly held out his Dixie Cup, as Leon poured. "Thanks, my brother. Thanks for everything you're doing for me, by the way—putting me up here at your own house tonight. I can't even begin to tell you how much I appreciate it."

Where else could Booker go, Leon thought, after the only innkeeper in town had turned him away? "I haven't done anything," he replied, pulling his sweatshirt down over his shirt. Though Booker had not mentioned it outright, Leon knew exactly what he could do to help him—dig that Bible out of Lily's grave, that's what. But he didn't offer to do it, didn't even hint at it, because it was such a drastic, off-the-wall thing to do, and at what cost? Opening up her grave would no doubt be traumatic for both

Willow and her brother Adam, not to mention for the townsfolk, who'd almost certainly find the whole thing appalling.

Still, Booker had spent a lifetime searching for that Bible, and the karma seemed far worse if Leon allowed it to remain underground. Besides that, Jack Trudeau, his own father-in-law and Willow's grandfather, was the one who had orchestrated Raymond Roberts' murder in the first place. They owed it to Booker, didn't they? He could almost feel Noël's tug on his sleeve, hear her whispering in his ear ... *Do it.*

"So what was it you did for a living?" Leon asked.

"I taught history at Loyola."

"In Chicago?"

"No, New Orleans."

Leon didn't realize there was a Loyola in New Orleans. "You were a history professor, huh?"

"I guess I thought of myself more as a student of history— a perpetual student." Booker tasted the sherry. "Oh, that's good. And what about you? What did you do?"

"Steel mills, that's what I did. Nothing fancy. I worked in the mills all my life."

"Good solid work. It makes the world go round."

The dark night was quiet, disrupted only occasionally by the sound of a passing car on the street out front. They were drinking their sherry out of Dixie Cups because Leon hated doing dishes and frequently used picnic ware instead. Earlier, in between their conversations, he'd gone out to the liquor store and bought the sherry after Booker disclosed it to be his usual nightcap. "Cheap brandy," Booker called it, and he was right. The sherry felt warm all the way down his throat, as good as the Courvoisier cognac Leon used to savor before he gave up hard liquor (damn that Dolly Schmidt). "I wish I could have a cigarette," he said.

"Why can't you?"

"I stopped smoking five years ago. And seven months."

"And how many days?" Booker chuckled, a raspy sound that seemed to emanate from deep inside his throat—an old smoker's laugh, to be sure. "Yeah, I gave them up too. So many times, I lost count. My daddy died of lung cancer, and that was the first time I quit. It was a bad death."

"So I've heard. I knew lots of guys from the mills who died that way." Leon lifted the Dixie Cup to his lips, recalling some of their faces in his mind, how the cancer had ravaged them.

"… You ever think about how you're gonna die, Leon?"

"When you get to be our age, guess it's only natural. My dad died of Alzheimer's."

"Alzheimer's." Booker whistled a single note, low and mournful. "Now that's a rough way to die. So how would you want to die—if you could choose, I mean?"

Leon held the sherry against his tongue momentarily before swallowing and letting the soothing liquid do its thing. "In my sleep, I guess. Or struck by lightning. Any way that I didn't see it coming. How 'bout you?"

"In peace, my brother. I just want to die in peace, however it comes."

Off in the distance, one of the neighbors was calling out to someone—was it Nancy Salvo? Leon took another sip. "You might as well just sleep in there!" she screamed. Yup, it was Nancy all right. She needled poor Telles day and night about spending too much time out back in that little red shed of his, his workshop. Probably his haven.

"My brother sure didn't have that chance," Booker said.

"What chance?"

"To die in peace."

The yelling next door stopped; Leon heard a door slam.

"Do you know what they nicknamed Ray back in divinity school?" Booker answered his own question before Leon had a chance. "The Love Pastor, that's what. But Ray called himself a *Jes-ist*. His ministry was based solely on the life and teachings of Jesus—pretty radical Christianity, huh?" He smiled. "Like Jesus taught, Ray knew that Love was synonymous with God—the supreme, transformative, transcendent force of all being. You know, as in 1 John 4:16?—'God *is* love. Whoever lives in love, lives in God, and God in him.' Ray built his whole ministry on that verse. He used to say that if love was the answer to every question we ask, the New Jerusalem would come right down from the sky, no apocalypse necessary."

Leon shuffled his feet beneath the chair. Besides not having a clue what any of that meant, preachy talk made him uncomfortable. When it came to religion—and pretty much everything else—he was a pragmatist. Thank God, he was reared on the Catechism of the Catholic Church where it was all thought out for him in advance centuries before. No touchy-feely stuff. No need to over-think things.

"When Ray was five years old," Booker said, lowering his voice. "He claimed he saw Jesus."

Leon took a gulp of sherry, a big one.

"He was climbing a tree out back of the house all by himself one day, fell out, and knocked himself out cold. The scar on his forehead never went away. Anyway, when he woke up, he was in Jesus' arms. Or that's what he told my parents, anyway."

Kids have active imaginations, Leon thought, but he kept his mouth shut. When he was five, he thought he could fly like Superman.

"Can I be square with you?" Booker asked. "This whole

thing—the whole reason I showed up here in the first place—it's all for my son, Cyrus, my only child. It's sad how something traumatic that happened a long time ago, before we were born, can show up again in another generation, isn't it? I swear, Cyrus carries my brother's murder in his DNA, and it's made him bitter. Living through Katrina only made it worse. No offense, but he doesn't have a speck of trust for white people."

"Where's he now?"

"In New Orleans. He'll never leave there. He's a lawyer. He really enjoys stickin' it to whites whenever he can."

Leon remained silent.

"Hate is no good, no matter which side it's on. Hate is poison. I thought that if I could find something that Ray had written, something Cyrus could read for himself, even after I'm gone ... I thought, maybe, it could heal his heart."

"I know what you mean," Leon said. "I worry about my daughter, Willow, too."

"I've been meaning to ask you. Is it a coincidence that her name is the same as this town?"

"Nope, no coincidence. That was Noël's idea ... Willow's my only natural child. I've got a step-son, Adam—at least that's the way I still think of him—even though Noël and I got divorced, the biggest mistake of my life, but that's another story. Adam and his wife and their boy moved here to Weeping Willow a while back. He's a retired pitcher from the Chicago White Sox."

"You don't say!"

Leon grinned. It always gave him a kick to tell that to people. "Is Cyrus married?"

"Oh, yeah. He met Vera in college and married her shortly afterward. They got two young boys, and they've been married for ten years now. A good marriage, solid as a rock—at least, as far as I know."

Leon poured again—a Dixie Cup could only hold so much, and they were on their way to killing the bottle. "A good marriage can heal you. A bad one'll kill you."

"Sounds like you're talking from experience."

Leon nodded. "I had pieces of both. My second marriage should never have happened."

"Second marriage? You mean, *after* Noël?"

"Yeah, after Noël. There couldn't be anyone for me after Noël, but I was too pig-headed to realize it back then. I ruined a hell of a lot of years of my second wife's life. And mine too."

"I hear what you're saying," Booker said. "Some loves are just unforgettable. Meant to be."

Leon noticed a faraway look in his eyes. "So … you ever been in love?"

"Me?" Booker stirred in his seat. "My Nettie died four years ago. She and I were married for fifty-one years."

"Fifty-one years?" Leon shook his head. "Must have been a good marriage."

"We had our ups and downs, mostly because I was pretty damned pig-headed too … but the good days were mighty, mighty good." He drank his sherry with what Leon recognized as a regretful expression. He knew the look, and the feeling, all too well.

A few moments of silence passed between them. "Life sure goes by fast, doesn't it?" Leon said. "I didn't even know my daughter existed until she was almost twenty-five. She just showed up one day—like a godsend. We were having a rough time dealing with my father's Alzheimer's, and Willow just happened to have training as a nurse, and … I swear to God, Booker, that girl saved me in more ways than I can tell you."

"Thank God for our children, huh?" Booker leaned over to give Leon a fist bump. "Since Noël died after Willow's birth, who raised her?"

Leon took another sip. "Steve, Noël's brother, the one that lives in California, and his wife, Betsy." He hated divulging that fact. Among his many self-recriminations, this was the biggest. "The thing about Willow is, she's had bouts of depression all her life."

"Depression? That's a difficult thing to live with. I'm sorry to hear it."

The crickets were out now, croaking in unison the way they did. Maybe it was the sherry, but Leon hadn't realized how much he missed being able to talk to someone the way he and Booker were talking right now. The two of them seemed to have a hell of a lot in common. Dead wives. Deep regrets. One child that worried them. Being in their seventies. Something about Booker was genuine, down-to-earth, like the old buddies he used to hang out with back in the day, like Ted Budzinski, the kind of guy you could tell anything to without fear of judgment or ridicule. It had been a long time since Leon had a friend like that. He and Ted used to wash their hotrods together on Saturday afternoons when they were in high school. He fingered the rim of his Dixie Cup. What the hell ever happened to Ted Budzinski anyway? Funny how people came and went from your life without any rhyme or reason. "You know what I miss most about being young?" he asked.

"What's that?"

"Records."

Again came the Booker chuckle, low and raspy, by now a familiar sound. "I miss them, too. Both LPs and 45s. Remember the scratchy sound of putting the needle down in the groove of your favorite track? Pure anticipation, excitement."

Leon nodded in wistful memory.

"Nowadays, there's Bluetooth and iPods and MP3, and who knows what all else? I need to get out a magnifying glass just to turn them itty bitty things off and on."

Leon raised his Dixie cup and clunked it against Booker's carefully so as not to mash it. "Here's to record players and to—" A sudden noise from around the front of the house interrupted his toast—the unmistakable sound of a car door closing in his own driveway.

Booker sat up. "Expecting someone?"

By the time Leon headed into the house, he heard a soft rapping on the front door. When he pulled it open, there stood his daughter. "Willow!" He could hardly assimilate the surprise of her unexpected appearance, especially given the lateness of the hour. She looked too thin—and a little lost. Her long, dark hair hung beneath her bony shoulders. Besides her purse, there was no other visible baggage. Throwing his arms around her, he asked, "Why didn't you tell me you were coming to visit?"

"I'm not here to visit." She lingered in his embrace for a few seconds. "I'm here for good."

For good? "Is everything okay?"

"Fine." She smiled in that evading way of hers, tight-lipped, no teeth showing. "I just needed a change of scenery, that's all."

Happy as he was to see her, Leon sensed something wasn't quite right about it, but before he could say another word, Booker's appearance in the room had engaged Willow's full attention.

"Oh, I'm sorry," she said. "I didn't know you had a guest. Maybe I shouldn't have—"

"Not to worry," Booker said. "Let me take a little walk, give you two some privacy."

"I wouldn't dream of it. Please stay, Mr.——" Eyebrows rising in expectation, she turned to Leon.

"Mr. Roberts." Leon filled in the blank. "This is Booker Roberts. His brother was a close friend of your grandmother's."

"Of Mary's?"

"God, no!" Leon laughed. He couldn't imagine his own mother befriending a Black man. "Your *other* grandmother."

SIX

HOMECOMING

HER *other* grandmother?

Frankly, Willow had never thought much about Lily Trudeau, her mother's mother, about whom she knew virtually zilch. Feeling a bit flummoxed, as if she had barged in on something, she refocused her thoughts on Leon's unexpected guest. "Very nice to meet you, Mr. Roberts."

"Mr. Roberts was my father. Please, call me Booker." Once again, he offered to take a walk, to give her and Leon a chance to reconnect. And, once again, she insisted he remain.

The truth be told, Willow was relieved to find that her father had company—it allowed her to leave the explanation of her homecoming, and any other weighty matters, alone for the time being. She wasn't ready to go there yet, and getting acquainted with this interesting visitor from her grandmother's past seemed the perfect buffer.

As Leon grabbed three cans of soda pop from the fridge, she and Mr. Roberts settled into the living room, he in a wing chair by the fireplace, and she on the sofa. Looking around the space, she cringed at the sight of one of her earliest paintings, an abstract sunrise, hanging on the main wall.

Leon doled out the refreshments before joining her on the other end of the couch. "How was the drive?"

"Uneventful … but let's talk later, Dad. Right now, I want to talk to Mr. Roberts about his—"

"Booker," he interjected. "Just plain Booker."

"Okay then, Booker." She smiled at him, already taking a liking to his calm and kind demeanor. "Please tell me more about your brother." She was eager to hear the story about how his brother came to meet her "other" grandmother. Uncle Steve never talked about his mom—any history beyond the current day's breakfast was taboo for him. "How did he know Lily?" She glanced at Leon, at Booker. The question seemed to elicit peculiar expressions on both their faces, their eyes darting away from one another's.

"Ohhh." Booker stretched out his response. "He knew her back in Louisiana."

"Yeah, your mom used to live in a little town there called Hyssop," Leon said. "They moved to Weeping Willow when she was seven years old."

"I don't think you ever mentioned the name of Hyssop before," she said.

"You never asked."

Touché. Fair enough. Willow noticed a bulging book sitting out on the coffee table—a shiny cover with big black and red magnolias—and she recognized it immediately. Uncle Steve had given her the old photo album when she left San Diego, and she had passed it on to Leon before she moved to New York—she could only take so much with her and it mostly contained photographs of unrecognizable people from the distant past. She reached over, picked it up, and began flipping through the album, pausing to look at a large photograph taken on Lily's wedding day. *That* photo she remembered well—she used to stare at it when she was a child because Lily looked so much like her own mother and all of Noël's pictures were small, amateurish Kodak shots, while this photograph of Lily was taken by a professional, large and clear enough to show the details of her delicate, heart-shaped face. In her lacy white bridal gown, she looked like a raven-haired princess or an old-time movie queen. Even in black and white, her translucent eyes intimated intense color. The kicker was, Lily also had to be the unhappiest-looking bride Willow had ever seen.

"Something happened to your grandmother a long time ago that ended up affecting the whole family," Leon said. "And Booker's family too."

Now he had her full attention. With the rapid dryness of a newscaster, he gave her a quick rundown about Lily's love affair with Raymond, their stillborn child, Raymond's murder, Booker's search for the Bible—and where it was now.

"So my grandmother is buried with your brother's Bible?" Willow said when Leon finished. The rest of the story, unbelievable as it was, was a gust of wind from a past she couldn't quite fathom and that couldn't be undone. All her life, Willow had tried to live by the wisdom of the Serenity Prayer: *Change what you can, let the rest go*—the first part decidedly easier of the two. The buried Bible was the only piece of the astonishing tale she could do something about. "Then we have to make sure we get it back to you, don't we?" she said to Booker.

Neither man responded. Booker looked down at his shoes, Leon at the clock on the wall. Evasive reactions, she thought; how strange. "It's their family Bible, Dad! What good is it doing anyone down there in the ground?"

"Hang on there, honey," Leon said. "That's not a simple thing to do."

"Why not? It seems pretty simple to me."

"Okay, then," he said. "Grab a shovel, and let's go."

The sarcasm was vintage Leon. "Come on, Dad, I'm serious!

I'm the next of kin. If I give my permission to exhume the grave, why can't it be done?"

Leon was getting fidgety, shuffling in his seat as if it were stuffed with needles, the way he often did when a topic he considered irrational was first brought up, like when his father Walt was newly diagnosed with Alzheimer's and Leon thought the doctor was out of his mind. "We'd have to apply for permission to do it, or something like that," he said. "And I have no idea where we'd apply or how difficult it might be."

Booker listened silently, his hands at his sides, his eyes shifting back and forth between them.

"So let's find out," she said.

"Actually, they'd need Steve's permission, not yours. As Lily's son, he's her next of kin."

"Well, then, we'll get it." She scooted forward in her seat. "Uncle Steve wouldn't care. He always rolls with the punches."

"Just don't go getting ahead of yourself!" Leon crossed his arms against his chest. "You're not in New York City anymore, Toto. I can't imagine digging up a grave in Weeping Willow. You can't even spit on the sidewalk without someone pointing a finger. Do you really want the whole town to know your family secrets?"

She glanced down at her grandmother's photo with a twinge of camaraderie, her depression fading away, at least for now. Willow never felt livelier than when she was on some kind of a mission, especially a mission like this, a grander cause in the scheme of things. Life was handing her an opportunity to do something good. Like the Twelve-step program advised: *Do the next right thing.* "Who cares what anyone asks, or says, or thinks? It's the right thing to do!"

"Besides, that Bible probably disintegrated a long time ago,"

Leon said. "Lily's been dead for almost fifty years, plenty of time for water and decay to seep into a coffin."

Crushed by the thought, she shifted her gaze to Booker.

"Do you happen to know if a burial vault was used?" Booker's voice was soft, his eyes downcast.

"They didn't just stick her into the dirt," Leon said. "She had to have a vault ... didn't she?"

"Not necessarily."

Leon scratched his head. "As opposed to what else?"

"As opposed to a lawn crypt or burial liner. They're much more commonly used."

"Beats me what they used." Leon shrugged. "Noël and her brother Adam took care of all that. Why? Does it matter?"

Booker sat up, cleared his throat. "It's just that I used to be a gravedigger way back when—one of my odd jobs to earn my keep while I was away at college—and I learned that a good burial vault is your best bet for waterproofing. Vaults are reinforced with a heavy gauge wire mesh and lined with copper or plastic. The cover's sealed on with a strip of tar. All in all, as opposed to lawn crypts or burial liners, that makes them pretty airtight. But a vault is pricey. It's what you might call the Cadillac option."

"Noël's family was on a tight budget," Leon said. "I seriously doubt they could afford *any* kind of Cadillac."

As the two of them tossed it around, Willow remained deep in thought. She was a believer in things happening for a reason; well, if not for a reason, then as part of some pattern, a pattern that seemed chaotic and random, like the underside of an embroidery, until things were over and done and it was flipped to the other side. Why would Booker have shown up here and stirred up this family history if they were meant to drop it without even trying?

"I've got something to say," Booker said after a pause. "I

know all of this is a longshot and way out of bounds. You're right, Leon—the Bible probably disintegrated a long time ago. Though I want to make it clear that I would pay for any and all costs to do it, digging up a sacred grave is no small thing." He stopped Willow as she tried to interject a rebuttal. "It's a big deal, Willow—it *really* is. It's too much to ask. And I'm not asking."

"I know you're not asking," she said. "But I'm offering. The funeral home must have records about whether or not Lily had a vault. Let's at least go there and find out."

Booker fell silent.

"You came all this way!" Her eyes shifted to her father imploringly, long enough for him to break into a grin.

"See, Booker?" He leaned over, kissed her on the cheek. "This here is my charger, her mother's child all the way. The two of them have always been my conscience."

†††

Willow found it difficult to fathom that finding an unoccupied bedroom could be so complicated in a home that used to have five of them, tiny as they had been. But when Leon had moved in, he remodeled the whole shebang—converting one bedroom into a master bath and knocking down a wall between the two smaller ones to create a man-cave of sorts, half-office, half-entertainment/exercise space. And, *voila*, it was a two-bedroom home. Well, three-bedroom, if you counted the half-finished room up in the attic. Though Leon had offered his room, and Booker had already begun to remove himself and his belongings out of the second bedroom, Willow would have no part of either arrangement. She was the usurper. Lugging her overnight bag upstairs (the rest of her stuff could be unloaded tomorrow) she entered the musty, dusty attic space and flicked up the button on the switch plate. A dim bulb, about to burn out, blinked from the lamp on the nightstand, covering the room in shadows.

Spooky.

Once, long ago, when she and Adam had both come to stay with Leon for the weekend, Willow had opted to sleep on the living room couch rather than up here, and now she remembered why. She glanced around at the pitched roof, the red brick chimney, the exposed wood beams on the walls and ceiling. Though half-finished, the space remained as rustic as a long-neglected cabin. The "half-finished" part was the darkly stained hardwood flooring and the drywall with a door that separated the finished part from the neglected original. She opened the door, shut it fast. Even in the flickering light, she could see that the unfinished room was a total mess, stuffed to the brim with junk.

She hoisted the suitcase on top of the double bed, neatly covered with a dingy, badly yellowed (originally white) chenille bedspread. The old furnishings added their own odd touch, a mishmash of eras from mid-century to early American brothel. The floor was covered with a 1960s-style braided rug in shades of browns and tans. A blonde wood nightstand beside the bed sported a lamp with a purple-tasseled shade. Near the window, stood a four-drawer dresser, with matching blonde wood. In the corner on the other side of the brick chimney, was an old rolltop desk that appeared to date back to the 1800s. One square window, overlooking the neighbor's house, was framed by tasseled curtains in the same purple hue as the lamp shade. Thank God, there was a central air vent up here. Otherwise, she'd suffocate to death.

A few minutes later, Leon appeared with an armload of freshly laundered sheets and the spread from his own bed. On top of the stack sat a lightbulb, a dust cloth, and a can of furniture polish.

"You don't need to make a fuss over me," she said, but he couldn't be deterred. She watched as he replaced the dying light-bulb, the brighter voltage casting dense, solid shadows between the overhead beams.

He stepped back. "It still looks creepy up here," he said.

Willow was grateful for the refresher, especially the comforter and clean sheets. Together, they assembled the bed to make it look as inviting as possible. "You want to tell me what this is all about?" he asked as they worked, not a shred of condemnation in his tone. "I mean, why you left New York?"

"Not tonight. It's late, and I'm dead tired." She yawned to emphasize the point. "We'll talk tomorrow. Besides, there's nothing really to say. I just got tired of living there, that's all."

He gave her a skeptical look, his eyes narrowing. "You're too young to get tired of New York."

"I always wondered why there's a bedroom up here," she said. Both she and her father were masters at changing the subject when they wanted to evade a topic; maybe they had picked up that trick during Walt's dementia—switching the subject to divert him had been a handy caregiving technique. "Those people who rented the house after Mom died … what was their name again?" It came to her faster than she expected. "The Richards, that's it. Dotty and Jerry, and their three girls. When I saw this house for the first time after they moved out, it still had five bedrooms, one for each of them. The furniture up here was the only furniture left in the whole house."

Leon shrugged. "All I know is that your mother's aunt used to sleep in this room."

"Really? Which aunt?"

"Aunt Clarissa, Lily's sister. They called her Aunt Clarry."

"Oh, yeah—the one on the tombstone. I forgot about her.

Hmp." She gave the space another scrutinizing glance. "Do you think this is the same furniture she used?"

"Probably. Especially since the house was totally vacant when you first saw it after those Richards people moved out—except for this stuff. Sure looks like it might be from the 1950s or 60s." Leon sprayed and dusted until the musty smell mingled with the distinct scent of manufactured lemon.

An improvement, she supposed.

"Get some sleep now," he said. "But tomorrow morning, you and I are having a long talk." He winked. "Unless the bats in the ceiling get to you first."

SEVEN

LEAVE ME ALONE

SHORTLY past eleven that morning, Adam Stephen Beauregard Ketchfield snapped the screen door shut behind him as he stepped into the kitchen, sweaty from the heat and hungry as a mountain lion. His wife Anne and their son Rocket had gone shopping at the supermall in Bedlington, leaving him alone to tackle the enormous yard, front and back, with the riding mower.

Pouring himself a glass of water from the tap, he surveyed his efforts from the window over the sink. The grass looked like green velvet. A prideful feeling always surged during quiet moments such as this. This home, on the outskirts of Weeping Willow, had more room than they needed, both inside and out, yet it felt grand to be able to stretch out on their own oasis—a fire pit out back and an old wishing well out front. The best part was the huge country kitchen with a stone fireplace. If they had remained in Chicago, a place like this would have cost them a frickin' fortune.

His cell phone chimed. He couldn't remember exactly where he'd laid it this time. Following the sound, he located it beneath the morning paper on the kitchen table. A quick glance revealed the caller's identity: *Cory.* He braced himself. "Yup," he said.

"Hiya, ugly!"

As usual, Adam's muscles tensed at the sound of his younger half-brother's voice. He replied with a soft grunt.

"I'm on my way over. Got something I need to talk to you about."

Click. He was gone. "Okay, then," Adam said to the disconnected phone. "Don't bother asking if now's a good time or anything. Just do whatever you damn-well please, the way you always do."

On his way into the living room, he passed the gigantic antique mirror in the hallway—he hated that ornate mirror, another one of Anne's treasured garage sale bargains. Maybe it wasn't the mirror he detested as much as where it was placed, huge and prominent at the end of the hallway, an unavoidable reminder that he was getting old. At fifty-three, his once-blond hair was fading to gray, though still thick with a hint of a wave. His brown eyes were a reliable shade of milk-chocolate. His Greek nose was admirably straight; his jaw square and strong. All in all, he supposed he wasn't bad looking for his age. The problem was, whenever he looked in the mirror, he saw Cory's face staring back—in the shape of his chin, in the color of his eyes—prompting him to avoid mirrors at all costs. Even when he shaved in the mornings, he tried to concentrate only on the precise spot, not his entire face.

He sat down in the living room, in his favorite chair in front of another fireplace, this one brick. The three of them—he, Anne, and Rocket—had lived here for four years already. Anne had been itching to move to Weeping Willow ever since she first got pregnant with Rocket—she was a small-town girl who had fallen in love with the town when they came to visit Leon during a rainstorm and the soaked, hanging tree branches appeared to be weeping. But Adam wasn't so sure that he wanted to return to his childhood town, heavy with memories of his dead mother, Noël Trudeau, and it took another eight years of cajoling before the move finally came to fruition. When they came across this perfect house online, they swooped in to buy it.

A year ago, Adam got hit with a shocker. Turned out, he had a half-brother. Out of nowhere, Cory just showed up one day and introduced himself. The sheer sight of him had been overwhelming—he was a hefty, beer-bellied, over-tattooed, over-opinionated guy, with a shiny shaved head, a strong, square jaw (same shape as Adam's), and two cocoa-brown eyes (same reliable color as his own). The glaring similarities in their faces freaked Adam out. It was like seeing a vision of himself had his life gone another way—had his mother not run away from Weeping Willow with Adam when he was two years old and hidden him away in Langston, Indiana, saving him from the father he remembered only by name: David Ketchfield.

He and Cory had talked for hours that first day—rather, Cory talked and Adam listened in what would become their routine ever after. As Cory's story unfolded, Adam learned that their childhoods were also eerily similar, except in reverse; Cory had the misfortune of being snatched away by the wrong parent.

Cory told him he had been born in Kentucky to David Ketchfield and Marybelle, his second wife after Noël. After David ditched Marybelle, or maybe it was the other way around (Cory wasn't certain which way it went), his father had taken him away at the age of three, kidnapped him, probably (Cory wasn't exactly sure of that part either) and raised him in a small town in Texas. For a time, Cory worked with his dad as a plumber until he branched off into his own landscaping business. Fifteen years ago, David Ketchfield had dropped dead of cardiac arrest, still holding a BLT. Cory laughed when he threw in that detail, but it wasn't a *ha-ha* kind of laugh as much as a painful one, or that's the way it seemed to Adam. Cory frequently laughed in places where others cried.

Life wasn't fair for men like him and his father, Cory had gone on to say that first day—they were solid guys who worked by the sweat of their brows with little to show for it; guys who struggled for everything they had, only to watch it get snatched away in the end, stolen blind by one thief after another—be it a nagging wife, the government, illegal aliens sneaking over the border, mandated insurance, or some other form of thievery. Cory had experienced them all, including an ex-wife who had the audacity to accuse him of battery. The growing rage in his eyes as he continued his diatribe had sent a shockwave down Adam's spine. "Those other landscapers hired all those goddamned illegal aliens, undercutting my prices! And the next thing you know, my business goes belly up. So what was I supposed to do? Have compassion for the aliens? Bullshit! This goddamned government puts everyone on the tit except their own people, the backbone of this country—they sit back with their thumbs up their butts and watch our jobs float away—let us fucking starve! How about some compassion for *us*?"

His bitterness had all but consumed him, Cory said, until he found a little white cement-block church—a converted gas station—and had gotten himself born again, dunked into a vat of water in front of the whole congregation. After that, the idea had come to him: He would head to Weeping Willow, back to his father's old hometown, start all over again, and so he jumped into his oversized pick-up, a U-Haul in tow, and drove across country. Once he got here, he discovered he wasn't the only Ketchfield in town. So here he was.

There he was, all right. And the peace of living in a quiet sanctuary like Weeping Willow was shattered for Adam.

He glanced at the clock on the wall, relieved that Anne and Rocket were still shopping. Whenever Cory dropped by, Anne found an excuse to go outside or upstairs. ("Something about him scares me," she confessed). Adam looked at the clock again. Cory would undoubtedly be late. It was his M.O. to call and say he was coming right over, then another hour or more would tick by, keeping them in limbo, holding up whatever plans they might have.

No use waiting around. He headed back to the kitchen and spread a heaping helping of Anne's chicken salad on a couple slices of bread, gazed out the window at the wishing well and gravel driveway as he chewed. Though he couldn't see it from this window, out back he had created a pitching mound, but Rocket wasn't much interested.

Adam and Anne had named their only child "Clemens" after Adam's favorite pitcher, Roger Clemens, and they ended up calling him by Roger's nickname, "Rocket." Clemens had been a contemporary of Adam's back in the day, a pitcher at the same time he was, only the original Rocket played for the Boston Red Sox, among others, while Adam had pitched one long stretch for the Chicago White Sox.

Their own Rocket was going on twelve, come December. Thank God, he resembled a full-blooded Trudeau, not a trace of Ketchfield, with near-black hair and periwinkle eyes. Rocket wanted no part of being a pitcher when he grew up. He had his sights set on something higher, and it didn't seem like a pipedream or passing phase that kids went through. Ever since some kid in his class had a brain tumor and the doctor was invited to give a presentation at the school, Rocket wanted to be a neurosurgeon. He had landed on that singular profession without wavering. That Rocket of his was a serious, determined kid, smart enough to do whatever he set his mind to, not a dreamer like Adam had been at his age—maybe still was. After he retired from pitching, Adam had grown more and more restless. Now, it gnawed away at him. Was it possible to have an identity crisis at fifty-three?

A good half-hour later, he heard the sound of a door slamming in the driveway, not a car door, but the heavier sound of a Cory-sized pick-up. When he looked out the window, sure enough, there was Cory, barreling up the curving stepping stone walkway dressed in a black t-shirt with huge, red-block letters, readable even from a distance: LEAVE ME ALONE. He bypassed the formal entrance and, without knocking, pushed open the screen door to the kitchen, the one they called their back door though it faced the front of the house. "Since when does Leon pal around with nigger boys?" he said.

Adam knew he should be outraged, but he had heard the despicable racial slur erupt from Cory's foul mouth so many times that he'd become desensitized, which bothered him all the more. "Most people say hello first," Adam said.

"Okay, then. Hello, First Man." Cory plopped into one of the kitchen chairs. "The trouble with you is, you live out here in the sticks, and you don't have a fucking clue what's happening. You're always the last to know everything."

First Man, that's what Cory sometimes called him—not only because of the Adam and Eve thing, but also because Adam was born first, six years earlier than Cory, to be precise. Adam sat down across from him. "As usual, I have no idea what you're talking about."

"Obviously." Cory got up and ripped open a bag of potato chips he had apparently spotted on the counter. "I'm talking about some old Black dude that turned up at the motel yesterday asking questions about your sister."

"About Willow?"

"You got another sister?" He jammed a fistful of chips into his mouth, kept right on talking. "The next thing you know, Leon is wining and dining this guy at the tavern. And guess the fucking what else?"

"I give up."

"He's stayin' with Leon now, at his own fucking house! You got any idea who this guy might be?"

"Not a clue." Adam reached into the bag, got his own handful. "You know what? You need a dog or something. You've got too much time on your hands for gossip."

"It's not gossip, asshole—it's real life. You're the one who lives out here in fantasy land. You mean to tell me you're not at all bothered?"

"Why should I be?"

"Niggers don't just show up in a white town for no good reason. Maybe he's holding Leon hostage or something."

"Man, you sure have a wild imagination."

Cory glared at him, as if he couldn't believe Adam's stupidity or naiveté. "Besides that, I'm plenty busy. Unlike you, I wasn't a fancy pitcher who retired to the good life in my late thirties. I still have to work my ass off."

Adam had to admit it; Cory *was* a hard worker. He had opened up a plumbing business as soon as he arrived in Weeping Willow, and it was going gangbusters from what Adam understood. The only problem was, it gave Cory endless entry into peoples' homes, and people talked too much, often about other people—not good in a town this size, and definitely not good for a semi-paranoid like Cory.

"How's church?" Adam changed the subject to a safer one. Cory was a devotee of the megachurch on Old Mill Road, nearer to Bedlington than Weeping Willow.

"Church? ... fine. Why do you ask?"

"Just wondering."

Cory grabbed the bag of chips, read the label. "Low salt. That's what I thought. Why does Anne buy shit like this when she must weigh all of thirty pounds? ... Like I told you before, you and Anne oughta give the church a try. Rev. Tommy is brilliant—a fucking prophet."

"And like I told you umpteen times, I'm not into that stuff." If even a megachurch couldn't straighten-out Cory, how great could it be? "I've never been much of a churchgoer."

"You got a kid to consider." Cory observed him the same intent way he'd beheld the bag of potato chips a second earlier. "Maybe you *should* be a churchgoer. It's never too late, you know. Get that boy baptized."

Adam returned the stare, thoughtfully. Face to face, Cory seemed more human than the thought of him while he was away, and when he said things like that, it gave Adam pause, a thin hope that underneath all that tattoo ink, bigotry, and blubber, a glimmer of a good heart might yet be beating.

"Is that what you came here to tell me? That Leon has a friend who just happens to be—" Adam slapped his own face in mock horror, "—*Black?*" He imitated the screeching violins from the shower scene in Hitchcock's *Psycho*.

"You're ignorant," Cory said, unsmiling. "Fucking ignorant. You don't get the way the world works. Rev. Tommy says we gotta protect what's ours, and believe me, he's a guy who knows the score. He watches out for us, tells us we gotta believe in ourselves, fight for what belongs to us ... I'm not the only one around here who's bugged by this Black dude hangin' out with Leon. Tongues are waggin' all over town."

"Thanks to you, probably."

"I hope it's thanks to me. Unlike you, I look out for my

neighbors. You spent too long in Chicago, that's your problem. You've still got city slicker mentality." He pointed to his head.

"You're forgetting I also spent a lot of my childhood right here. And in sunny southern California too."

"California. Hah! That's why you got alfalfa sprouts in your brain." Cory stood up, hopefully to leave. "Be that way. But don't say I didn't warn you, butthead."

"Consider me warned, Beevis."

As Cory headed for the screen door, Adam crossed his fingers that he would be out of there before Anne returned home, but Cory stopped suddenly and turned around. "By the way, I'm giving myself some time off next week, maybe two whole weeks. I decided to take a little road trip."

"Oh yeah?" Adam said. "Good for you. To where?"

"Heading up Virginia way. Thought I'd see what Charlottesville is like." A car door closing in the driveway halted the conversation. Cory's eyes widened as he looked outside. "What have we here? You got yourself a sweetie on the side or something, First Man?"

"What are you talking about?" Adam stepped over to the window above the kitchen sink. Willow was walking toward the back door. What was she doing here? There was no holiday coming up or anything. He nudged Cory out of the way, swung the screen door wide open. "Hey, sis!" he called out. "What a surprise!"

Willow smiled at him, quickening her pace.

"Well, well," Cory said after she entered, ogling her up and down, the same way he sometimes ogled Anne and any other woman within proximity. "So this is the famous Willow. I knew there'd come a day we'd finally meet face to face. Lucky for you, your face doesn't look anything like this ugly brother of yours. Well, half-brother. You definitely got the better half!"

Willow glanced at Adam in confusion for a second before it registered. "Are you ... *Cory?*"

He flashed a full-toothed smile. "In the flesh."

Adam stepped in front of him, hoping he'd catch the hint, though Cory seldom caught the hint about anything socially appropriate. "Great to see you." Adam kissed her on the cheek. "How long are you here for?"

"A while," she said. "I'm moving here."

"You mean you left New York?"

"Moving here, huh?" Cory interrupted, reasserting himself in front of her. "Maybe you and me can get together once you settle in, you being unattached and all. There's not too many single people our age around this town. Like zero."

"Give me a break, Cory," Adam said. "She's *family!*"

"Not *my* family! There's not one drop of shared blood between her and me." He grinned at Willow again. "Is there, honey?"

"If it's all the same to you," she said, moving away from him and taking a seat at the kitchen table, "I think I'll take the advice on your t-shirt."

†††

An hour later, Cory long gone, Adam and Willow remained at the kitchen table catching up on each other's lives. Neither was comfortable talking about themselves, so each kept shifting the focus back to the other. Or to Anne and Rocket, or Leon. Or to Cory, the eccentric. "What a piece of work," she said.

She looked well, Adam thought, though too thin, as if she could be cracked in two under the slightest pressure. Middle age had softened her features in a pleasant way, but he could still see traces of the sad little sister he used to know, especially in her eyes.

Her news about leaving New York didn't sound good. Though technically true, as she insisted, she could do her magazine work from virtually anywhere, the sudden move seemed a failure of some sort that he couldn't quite put his finger on.

Willow, nine years younger than Adam, had always been a bit of a puzzle to him. Growing up in San Diego, they had been closely knit but, after that, they drifted apart. Slowly, they reconnected, and by the time he and his family had moved to Weeping Willow, they were back in regular communication via text, Skype, email, not to mention her in-person visits a few times a year. Sometimes Adam felt sharp pangs of regret for leaving her behind in San Diego after he was offered a slot in the minor leagues when he was eighteen and she just nine—the way she had cried and carried on the day he left, begging him to take her with him. It wasn't a memory easily forgotten. On her deathbed, his mother had told him to look out for Willow, but she also made him promise not to give up on his own dreams. "Go be a ball player"—those were her exact words. After he left San Diego, he called Willow every week, even got her a plane ticket a couple times to come see him play ball at Comiskey Park once he joined the White Sox. But he never returned to California. Living under Aunt Betsy's and Uncle Steve's guardianship had been intolerable for him.

He watched his sister's delicate fingers stroke the placemat as she talked about Booker, what a nice man he was. "So he's an old friend of Leon's?"

"Not exactly ..." Willow's fingers stopped moving. "Did you ever meet our grandmother, Lily?"

Their *grandmother*? Why had she suddenly switched topics to such a remote one? She might just as well have asked the name of his kindergarten teacher. But that was Willow; her brain operated on a different track. Trying to recollect his fuzzy memories of Lily, he formed the vision of a black-haired woman, a scary woman at that, hollow-eyed and mute, but it was like seeing her through a thick, dense fog. For some reason, the woman in his head was wearing a big straw hat. "I think she was crazy or something," he said. "But I don't really remember. She died when I was small. All I know is, she didn't talk."

"What do you mean, she didn't talk?"

"I mean, she didn't talk."

"Never?"

"Not that I ever heard. She was like a mannequin."

Willow's face scrunched into a frown. She began sharing the real reason Booker Roberts had come to town, about some missing Bible buried with their grandmother, about possibly exhuming her grave to retrieve it. "We've got an appointment at the funeral home later this afternoon to find out more about it."

"Holy cow, Willow! That's a big deal. Isn't it? I mean, digging up a coffin?"

"Do you object? Uncle Steve is the main one, but we might need your approval too."

"No … I wouldn't exactly object. Not really, I guess." If he came across sounding lukewarm to the idea, it was because he was. "Not if you think it's the right thing to do. It just sounds kind of … I don't know … weird, that's all. How did this Black guy's family Bible end up in our grandmother's grave anyway?"

"Another story. A long one."

He shot her a quizzical look. Fortunately, she gave him the short-and-sweet explanation. "Man," he said at the conclusion. "That's a lot of stuff to take in."

"You're telling me." She twisted a strand of her hair, a nervous mannerism she had inherited from their mother. He pictured his mom sitting on a sofa, drinking a bottle of soda pop, her legs curled beneath her. Since she died at twenty-eight, a youthful image of her was the only one there could ever be.

"I don't know why I didn't ask anything about Lily before," Willow said. "Or our grandfather, Jack, for that matter. Or our great-aunt, Clarissa. Or any of our uncles. I mean, who *were* they? They're part of us, you and me. But I never bothered to ask Uncle Steve, or Leon, one thing about them … did you?"

Adam shook his head. The only one he remembered was his mother's youngest brother who he was named after, Uncle Adam, the one-armed war veteran he adored as a child. Uncle Adam had a special way of swinging him around in the air, and the one-arm hold made it that much more exciting. Later, when he was older, he relished his conversations with Uncle Adam. He talked about interesting stuff, adult kind of stuff the others didn't talk to kids about—like having dreams and goals. He made Adam feel excited about growing up.

He died when Adam was eight. "There was nothing else he could do," was how his mother had explained it. It was only after Adam discovered the old newspaper article among his mother's things that he found out Uncle Adam had killed himself when he was twenty-four. A drug overdose.

Beyond that, Adam had little interest in knowing anything about the rest of his Trudeau predecessors, despite the fact that his own name, Adam Stephen Beauregard, was a literal roll call of Trudeaus, the names of all three of his mother's brothers in descending order of birth. As long as he was part Ketchfield, gene-alogy was a frightening prospect. Let sleeping dogs lie. Let the dead remain buried.

EIGHT

GREEN'S FUNERAL PARLOR

BACK in high school, Christopher Green's favorite joke was that he would rather be caught dead than join his family's funeral home business. It always got big guffaws from his friends. All kidding aside, he felt he had dodged a bullet by being gifted in sports, especially basketball, not to mention by turning out tall and lanky, like his grandfather on his mother's side, rather than short, rotund, and neckless like all the Green men, including and especially his father Ben. Without other options, they had no choice but to become morticians.

Christopher had felt destined for a more lively, glamorous career—maybe even becoming a pro player like Adam Ketchfield. Then, in his junior year in college, his world caved in. While still in his late forties, his father had a stroke, and his mother pleaded with Christopher to change colleges, to leave his basketball dreams behind and switch to an associates' degree in mortuary science to save the family business during his father's long recovery. Before he could say "embalming," Christopher became the fourth generation to sit at the helm of Green's Funeral Parlor.

As he tidied his office for the four o'clock appointment with Leon Ziemny and his daughter, he wasn't certain how to prepare for it. It wasn't as if they were coming in to do pre-planning, his favorite part of the job (no one fell apart during a pre-planning). No, the Ziemnys were coming to ask questions about some old burial that had occurred back in 1968, three years before Christopher was even born. He hoped it was nothing untoward; that is, that his family hadn't fucked up the burial somehow and Leon Ziemny was planning to sue or something. He said he was bringing his daughter along to the appointment, a New Yorker. And didn't New Yorkers like to sue?

Fortunately, Christopher's father and his grandfather before him had been meticulous file keepers, an attribute he sorely lacked, and so he farmed out the task of retrieving the old records to Mrs. Nichols, his elderly assistant. Mrs. Nichols had placed the average-sized file on his walnut desk a few hours earlier, and he thumbed through it now. *Lily Trudeau*; no middle name. After a quick scan of the papers, nothing seemed out of the ordinary, except maybe the cause of death listed on her certificate, *natural causes*, when she was only forty-two. Other than that, he could think of no reason that would necessitate a meeting nearly fifty years after the fact. He pulled at his cuffs, a familiar habit. A mortician was forced to wear a suit, and it was difficult to find one with sleeves long enough for basketball-player arms.

He heard familiar sounds outside his office, the flurry of sudden commotion that accompanied guests entering the front doors on otherwise noiseless days when there were no viewings—followed by the high-pitched greetings of Mrs. Nichols and the indecipherable murmurs of the newcomers, their voices growing slowly louder and more distinct as they approached his office at the end of the hall. When he got up from his desk and entered the hallway, he was surprised to see that there were three of them. He had been expecting Leon and Willow, of course, but the sight of the elderly Black man leaning on a cane beside them—the one

Cory Ketchfield had been ranting about when he came to fix the
leaky faucets in the Ladies' Room yesterday—stumped him. *This*
was an unforeseen development.

†††

Willow could have guessed that the gloomy office they were
led into would look exactly the way it did. Typical funeral home—
burgundy walls; a mahogany (or was it walnut?) table in the corner
of the room; a single lamp on his empty mahogany (or was it
walnut?) desk, with a Frank Lloyd Wright style lampshade; a wall
of classic, darkly stained bookshelves spoiled by rows and rows of
ugly black binders. As Christopher Green introduced himself to
her and Booker, he placed a file folder on the table in front of his
own chair before inviting them to sit down. "Please make yourselves comfortable," he said.

"Comfortable" was not even remotely on her list of emotions
when it came to this unusual meeting. Her hands felt clammy.

"This is my daughter, Willow," Leon said. "And this is Booker
Roberts."

Christopher nodded at Willow, extended his hand to Booker.

"How're your dad and mom doing?" Leon asked.

"Good. Thanks for asking." Christopher smiled; a smile
Willow observed to be a rather lopsided, half-hearted attempt,
with one side of his mouth rising slightly while the other side
remained flat. "They're enjoying the high retirement life in Florida.
No more worries—for them."

Leon nodded. "Yup, Florida's the place to be. Your dad still
feeling good?"

"Can't keep him down. In fact, he's too busy to track down

most of the time. He's still on a boatload of meds, but so far, so good." Christopher knocked on the wood table.

"Good to hear." Leon nodded a second time.

After the pleasantries, the room got quiet, quiet enough for Willow to notice the sound of the central air kicking into higher gear. Outside, another scorching August afternoon raged on, temperatures soaring into the high nineties, but not in here. In this dark room, she felt a distinct chill. She watched Christopher's thumb and index finger play with the edge of the manila folder in front of him. "Tell me what brings you in here today," he said.

For some reason, both Leon and Booker turned to her for the response. "Well," she began slowly, gathering her wits for the best way to phrase it. "It appears that my grandmother, Lily Trudeau, was buried with something of value. Not money-wise, but—" her voice trailed off. She glanced at Booker, who looked down at the sports cap he had removed from his head and was now twisting between his fingers. "She was buried with a family heirloom."

"A family heirloom?"

"A Bible."

"A Bible?"

Why was he repeating everything? "Yes, a Bible," she said. "And we'd like to get it back."

This line seemed to stop Christopher cold. His eyes enlarged; he pulled at his sleeves. "Do you realize what you're asking?" he said. "That would amount to exhumation of a gravesite. I don't think it's typically done—maybe it's *never* done—just to retrieve an item. One thing I do know for sure—we've never done an exhumation of a grave in Weeping Willow. This is new territory for me." He got up from the desk and began to scan the rows of black binders on the higher shelves of the bookcase.

"Can you give us some details about how she was buried?"

Booker asked. "I mean, can you tell us if they happened to use a burial vault?"

"A vault?" Christopher stopped his searching, seemingly flustered by the question. He returned to the table, back to the manila folder, and thumbed through the papers. "Damn," he said when he reached the correct sheet, "my dad gave her a concrete burial vault. And he didn't even charge them anywhere near—" Christopher stopped in mid-sentence.

Booker pumped his fist. "The Cadillac," he whispered to Willow.

The Cadillac, yes—she knew what that meant. It meant there was half a chance that the Bible might still be intact. Her heart was hammering. The exhumation was starting to feel real.

Christopher stood up, again scouring the bookshelves until he located the right binder. He stood on a small stool to fetch it, then brought it over to the table and opened it up. Within seconds, he began reciting a laundry-list of legal requirements and procedural steps, enough to make Willow's head spin. The more he read, the more animated his face became, as if the prospect was becoming exciting to him. Willow looked at her father, and his features seemed livelier too, but not from excitement. That telltale muscle in his cheek was throbbing. This wasn't going to be easy or inexpensive. They had to apply for a disinterment order from the probate court to be authorized to exhume the grave, get consent from the owner of the burial grounds and the next of kin, enlist the services of a plethora of people, including cemetery authorities, environmental health managers, various authorized officers. Then there was the costs of disinterment and reburial. On and on it went.

"Who owns the cemetery?" Willow asked.

"Fortunately, that one is easy," Christopher replied. "Our

funeral home does. But, again, I don't know if you can exhume a grave just to retrieve an object."

"What are reasons you *can* exhume a grave?"

He glanced at her blankly, as if he didn't have a clue. He flipped to another page in the binder. "It does list family choice as a reason," he said. "But the more common ones are things like … to do a medical examination into cause of death, or a police investigation for DNA, or to transport the body to another burial place, that kind of stuff."

"Does your file list Lily's cause of death?" Willow asked.

"Natural causes."

She was surprised that he didn't have to look that one up. "Natural causes? She was younger than I am now when she died. How can that be natural?"

He shrugged.

"As long as we're opening the grave," she said, "maybe we should exhume the body too."

"Willow!" Leon reached over to clutch her arm, as if trying to restrain her latest insanity. "What are you thinking? What difference does it make? No matter what she died of, she'll still be dead."

"But what was wrong with her exactly? Why couldn't she even talk?"

"I don't know, honey."

"I mean, how did she exist? How did she bathe? Could she eat by herself?"

"She ate if they fed her," Leon said. "They had to do everything for her."

"I just think it's kind of important to know exactly what she had." She looked into her father's eyes with the kind of intensity she hoped revealed the gravity of her concerns. "I mean, was it all mental? Was it physical? Did she have Alzheimer's like Walt? You can get early-onset dementia, you know, when you're still young like Lily was."

"Hold on there," he said. "I said I don't know."

"I've read that early-onset dementia is usually genetic, especially to a grandchild—that it tends to skip a generation. It might be good to know what's hiding in Adam's and my genes."

"Stuff hides in all our genes—that's just the way it is," Leon said. "As for me, I'd rather be surprised."

Christopher cleared his throat, seemingly to redirect their attention to the matter at hand. Willow watched him pick up the shiny black phone on his desk and ask his assistant to retrieve a disinterment packet from the files. "We have the application right here in the office," he said, hanging up. "After it's approved, along with the payment of the disinterment costs, we would have to go ahead within thirty days."

"How long will it take to process the application?" Booker asked.

"Shouldn't take too long," Christopher replied. "Unless you have to have additional hearings."

Booker frowned. "Additional hearings?"

"Yeah." Christopher drummed his pen against the folder. "Like if someone files an objection to the disinterment or something like that."

From the corner of her eye, Willow saw her father shifting in his seat.

"And the cost?" Booker moved forward to the edge of his chair. "Can you give me some idea of the cost? I'll be the one paying for it."

Christopher shifted his eyes toward him, a look of puzzlement on his face. "Oh. Okay …" he said. "Well, I can calculate the exact costs for you and give you a call. But it won't be cheap, that I can tell you." When the assistant entered the room with the papers, Willow saw that it was a relatively slim packet, which seemed a good sign. Retrieving the papers from her hands, Christopher held them out in front of him—to any one of them who might grab them first.

Booker seized the papers. "Here's my cell phone number." He slid a business card toward Christopher. "I'll wait for your figures, Mr. Green, and we'll see what we got." After planting his cap back on his head, he leaned on his cane to hoist himself from the chair.

Christopher escorted them to the door, then turned to face them. "Okay, I gotta ask." He looked at Booker. "Why are *you* the one footing the bill to retrieve *their* family heirloom?"

"It's a long and winding story," Leon said, slapping him on the back. "And I know what a busy man you are."

†††

As they crossed the parking lot toward Leon's car—Willow's Subaru was still loaded with her belongings from New York—Leon leaned in close to her ear.

"Tell you what," he said. "I'll give Joshua Wharton a call—he was the doctor here back in 1968. He's got to know something more about why Lily died. Maybe that will put your mind at rest."

Willow smiled, looped her arm through his as they walked. Every time she thought Leon wasn't hearing what she was saying, he showed her that he was. And every time she thought she loved him as much as a daughter could, he went and gave her another reason.

NINE

THE DOCTORS
WHARTON

J **OSHUA** Wharton was just about to leave for his daily jog when Leon Ziemny's enigmatic phone call came. Leon's voice sounded strained, a trace of urgency even, but he gave no clue as to the reason he was calling. "Can Willow and I talk to you as soon as possible?" That was all he said.

"It'll be nice to see Willow again," Joshua replied. "How about six o'clock?" He had met Willow only once before, briefly, but before he could ask how long she planned to be in town, Leon ended the call.

Joshua sat down, mulled things over. Earlier, he'd heard from Dolly Schmidt at the tavern that Leon had showed up there the other day with some stranger, and he wondered if this meeting had anything to do with that.

Joshua and Leon had grown friendly over the years. Born the same year, 1943, they had a similar frame of reference about the world, and they sometimes car-pooled to Bedlington when needing merchandise unavailable in Weeping Willow. Besides that, Joshua had a long history with the Trudeau family. He was the one who had nursed Noël through the fatal pregnancy that had resulted in Willow. Prior to that, he'd grown up alongside the Trudeau kids—Noël, Bo, Steve, and Adam, the youngest, whose memory troubled Joshua the most because it was Adam who

Joshua's beloved grandfather Harley had chosen as his protégé, not Joshua, to follow in his doctoring footsteps. Given all that, Joshua felt a complicated kinship with the family. How could he not?

Retired as of six years ago, Joshua sported a tidy, gray-streaked beard, a fringe of gray hair, and 1960s-style, wire-rimmed glasses that he kept pushing up to the bridge of his nose, a reflexive habit that now irritated his wife Melissa. Retirement had been an adjustment for both of them, mostly not a good one. A physician's wife learned to become independent early in the marriage, and now that he was no longer practicing, he was underfoot. With the exception of Joshua's father, three generations of Wharton men had chosen to become doctors. Harley was the first dedicated family physician in Weeping Willow. After him came Joshua, and now it was Joshua's son, Aaron, who assumed the mantle, though Aaron no longer practiced in Weeping Willow. Times had changed too much for that—running an independent family practice in a small town belonged to a bygone era. Aaron was now part of a larger practice of family doctors in Bedlington, affiliated with the hospital there.

He glanced at his watch, decided to skip the jog. Leon would be arriving in an hour, and he was always punctual—another thing Joshua liked about him. You could count on people who kept their word, who were reliable in small things. Even mediocre physicians like himself came to appreciate punctuality; it kept the flow of patients humming.

He and Melissa shared the old two-story home, first purchased by Harley Wharton back in 1939. The house was large enough for both to have their own space and privacy—he remained downstairs for the most part, while Melissa roamed the upper rooms. They got together in the kitchen at night, for supper.

As the story went, Joshua's grandparents, Harley and Lydia Louise, had moved to Weeping Willow from New York City after craving a softer existence, and they had been beguiled by the town during a coast-to-coast driving vacation they took back when their three children were teenagers. The shingled house was white when they'd found it, perfect for their needs, with ample space downstairs for a doctor's office, complete with its own side entrance. Lydia Louise was the one who insisted they change the exterior color to robin's-egg blue.

And robin's-egg blue it remained.

†††

At six o'clock sharp, Joshua was waiting at the side entrance when Leon's car pulled up, on the dot. Giving him a wave through the glass door, he watched Leon come up the sidewalk alone; no Willow. Once he entered, Joshua led him into the room that used to be his private doctor's office, a bright space with large windows, the summer sun streaming through.

"How's that little surgeon of ours doing?" Joshua asked.

"Rocket?" Leon grinned. "I swear he's gonna be the next Christiaan Barnard or whoever the hot doctor is nowadays. That kid doesn't play with balls—he plays with scalpels." He settled himself on the green leather sofa, and got right to the point. "Okay, Josh, this is the deal. We need to find out what Willow's grandmother died of, and we're hoping you can help."

Joshua was taken aback. He hadn't expected a reason like this for Leon's visit. Pushing his glasses against his nose, he sat down in the matching leather chair across from Leon. "What year did she die?"

"1968."

"Well, that's a problem," he said. "I wasn't the doctor here in 1968."

"You weren't? Well, it was your granddad then, right?"

"No. He died the year before."

Leon looked puzzled. "Then, who was?"

Joshua crossed his legs—another bad habit, bad for circulation. "For the last couple years of the sixties, there was another guy, a Dr. Young from Bedlington, who filled in as physician and coroner until I graduated medical school. He died a few years back."

"Then we're fucked," Leon said, folding his arms. "I thought there was *always* a Dr. Wharton in Weeping Willow back in the old days."

Joshua smiled. "For one rare moment in time, it wasn't so."

"Just my luck." Leon heaved a sigh. "So that's why Lily's death certificate said *natural causes*. That doctor probably knew shit about her history. Well, I guess that's that. Sorry to waste your time. I should've told you what I needed before I came rushing over."

Joshua's gaze drifted to the window. A cardinal sat in a low limb of one of the magnolia trees. When he occupied this office, he used to stare at those cardinals while writing his case notes, a task most physicians detested but that he actually enjoyed. His grandmother used to say that cardinals were visits from the dead. "You know, I remember Lily well," he said. "Poor woman. Those vacant, vacant eyes. Granddad said she had mental problems and left it at that." Another image entered his brain: Lily in her coffin, how oddly lovely she'd appeared—the loveliest corpse he had ever seen as a matter of fact, lovely enough to be memorable, even to a university student in the midst of feckless youth.

"I know what you mean." Leon nodded. "I never questioned what was wrong with her either. But you know my Willow. Once she gets a question in her brain, she's like a dog on a bone. She always needs to find out *why*."

Willow. Yes, Willow, the baby Joshua had urged Noël to abort to spare her own life, the person who wouldn't exist if Noël had listened to him. That Willow. Another Trudeau who haunted his conscience. And her brother too—little Adam Ketchfield, left without a mother at nine years old after Noël's avoidable death. There was no winning in that situation. "Is Willow in town for long?"

As he stood up, Leon gave a half-shrug in reply. He wasn't one to elaborate much; he held his personal life pretty close.

As Joshua led him slowly back through the hallway toward the old waiting room, he debated whether to ask the question floating around in his brain, then decided he knew Leon well enough to do so. "Listen, I've heard that you have a visitor at your home. Does Willow's need to find out about her grandmother have anything to do with that?"

"Nothing gets past the rumor mill around here, does it?" Leon shook his head.

"Sorry, I didn't mean to pry. I just thought maybe your visitor was some relation to Theckla Chavis, that's all." Prior to Leon's current houseguest, Theckla was the last Black person seen in Weeping Willow; she had come to town in the early seventies to tend to Noël during her pregnancy. Joshua recalled the endless scrutiny Theckla used to get from Willowites while shopping for groceries, curious more than malicious, as if they were seeing snow for the first time. No doubt about it, this town was as white as brand-new underwear. Without a chromosome of diversity, it had become a dusty collection of Protestant-type white people stuck in their ruts. Well, not so much Protestant anymore, but a mongrelized mixture of whatever was now being taught in that megachurch.

"No relation," Leon said. "I wish there was. Theckla was like a second mother to me."

The comment was a rare window into Leon's emotions. Every time Joshua happened to mention Theckla's name or anything remotely connected to Noël's final days, he couldn't help but notice the profound sadness that darkened Leon's face as if an inner light had been switched off.

"Booker's just a friend," Leon added. "He came all the way from New Orleans."

Eager to atone for dampening Leon's spirits, Joshua changed the subject to a brighter one. "Great city!" he said. He'd been to New Orleans many times for medical conventions, and he adored the city. Last year, he took Melissa there for her birthday, and she was uncomfortable the entire time because of the crime rate, clutching her purse against her belly like one of *The Golden Girls*.

Distracted, he shook Leon's hand before letting him out the door. Like it or not, the Trudeau family's history was all tangled up in the Whartons' sense of responsibility. As physicians, it came with the territory to carry a certain load of guilt whenever a heart, on their watch, stopped beating.

He plunked down into one of Melissa's fancy reupholstered chairs that adorned the old waiting room, his elbows on his knees, his head in his palms. His grandfather Harley had been a legend in his own right, to this day still revered by anyone in Weeping Willow who remembered that far back. Harley had spent decades caring for the townsfolk, including the Trudeaus, through one tragedy after the next. After Harley died, that weighty role had fallen on Joshua's shoulders. What he hadn't told Leon was that Harley's old files were still stacked in boxes in the basement. Most physicians kept medical records for as long as seven years, but he and his grandfather had held on to theirs, God knows why.

He knew why. The Doctors Wharton considered their patients to be extended family—it was part of being a small-town doctor. You were always on the clock, constantly on call, every weekend, every evening. Even when he went to dinner at The Seashell Supper House, someone would invariably stop by his table, point to where they had their latest pain, or take a seat to discuss their bursitis. The Seashell Supper House was long gone, but they still did it wherever they ran into Joshua, even though he couldn't do a thing to help them anymore. That was okay with him. They were family, and their health charts weren't dry, obsolete records; they were personal, a panorama of life history, of Weeping Willow history, and he couldn't just toss them away like empty milk cartons. He *had* to keep them. How could he not?

Joshua stood up, pushed his glasses against the bridge of his nose. He knew he was going to do it, though he pretended to himself he was still considering it. Maybe even as soon as tomorrow. He was going to go down into the basement and start hunting through those boxes, see what he might be able to dig up about Lily's medical diagnosis, for his own curiosity, and … for Willow's sake. He might have been a mediocre doctor, not the kind of legendary doctor his grandfather was, not the kind of legendary doctor that Adam Trudeau might have become had he not lost an arm in Vietnam. But he could do this for Willow, couldn't he?

He headed through the back door of his old office which led to the living room of their home, stopped suddenly, cursing softly under his breath. There was a problem with the plan, a glitch. HIPAA protected health information for fifty years after death. Whatever he might find down there in the basement, he was forbidden, for one more year, to share it with Willow.

Any secret he discovered would have to hold itself until then.

-TEN-

THE TO-DO LIST

THAT evening, Willow put on her reading glasses and began tackling the assortment of papers that Christopher Green had provided. She soon discovered that it was the first document, the *Application for Order to Disinter Remains,* that required her immediate focus. As Leon whipped up a dinner of ground-beef tacos and Spanish rice, she and Booker sat together at the dining room table to review the eleven items on the application—their "to-do" list, as she saw it. Each of the items had to be sworn to be true statements. "We're going to need a notary," she said.

Besides that, they had to compile a fair amount of accompanying material to go along with the application, including a copy of Lily's death certificate, a health certificate stating that she hadn't died from an infectious or contagious disease, a batch of notices and waivers, and who knew what else would crop up the more they got into it? "Do you think we should find a lawyer too?" she asked Booker.

"That would probably be a good idea. I know how complicated these things can get. I'd ask my son to do it, but we need a lawyer familiar with Ohio laws. Besides that, Cyrus doesn't even know I'm here—he thinks I'm vacationing on the Carolina coast."

Why the secrecy? Willow wondered, but she didn't feel it her place to ask. Inhaling the aroma, she turned around to glance at

Leon, who was chopping an onion at the kitchen counter, the Spanish rice already simmering on the stove.

"Leon, my man," Booker said. "You know any good lawyers around here?"

He shook his head. "I only needed a lawyer once since I moved here … and he died last year."

"Well, I guess that counts him out."

"But I'm pretty sure Clement Fitzpatrick, my insurance agent, has a law degree," Leon said. "I think he got it online."

Booker chuckled.

"You'll probably have to go to Bedlington to find one," Leon added.

"Bedlington?"

"The county seat."

"How about a notary, Dad?" Willow drummed her pen against the papers. "You know any of those?"

"Clement Fitzpatrick."

"He's a one-stop shop, isn't he?" She smiled. "Christopher Green can probably help us find the others who need to get involved, not only for the certificates and waivers, but the ones who have to be at the cemetery the day it happens." Adjusting her glasses, Willow tried to concentrate on the document, but the noise in the kitchen was distracting. Leon was making a real racket in there, rattling the pots and pans, ostensibly to find the right size to fry the onions, but she recognized the unnecessary clatter and clang as something else—a warning sign that he was getting upset. She watched him scrape the onions into the pan with daunting vigor.

"Is the whole town going to have to get involved with this thing?" he asked.

"Not to worry, brother," Booker said. "I'm paying for all of it, whatever it costs. Every last cent."

"It's not the money I'm worried about—especially if you're not." He removed the package of hamburger from the fridge, unwrapped it. "It's just that, I know what it's like to live here, and the less people know about your business, the better. ... And you, Booker—" He pointed a large wooden spoon at him. "You shouldn't have blurted out to Christopher Green that you were the one footing the bill."

Was *that* the reason for her father's sudden uneasiness? Willow noticed the careful way Booker was observing Leon, as if he too were trying to figure out his mood shift, though he said nothing in reply. Leon had been a very private man since the day she met him, and she'd observed the way he fought to keep his life here in Weeping Willow as quiet and unobtrusive as he could, which made it even more incredible when he had decided to reseed the willow trees for all to see.

Maybe he was right to feel uncomfortable. Though Booker was paying all the expenses, Willow was the actual *Applicant* on the paperwork, and she had no clue what she was getting into, legally or otherwise. But it was the right thing to do, and there was no turning back.

She looked down again at the application in front of her, read the first item out loud: "'Applicant is an interested person of sound mind who is at least eighteen years old.' ... Sound mind?—uh, oh. We've already got a problem." She hoped to lighten the mood with her joke, but neither man cracked a smile. She read the next few items, straightforward enough, silently. The fifth item on the list presented the first real complication—it required them to list all *legatees* and *devisees* named in Lily's will.

"What's a legatee?" she asked Booker. "A beneficiary?"

"Yup. You got it."

"How about a devisee?"

"That means anyone who might have inherited any real estate from your grandmother."

Real estate? Did this house count? "Okay, Dad. Here's another one for you. Did Lily have a will?"

"Hell if I know."

"Well, we have to find out. Maybe Uncle Steve knows." She jotted a note down on the legal pad beside her—another thing to ask when she called him tomorrow. The next few items on the application dealt with more will-related questions. Any legatees and devisees named in the will had to receive notice of the application by certified mail. If there was no will, notice needed to be given to all those who were entitled to inherit.

"The family was pretty small when Lily died," Leon said. "The only ones left were Noël, Steve, and Adam—and old Jack, of course. Frankly, I doubt he put anything in his wife's name, given her ... condition." He whirled his index finger around his ear, making the sign for "crazy." "As far as I know, Noël got nothing from her mother. Nada. Except one of her old paintings."

"One of her *paintings*?" Willow put down her pen. "Was Lily an artist?"

"That's using the term loosely," Leon said. "She dabbled in it, nothing like you and Ricky."

She rested her chin in her hand, distracted by this major piece of news Leon had just thrown into the mix. Well, at least *she* considered it to be major. "What happened to that painting? Do you know?"

"I found it leaning against the wall in the attic when I moved in. On the side where I store my junk. So I left it there, face down, where it belongs."

The diversion caused Booker to get up from the table and join Leon at the counter. After they returned from Green's Funeral Parlor, he had made a solo trip to the grocery store and local bakery to purchase a boatload of groceries and various assorted goodies to stock Leon's kitchen, another one of his ways to repay them for their hospitality.

Knowing how much Leon hated cooking, Willow was glad to take over the chore—starting first thing tomorrow. It was the least she could do after barging into his life. Come to think of it, maybe that's another reason he was getting pissed. They were sitting around while Leon was doing all the work in the kitchen.

Resting his cane against the cupboard, Booker leaned into the fridge. As he took out three bottles of premium beer, Willow couldn't miss the prohibitive look that Leon flashed his way. "It's okay, Dad," she said, shifting her eyes toward Booker. "I used to be an alcoholic. Well, technically, I guess I still am, according to the—experts." She put air quotes around the last word.

Nodding, Booker set all three bottles back inside the refrigerator.

"That doesn't mean you two can't have a beer! It won't bother me in the least. I gave it up years ago. Please, go right ahead."

"I have that in my family, too," Booker said, returning to the table. "Besides, I shouldn't be making my head fuzzy while we're in the middle of this." He sat down beside her, laid his hand over hers for a few seconds. "Now, where were we?"

Item eight, that's where they were. She read it aloud. "*Applicant states that the disinterment is not against Decedent's religious beliefs.*" She sifted through the accompanying papers. "This says we might need a written agreement from her church. Or from a church that the cemetery might be affiliated with … Did Lily go to church, Dad?"

"Lily didn't know a church pew from a toilet seat."

Yup, he was annoyed all right. Glancing at Booker, she raised her shoulder in a half shrug.

"Tell you what." Booker gathered up the papers, stuffed them back into a folder. "Why don't we give this a rest for a while? That Spanish rice smells too good to concentrate on anything but eating."

†††

Later, Willow went up the stairs to the attic for the night, switching on the lamp with the purple-tasseled shade before opening the door to the other half, the unfinished side. Feeling for the switchplate cover, she flicked on the light. A single overhead bulb dimly illuminated the space, and a distinct musty odor hung in the air along with a heavy dose of cedar.

How did Leon manage to accumulate all this junk? She scanned the space for a quick inventory—assorted Christmas decorations, including a fake tree covered loosely by a jumbo trash bag; dozens and dozens of stacked cardboard boxes; a man's bike, old enough to be an antique (since when did Leon ride a bike?); a couple of old cedar chests (so that's what accounted for the smell); and a dizzying array of other miscellaneous objects.

As she stepped through the mess, Willow visually hunted for anything that might resemble a canvas. She stumbled on some unidentifiable woodworking pieces as she noticed the Virgin Mary statue that used to stand against the garage in the backyard of her grandparents' home in Langston, Indiana; the nose had broken off again. She'd never known Leon to be a packrat, but here was the undeniable proof. Beneath the diffused lighting, the room was alive with shadows, like ghosts dancing between the rafters as she edged her way toward the back wall.

Finally, she spotted the canvas. Resting behind the Christmas tree, it was much larger than she had anticipated, maybe four feet by four feet. The painted side was turned against the wall, prolonging the mystery.

She continued maneuvering through the maze of junk. The only way she could extricate the canvas was to move the Christmas tree, and that wasn't going to be easy, given the densely packed space. Painstakingly rearranging several items one by one, she strained to do it quietly, so as not to awaken Leon or Booker. A little at a time, she managed to push the tree far enough away to rescue the painting.

In addition to being larger than she expected, the painting was also heavier. Gripping it at the top, Willow inched her way back to the entrance where she set it down, leaning it against her hip. She opened the door to the finished room, pulled it inside, and rested it against the wall. *Phew*, that was a work-out.

Now came the moment of truth. Sinking to her knees, she had her first look at Lily's artwork. She stood up, moved back, as far away as possible, to get the panoramic perspective. Either way, close or further back, the image was startling, shocking, disconcerting: A beautiful red rose being devoured by flames.

✝✝✝

Unable to sleep, Willow lay on the bed, staring open-eyed into the vaulted space. She was thinking that an attic had a much different aura than a basement. If a basement was the practical space for storage, the place to stow reliable things used more often, like old paint cans, tools, and the like—the brain of the house, if you will—then the attic was the soul. Arched to an apex like a cathedral, an attic was reserved for the rarer finds, the seldom-seens, the forsaken and forgotten treasures, the secrets.

She lifted her head to get a better glimpse of the painting. Yes, it was rather amateurish, but it was undeniably gripping. Lily had managed to convey the troubling emotions she must have felt while bringing it into creation—the well-defined brushstrokes, her nuanced choice of vibrant colors for both the delicate rose petals and the surrounding flames, juxtaposed against a stark, ominous, black background. This painting was very much alive. It jarred the senses. Who *was* Lily, really, to have painted such an unsettling work?

Her grandmother heavy on her mind, so was Lily's sister, Clarissa, the one who used to sleep up here in this very space. Save for her tombstone, Willow might not have known she even existed. Glancing around the room—at her choice of lampshade, her dresser, her desk—she searched for clues as to what Clarissa might have been like. The drawers in the dresser and the rolltop desk were empty; the rolltop part locked up tight, unable to be pried open. Willow had already attempted that last night, her first night up here. The key was nowhere to be found.

Her eyes refocused on the painting. She had taken a poetry appreciation class in college, so she knew a little bit about classical poetry, enough to know that Lily's tombstone epitaph about the fire and the rose had been taken from a famous poem, but she couldn't recall the title or the poet. Was this important in any way as far as her grandmother was concerned? Willow's mother, Noël, was the one who had chosen Lily's epitaph—Leon had told her as much. Maybe this painting had merely reminded Noël of that poem too, the same way it came to Willow's mind. No obscure message, no clandestine meaning. Lily probably didn't even know the poem existed when she painted it.

Willow reached for her phone on the nightstand, Googled the tombstone quote, and up popped "The Four Quartets" by T.S. Eliot. She read through the entire lengthy poem. "Wow," she whispered. "What a masterpiece." She had forgotten its richness and complexity, its depth and breadth in scope and subject—from the passage of time through seasons and generations, to war, to our connection with the dead, to salvation. She hadn't yet lived enough life to understand it in college, and she still couldn't fully comprehend its many layered meanings.

She read through it a couple more times, but the hour was too late for clear-headedness and deep thinking, particularly after such a long, peculiar day as this one had been, beginning with meeting Cory, the eccentric, followed by the trip to Green's Funeral Parlor, the disinterment application, and ending with this, Lily's distressing painting.

She switched off the lamp, rested her head on the pillow, closed her eyes.

It was no use. Tired as she was, any trace of a sleepy feeling eluded her. Reaching for her phone, she reread the poem in the dark room. Her imagination was working overtime. She sensed Clarissa's presence, not in a spooky way, but in a compelling one, as if Clarissa were dropping a trail of breadcrumbs for her to find. "Are you there?" she said softly. As she lay there on her back, she read a few of Eliot's lines aloud to the shadows in the vaulted ceiling—or was it to Clarissa?

We die with the dying:
See, they depart, and we go with them.
We are born with the dead:
See, they return, and bring us with them.

ELEVEN

UNCLE STEVE

WHEN Stephen Trudeau was just a boy, he loved to take baths. Unusual, yes, especially for a male child, but he craved the feeling of water, of pure cleanliness, soaking into his skin. Ever since his family fled Hyssop when he was only six years old, he had taken baths all alone, no mother there to supervise him, because she was incapacitated in the strangest way imaginable; still there, yet gone. But as long as he was sitting in water, he felt brand-new, like a clean, wet blackboard before the world could scribble all over him again.

Much of San Diego County was a desert, yet the city itself was a lush paradise with a perfect Mediterranean climate, and that was as good a reason as any for Steve to settle there nearly fifty years ago, when he left the US Navy. That and Betsy McGill, a quintessential California blonde who lured him straight from the ship into her beautiful golden-tanned arms, and he never looked back, not even once, to the life he'd led before, back in Weeping Willow, or even further back, in Hyssop. San Diego and Stephen Trudeau were completely simpatico: sunny with cool coastal breezes blowing through their wide-open spaces.

When their landline rang that Thursday morning and he saw Leon Ziemny's name on the caller ID, he didn't want to pick up, except that Betsy made it clear there was "No way José" she was going to be the one to answer that phone. As far as she was

concerned, Leon had stolen Willow and Adam away from them—
and after they had sacrificed so much to raise them, right along
with Amy, their flesh-and-blood daughter. Children cost money,
and taking in two orphans had meant they could no longer afford
to have more of their own. To compensate for cheating Amy, just a
year-and-a half older than Willow, Betsy felt it only right to shower
their own daughter with extra love, extra attention, extra devotion.
Still, after all they'd done for them, Willow and Adam remained
ungrateful, and she wanted no part of Leon Ziemny, the long-
missing father who had abdicated his role and then so easily won
Willow's affection as a grown woman.

Reluctantly, Steve picked up the receiver and found it wasn't
Leon calling—it was Willow.

"How're you doing, Uncle Steve?"

She sounded cheerful enough. The last time he had spoken
with her—a year ago?—she didn't sound so chipper. "I'm good,
kiddo." He smiled. "Great to hear your voice. How are you?"

She launched into a little spiel about doing just fine, adding
that she had moved to Weeping Willow, but she said it all so quickly
that Steve couldn't really insert any questions, nor did he want to.
Chipper or not, it sounded pretty not-okay for her to abandon
her life in New York City for a smudge of a place like Weeping
Willow. Before he could assimilate it, she was on to another topic
altogether, an unnerving one at that, something about needing his
permission to open up his mother's grave.

"What in heaven's name for?"

Her response was indecipherable, until she went and
mentioned the name "Raymond Roberts." Hell's bells! The sound
of that name, unspoken for decades, stunned him. Who could ever
forget a man like him?—the man that caused their family to run
away from Hyssop like bandits in the middle of the night? They

had seen and heard the way Raymond Roberts died, an abomi-
nation no one should see and hear, let alone children. Why was
Willow bringing him up again after so much time had passed?

She prattled on about Raymond Roberts' Bible being in the
same grave with their mother. Steve couldn't fathom such a thing.
His mother used to take him and his siblings to the tent revivals
when they were small, but other than that, he knew of no direct
connection between Raymond Roberts and his mother. As he
listened, Betsy kept asking, "What? What?" Judging by her own
expression, she'd probably caught the horrified look on his face.

"Well, if you think it needs to be opened up," Steve said, "then,
sure, you have my permission."

He desperately wanted to hang up. What more was there to
say? But Willow went on with another question. "Did your mother
have a will?"

A will? He tried to remember. He was still in the Navy when
his mother died, and he didn't (couldn't? wouldn't?) make it back
to Weeping Willow for her funeral. "I don't remember getting
anything," he said. But what would there have been to get? His
mother was an empty shell. His father had called the shots. Having
her own will, on paper or anywhere else, didn't fit. "No, I'm almost
positive she didn't have a will."

"Do you know what killed her?"

Steve rubbed his perspiring forehead. All these upsetting questions, coming out of nowhere. "Old age, I guess."

"She was only forty-two!"

"She was?" It sure seemed to him like she'd been much older
than that.

"What? What?" Betsy kept saying.

"Would you object if I had them exhume the body for cause
of death?"

For the love of Pete, what had gotten into Willow? Why was she, all of a sudden, so unwholesomely fixated on his late mother? Let the poor woman rest in peace. Part of him wanted to say that. "Do what you want," he said, instead. "I'll sign whatever you need me to sign, or a POA to give you the right to act on my behalf. Okay, kiddo?" That seemed to satisfy her, and the call ended there.

Betsy stood in front of him, hands on her waist. "What was *that* all about?"

He told her the basics—that Willow wanted to exhume his mother's casket, apparently because she was buried with a Bible that happened to be someone's family heirloom.

"Is it valuable or something?"

"Valuable? How valuable can an old Bible be?"

"I guess it depends on how old it is," Betsy said. "Is it some kind of ancient relic or something?"

"I don't know. I doubt it."

"Whose family does it belong to?"

"Someone we knew back in Hyssop."

"Back where?"

"Hyssop. The place in Louisiana where I was born."

When he saw the funny look Betsy gave him, he decided it best not to go into the part about exhuming the body too. Like him, Betsy wasn't much interested in long explanations about unpleasant subjects, and she sure didn't need any more fodder to hold against Willow. "Well, if it's worth money," she said, "I certainly hope you get your share. After all, you're the only direct descendant."

A few minutes later, she joined him in the backyard, wiggling her toes on the chaise lounge as he jumped into the pool with a splash. Amy and her two children were coming over later. Amy's first marriage had been childless, but she was in her second marriage now, her kids still small, and they loved to frolic in the pool. Later, he would grill hamburgers and hotdogs and make a party of it. They got together at least once a week like that. Sometimes more.

Steve loved his life here in San Diego, and he hated looking backward. The future was a clean slate, the past unchangeable. He dove again, submerging himself for as long as he could hold his breath under the cool water. It was a pity, a real pity, that Willow and Adam had never felt like part of their family after he and Betsy had tried so hard, making sacrifice after sacrifice for them. It sure hadn't been easy providing for two extra kids. California was an expensive place, money was tight, and Betsy had to go back to work again, get trained as a hair stylist, but even that wasn't enough, and so they had to dip into the bank accounts that the original Adam, Steve's youngest brother, had willed to Noël and her son. And dip, and dip, and dip, until both accounts were depleted. Was that what the younger Adam was so burned up about? When he had left San Diego, and Willow did too a few years later, they simply dashed away one day, like the wild fox squirrels Steve fed in the backyard—ate up his food, then dashed away, never to return. Since then, Willow had come to visit them a total of three times. And Adam? Never.

Betsy got bitter whenever she thought about it, but bitterness was not an emotion in Steve's repertoire. After Adam had left them at the age of eighteen, Betsy had boxed up his belongings—his globe, his old lucky baseball and collection of baseball cards, the baseball poster he'd hung on his bedroom wall—but he never came back to claim them. Betsy wanted to toss them out, but Steve couldn't bear to do it, so instead she stuck the box in their storage unit, where it sat to this day.

As Steve lay back on a rubber raft shaped like a duck, his hand stroking the cool water, he recalled the last time Willow came to visit, a few years back. They were walking on the white sand of Coronado Beach together, just the two of them, the ocean waves lapping to the shoreline, and Willow had asked him what he was thinking about as he looked at the sun setting on the water. "I guess I'm thinking about getting wet," he replied. Though his answer seemed to disappoint her, he felt no need to elaborate, to add the fact that he had craved the feel of water ever since he was six.

TWELVE

A SUMMER'S NIGHT

LEON sat at the dining room table, finally getting around to his monthly bills. His habit was to pay them on the first of every month, like clockwork, taking them out from the shoebox by the back door, checkbook in hand, the house totally quiet except for the bird clock. But not this month. Since Willow and Booker's arrival eleven days ago, his routine was shot, the little chores and odds-and-ends gone to hell. Two days ago, Willow's crated-up paintings had arrived from New York, and the two of them (though he tried to help, Booker's mobility counted him out) spent the afternoon hauling them down to the basement, a grueling task, yet one that gave a sense of finality to her move.

Things seemed to be settling down into some semblance of normality again. A new normal, a better normal; certainly a fuller one. Leon's life now included his daughter living under the same roof with him for the first time in either of their lives, and, for now anyway, Booker too, who was staying with them longer than either he or Booker had anticipated. Driving back and forth to New Orleans while waiting for approval of the disinterment application didn't make much sense, especially since Booker had fibbed to his son about where he really was. Besides that, Booker proved himself to be an affable and thoughtful houseguest who had morphed into a solid friend. Their nightly talks on the back deck were one of the best parts of Leon's day.

Leon hadn't realized how lonely he'd grown over the past few years. Loneliness, he guessed, was one of those things that crept up on you like wrinkles, slowly, gradually, until ...*holy shit!* One day he caught his reflection in a store window and thought he'd seen his father.

Booker was good for Willow too. She was a thinker, and Professor Booker gave her plenty of deep contemplations to mull over, not to mention her holy mission of assuring the exhumation happened.

Leon listened to the sounds of Willow preparing dinner in the kitchen, Booker sitting nearby on a tall stool, coaching her about New Orleans cuisine. She had been itching to give it a try and make a special dinner of it—an ambitious menu of both jambalaya and beignets. Admittedly, Booker was no cook, but he was glad to offer the benefit of years of experience with "N'awlins" dining.

As far as the exhumation, arrangements seemed to be on track there too, all the players finally added to the mix. Booker and Willow had located a competent attorney in Bedlington to facilitate the process, and he was able to confirm that Lily left no will. Christopher Green obtained a written statement from the pastor of the church affiliated with the cemetery, which turned out to be the First Methodist Church. Yesterday, they received Steve Trudeau's waiver in the mail, and the application had been filed.

Leon had been surprised to learn that the cemetery was still affiliated with the First Methodist Church. He'd heard the old church was in danger of closing. Attendance at all the small churches in town was suffering because of the megachurch, the one Leon passed on his way to Bedlington—a mammoth, pure-white structure with gold-embossed, arched doors, a tall white spire, a pond out front. Only thing was, they forgot to hang a cross on it, so it looked more like a country club than a church.

Maybe that was the point—to cast a wider net, including Telles and Nancy Salvo next door, Dolly Schmidt, Jeff and Linda Miller, Cory Ketchfield, and a batch of others who seemed to think their pastor could transform water into champagne. Leon had seen the guy shopping in Rose's Drugstore a time or two, a pompadour of silver hair on his head, a smile full of pearly-white veneers, a big, fat sparkly diamond ring on his pinky finger. Saving sinners must be a lucrative business nowadays.

As Willow prepared the meal, Booker shared Mardi Gras stories, getting up from his stool occasionally to help her do this or that. While they cooked, they played music, mostly jazz, from some public broadcasting station on Leon's radio, not his usual rock and roll oldies channel. "My brother, Ray, played jazz clarinet, just like that one," Booker was saying. "When he was in college, he was in a band—they called themselves The Mellows."

His bills paid, Leon opened his laptop and sifted through his emails, the majority from companies he had purchased items from, enticing him to reorder. Punching the delete button one by one, he tried to whistle along to the music without the foggiest idea of the tune—the crazy way jazz music zigged and zagged. He was feeling pretty damned good. Later on, Adam, Anne, and Rocket were planning to join them for dinner and they were making a party of it.

Leon checked the online version of the *Langston Sentinel*, the newspaper from his old hometown in Indiana. He looked it over every day, mostly to keep up on the obituaries of people he used to know. An article in the metro section snagged his interest—the city was planning to tear down several blocks of buildings in the neighborhood where he and Noël lived during their marriage, including their old apartment building—the place to which Noël had run away with toddler Adam to escape David Ketchfield.

The place where Leon had first met her, and later Theckla and Freddie Chavis, who lived in the apartment one floor below. The place where Leon had spent the most magical days of his life. The thought of it being imploded was a sucker punch.

†††

Adam enjoyed being over at Leon's for dinner, and the food was delicious—all that sugar and sizzling-hot spice a welcome change from Anne's skinnied-down, healthy fare. It was their first opportunity to meet Booker. Adam observed him to be a gentle, intellectual man who gave whoever was speaking his undivided attention. After dinner, they sat around watching the small television in the corner of the dining room until Leon suggested they go out back to the deck. As each person picked up a second, or third, helping of beignets, and their drink of choice, Leon turned the TV volume down low. Adam chose chardonnay.

Another hot evening, the shadows were growing long across the lawn. In a half hour or so, give or take, it would be nightfall. Adam loved summer nights, including the soothing sounds of crickets in the bushes, the twinkling dots of fireflies in the darkness. Settling into his chair, he glanced around contentedly—full belly, full heart. Rocket, sitting cross-legged on the deck beside his chair, was even more talkative than usual. Booker seemed to know how to draw kids out. Adam presumed it was because of his training as a professor, or maybe he simply knew how to ask the kinds of questions kids wanted to answer. No small feat. Pretty soon, Rocket was sharing his goal of becoming a neurosurgeon.

Booker whistled, impressed. "That's a mighty fine calling, young man. Not an easy one, either. How are your grades in school?"

"Good!" Rocket looked at his mother, paused. "Well, most subjects."

"You enjoy science?"

"Yeah!" His eyes lit up. "That's my favorite! For the science fair last year, I made a replica of the lobes of the brain to show how each part does different things. It was really cool! I won first prize!"

"I'll just bet you did. The lobes of the brain are fascinating." Booker brushed some flecks of powdered sugar from his shirt, a casualty of the beignets. Adam peered down at his own shirt, frosted like a Mini-Wheat, and wiped himself clean. "What subjects don't you care for that much?" Booker asked.

Frowning, Rocket glanced at Anne again. "Mostly English."

"English is sure different from science, isn't it?" Booker agreed. "It requires a whole different lobe of the brain. You know, you're gonna have to keep up *all* your grades, if you want to become a neurosurgeon. You want to get into a good medical school, don't you?"

"The best one!" Rocket nodded. "But there's lots of time for that, Mr. Roberts."

"*Doctor* Roberts," Adam corrected. "He's a college professor with a PhD."

Booker waved his hand. "Just plain old Booker is fine with me." He took a sip of sherry. "Time goes by fast, young man, trust me. The time to develop good study habits is when you're young. Then you're ahead of the game. English can be exciting, too. A good book can open up a whole new world, like growing a deeper set of eyes ... You ever read *Complications: A Surgeon's Notes on an Imperfect Science?*"

Rocket shook his head. "There's really a book like that?"

"There surely is. You might want to read it sometime—I think you'd like it. It's hard, but reading over your age is a good thing."

Adam leaned over to tousle the top of his son's head. "Maybe we can go to the library tomorrow and look for it. What do you say?"

Rocket smiled up at him, nodded.

Adam stood from his chair, stretched his arms high into the air. "Can I get anyone a refill?" Having no takers, he slid open the glass doors and stepped inside into the dining room. Willow had spread a full array of food and drinks on the table. Locating the chardonnay bottle, he poured himself a fresh glass. The TV was set to a news channel, the sound still off, and they were showing some march somewhere, with throngs of angry people, both the marchers and those on the sidelines. The "breaking news" tagline on the bottom of the screen read, "Unite the Right rally continues."

Heavy-eyed, Adam stared at the chaotic scene; he'd eaten too much and the wine was starting to make him drowsy. Too much of a good thing. Setting his glass down, he grabbed another beignet off the platter, his third. Weight wasn't ever much of a problem, and he could work it off tomorrow on the stationary bike that Anne had gotten him for his birthday. He glanced back at the screen. The tagline had changed:

"Live from the white nationalist rally in Charlottesville."

Adam's thoughts raced. He struggled to pull them together. Cory was a racist. And Cory was in Charlottesville—that's what he had told him last week, wasn't it? He did say "Charlottesville," didn't he? That rally couldn't possibly be what he'd gone down there for. Could it?

He tried to convince himself otherwise, but he already knew the answer. "Oh, my God," he moaned. The beignets and spicy food were churning. Seized by a sudden sick feeling, Adam leaned against the counter.

†††

That evening, Joshua Wharton located the boxes among the vast collection in the basement, the ones marked by the letter *T* and the decade dates, *1950s* and *1960s*. It took a while, but he thumbed through the files until he found the right ones, three fat folders, labeled with the name *Lily Trudeau* in his grandfather's unpretentious handwriting, unusually legible for a physician. He pulled the files out of the boxes, relocated to the wooden chair in the corner, and took a seat.

Setting the other two folders down on the floor, he opened the most current one first, *1964-1967*. Harley's notes were assembled in chronological order, with each latest examination on top of the rest, two-hole punched and held with a clip, easy to peruse.

Joshua took a breath, pushed his glasses against the bridge of his nose.

Lily's final examination was dated *Monday, November 13, 1967*, a month before Harley's death. Along with Lily's medical stats, blood pressure, heart rate, weight, body temperature, the top page included his grandfather's handwritten notes: "Lily appears to be digressing into malignant catatonia," he wrote. "Her blood sample, i.e., her sodium, potassium, urea, and glucose levels, indicate increasing dehydration and kidney failure."

Malignant catatonia. So there it was.

Joshua set the file down, picked up the oldest folder, *1953-1958*, this time flipping back to the last page, to the first time Harley had ever examined Lily, dated *Friday, August 28, 1953*: "Patient is a twenty-seven-year-old woman. Her husband reports that she is four months pregnant with their fifth child, though she has gained little weight. Presenting symptoms include extreme agitation and confusion. She clutches at her abdomen sporadically and moans. My observations are that she appears to vacillate between akinetic catatonia—where she does not respond to stimuli and stares blankly as if in a daze—and excited catatonia, when she moves around in a state of delirium and mimics my movements during examination, though she does not speak. Her husband states that these symptoms first appeared two weeks ago, when the family left Hyssop, Louisiana. Husband does not understand what might have contributed to the onset of these symptoms, other than the fact that she was upset by the move. He further reports that she has had a lifelong history of melancholia, sometimes severe enough for hospitalization. He reports there is no history of drug or alcohol abuse. Will follow-up with complete physical, psychiatric, and neurological workup."

Flipping to the summary of Lily's second examination in 1953, a few days later, it was confirmed in Harley's handwriting: "Tests conclude patient is fifteen weeks pregnant. Pregnancy appears to be on track, though patient continues to rub her stomach repeatedly."

Joshua closed the file, contemplating the implications. If Lily was twenty-seven in 1953, she was only eighteen when she'd had her first child, Beauregard, the one they called Bo. Joshua knew that without the need to calculate the dates, because Bo had been a year ahead of him in school, Noël two years behind him, then Steve and Adam bringing up the rear, three and four years later, respectively. That certainly was a gaggle of babies for Lily to carry right in a row—bang, bang, bang, bang—especially for one who suffered from depression. And now here came one more. Joshua flipped through Lily's folder until he found the record of her youngest child's birth, Monroe. It was dated Christmas Eve, 1953. His grandfather's notes were uncharacteristically sparse: "Patient went into unexpected early labor. Stillborn male, weighing four

pounds, one ounce, born three weeks prematurely, at 10:07 p.m.,
in the patient's home."

He gazed down at the open folder balanced on his knees. He
had never thought of it that way before, but Jack Trudeau must
have been a bit of a brute to make his wife bear all those children so closely together. Though Harley didn't notate the cause for
the stillbirth, it could have been attributed to a condition called
preclampsia, high blood pressure that can begin around the thirty-
fourth week of pregnancy. One of the risk factors for developing
preclampsia was having had multiple children less than two years
apart.

Joshua shook his head. When he was young, he'd been quite
impressed by Jack Trudeau—perhaps "intrigued" was a better
word. Then again, most everyone was intrigued by Jack. Certainly,
he was an anomaly in Weeping Willow, a dashing figure, a defi-
nite cosmopolitan air about him. Customary male attire in town
was work clothes, flannel shirts, suspenders, jeans, but Jack favored
silk ties, tailored suits, and wing-tip shoes, tangible vestiges of a
mysterious occupation that took him regularly to large cities on
the East Coast. After the stillbirth of Monroe, Lily's sister Clarissa
Montgomery moved from New Orleans to care for Lily and her
children. And after she died, Lily's care fell squarely on Jack's shoulders. His traveling days over, his personality eroded over time, the
fancy trappings slowly falling away. Jack Trudeau seemed a broken
man after Lily's death. Not too much later, he suffered a fatal heart
attack, all alone, while shoveling snow.

Joshua redirected his attention back to the files. Flipping
through the myriad pages, he gave them a cursory glance—docu-
mentation from year after year of his grandfather's valiant and
fevered attempts—including an endless array of tranquilizers such

as Miltown, sedatives, homeopathic treatments—to rid Lily of her gripping catatonia. But in the end, he failed.

Joshua closed the file folder. Sad story, sad ending. Well, at least he had found the answer. He now knew what killed Lily Trudeau.

✝✝✝

Adam was taking too long, Leon thought. Over twenty minutes had gone by since he had gone inside to pour himself another drink. By then, the conversation on the deck was in full swing among the rest of the group, especially Rocket, a little talking machine this evening. Leon glanced at his watch again. Rising from his chair, he went back inside the house to check on Adam.

Leon found him sitting alone in the living room, head in hands, staring at nothing. Something was definitely up. Had he had too much to drink? Leon sat down across from him.

"You know, when I was a little kid," Adam said, without looking up, "I believed in angels. Kind of a sissy thing, huh? They were like my superheroes. But I stopped believing in them, and in a whole lot of other things, on the day Mom died. I needed a mother, not an angel."

Uncertain what to say and afraid he'd say the wrong thing, Leon remained silent. It was best to let Adam get out whatever was bothering him in his own way.

"Maybe I loved angels because I knew there was a curse hanging over me."

"A curse? Come on, Adam. That's crazy talk."

"Is it?" Adam's eyes met his. "I'm part Ketchfield, aren't I? That's curse enough for me."

Was it the wine that had deteriorated Adam's mood into this dark place? "You're nothing like Cory," Leon said, "and you know it." He waited for him to say something. Adam lowered his head. "Where's this coming from?" Leon asked. "What's *really* bothering you?"

"What's bothering me." Adam repeated it as a monotone statement, not a question. "Hmmm. Let's see." His eyes skittered to the back deck. "Did I tell you that Cory took a trip to Charlottesville?"

"Good." Leon nodded. "I mean, good riddance. Enjoy the vacation while you can."

Adam picked up the remote from the coffee table, the one for the gigantic, curved screen over the fireplace, Leon's pride and joy, and switched on the television. His back to the screen, Leon assumed he was trying to change the subject, end their talk, but the sight of Adam's unblinking eyes riveted to the screen was enough to make him twist his head around to look.

Leon tried to assimilate the scene unfolding on TV. A steady stream of white men carrying tiki torches as they marched through the University of Virginia campus, chanting white supremacist and Nazi slogans, but he didn't understand its direct relevance to Adam's dismal mood until the television screen flashed the tagline: "Breaking News: White Nationalist Rally Continues in Charlottesville."

"Holy shit!" Leon sat up. "You're thinking Cory's in that crowd?"

"That's exactly what I'm thinking."

Leon resettled himself on the sofa beside him. They were both searching each face that passed in front of the TV cameras—too many faces to show them all—but there was no sign of Cory among them. The coverage switched to another news topic.

"Maybe you got it figured out wrong? Maybe Cory went there for something else."

"Maybe so," Adam said. "Maybe he just moseyed on down to Charlottesville to soak up the ambiance and just happened to run into a mob who hates Black people as much as he does." He ran his fingers through his hair in agitation. "And maybe pigs fly."

Leon nodded. It was unlikely that it was a coincidence. "Holy shit," he said again. Clicking off the TV, he tried to figure it out, what it meant for them, what their next step should be. His first thought was of Booker, the only Black person in Weeping Willow, sitting out there on his back deck. "When's Cory coming back?"

"In a couple days, I guess." Adam shrugged. "He didn't say much about it. Just that he was going down to Charlottesville, that's all. He spends a lot of time on that computer of his, and God only knows what kind of crap he's been filling his brain with. But this Charlottesville thing jacks it up to a whole new level. Especially as long as Booker is in town."

"We've got to give Booker a heads up, that's all. Make sure he stays safe while he's here."

As the bird clock erupted in ten shrill tweets, Adam visibly jumped. When the room was quiet again, he spoke. "You know, I never understood racism."

"That's because you had a good mom."

"And I had Theckla Chavis. And Freddie."

"Yup, them too."

Leon went into the kitchen and poured both of them a splash of wine. He came back to Adam and handed him a glass. "Before Theckla and Freddie came along," Leon said, "I used to be a bit of a bigot myself. Not a certifiably crazy Cory-type. Just your average, run-of-the-mill, second generation bigot—on my mother's side."

"Not you."

"Yeah, me." Leon sat down. "People like my mother, like I was, like a lot of people in this town—I think they're ignorant more than racist. People are afraid of what they don't know, and if you don't know any Black people, or yellow people, or brown or red people—or Polacks like me—then you stay ignorant. There used to be a couple guys at the steel mills who called me 'the dumb Polack with the unpronounceable last name.' After they got stuck working with me on the same shift, they eventually got past the Polack thing. I think that's why they try so hard to keep Blacks and Whites apart—they're afraid we might start *knowing* one another and, next thing you know, God forbid, we might start *liking* each other … But people like Cory? He's the highest notch of ignorant. White nationalism is some scary Nazi shit … Maybe we should call the police."

"And say what?" Adam threw up his hands. "That he went to a rally? That's not against the law."

Leon looked in the direction of the back deck, toward the sound of laughter. "Here's what I think we should do. I'll tell Booker and Willow tonight. You tell Anne when you get home. I have a pretty good feeling Booker will still want to stay here 'til this disinterment thing is done. He and Willow found an attorney in Bedlington who's trying to speed up the process so he can get back to New Orleans as soon as possible. Until that happens, we'll just have to make sure he sticks close to the house, just in case Cory has some crazy ideas in his head … You think he might?"

"I doubt it," Adam said. "I doubt he'd stoop *that* low." His eyes looked haunted. "Then again, I never thought he'd stoop low enough to go parading around with white nationalists either."

Leon drained his glass, punched him on the knee. "Don't worry, kid. It'll be okay. We're in this thing together."

†††

Sitting outside on the back deck after Adam and his family had gone home, Booker took the news with much less trepidation than Leon had imagined. "Welcome to my world," was what he said. "When you're Black, it comes with the territory. Every morning you wake up, you learn to live with the possibility that someone could be out to get you."

Leon shook his head. "That's a hell of a way to have to live."

Willow's eyes filled with tears.

"Listen, Leon, I won't take any stupid chances," Booker said. "But finding my brother's Bible is too damned important to me. I can't stop living just because of some fool."

-Thirteen-

FLESH AND BLOOD

THECKLA Chavis was sitting at the dining room table beneath the bird clock, arms folded, obviously angry with him, and Leon understood why, though no words were spoken. She was angry because Leon hadn't come to Noël when she was pregnant. Theckla, on the other hand, *was* there. She was there when Noël left this world. She was there when Willow entered it. And he was not. Theckla's unforgiveness was the verdict he deserved without even trying to dissuade her otherwise. He had been here before.

Suddenly, Theckla got up from the table, came toward him, arms outstretched. Leon had no idea how bad he looked until he saw the pained scrutiny with which she observed him. Cupping his face in her palms, she said, "Listen to me, baby. It was beyond your control. I know that Noël wasn't able to find you to tell you she was pregnant." Her fingers felt warm, like a lifeline. "It's time to forgive yourself."

Leon sat up in bed. He'd been here before, the dream a recurring one in which Theckla was always seated at the table, arms crossed, brows creased in anger. Sometimes his mother joined the dream, parking herself beside Theckla in the exact same pose. He'd had this dream for years, except this time it had a surprise ending. This time, Theckla had absolved him.

Leon glanced at the clock on the nightstand: six a.m. He knew why he was dreaming the dream again now. It always came when he was stewing over something, and lately he had been stewing over good and plenty. Nearly two weeks had passed since his conversation with Adam. Cory had returned to town without incident, and so far, he hadn't even contacted Adam, which wasn't unusual. They knew Cory had resurfaced only because Christopher Green had mentioned in passing that he was doing another plumbing job at the funeral home. Added to that, the disinterment application had been approved, as of yesterday, and they had only thirty days to go through with it. And added to all of that, Leon and Noël's old apartment building in Langston was scheduled to be demolished later this afternoon.

Leon got out of bed, stumbled into the bathroom, splashed cold water on his face. Willow was foremost on his mind too. With both feet, she was throwing herself into this Lily thing, but what would happen afterward, after the exhumation took place and she had no more rescue efforts to distract her? It had been the same with his father's Alzheimer's, way back when. Willow had swooped into their lives like Florence Nightingale to tend to him. That's the way his little girl was. Without a worthy mission to engage her, her spirits sank like a rock.

He wiped his face with exaggerated vengeance, trying to rub it all away, then stared at his own reflection in the mirror, his hair disheveled, standing up every which way. Willow wasn't doing her art anymore. Her art grounded her, an outlet for her emotions. Now that she lived here, he would hook her up with Dr. Aaron Wharton for when the time came to get her depression medications renewed. He couldn't just stand by and watch her slide into depression again—not that deadly Trudeau depression.

He heard Booker moving about in his room, readying himself for the final meeting in Bedlington with the attorney. Adam and his family were planning to ride along with Booker to do some shopping in the mall; afterward, they hoped to grab a late lunch together at Rocket's favorite pizzeria. Willow had opted to skip the meeting with the attorney and spend the day holed up in the attic working on her next assignment for the art magazine.

Everyone else occupied, Leon was thinking about taking his own little road trip. It had been too long since he'd groomed the graves of his family in Langston and, while there, why not have a last look at the old apartment before it was blown to smithereens? With Booker underroof and all these other complications, he and Willow hadn't really had the chance to have a heart-to-heart talk since her arrival, and it was long overdue. Maybe he could convince her to play cyber hooky and ride along with him.

†††

As it turned out, Willow was eager to ditch her work and join him for the nearly two-hour drive. Thirty minutes into the trip, they stopped at a diner formerly known as the Crossroads Café, now renamed Vera's Vittles. Vera offered one of those ridiculously extensive menus—breakfast, lunch, and dinner served anytime— too many goddamned choices as far as Leon was concerned. A simple ham and cheese sandwich, with a side of fries, would do him just fine.

Willow couldn't decide on anything. "I guess, I'm not really that hungry," she said.

"You gotta eat sometime. Might as well be now."

She shrugged. "I'll have the cheese blintzes, then."

After their orders arrived, Leon tried to prime the pump. "So tell me," he began, "how do you like living in Weeping Willow so far?" The conversation-starter sounded unnatural, rehearsed, which, of course, it was.

She picked at one of her blintzes, eyeing him with that curious, albeit suspicious, expression she sometimes made. Whenever he started probing into her life, she tended to get defensive, same as he did. "It's been good," she said.

It took a few more tries of stiff openers before the conversation got rolling on a more authentic level. She confessed that she'd been "sort of" depressed when she decided to leave New York, but that it was behind her now, the fog had lifted. Nevertheless, she agreed to set up an appointment with the younger Dr. Wharton. Quickly, she redirected the topic to Cory. "He causes Adam so much grief," she said. "Maybe we should all leave Weeping Willow—together. Find another place." Her eyes brightened. "Maybe somewhere surrounded by mountains."

"Mountains? Yeah, sure, that'll be nice and cheap. How about Rio de Janeiro, while we're at it?" A bad attempt at humor, but Willow could be impractical at times. Packing up and starting over might be easy for her, but a big move to another city in this phase of life—surrounded by mountains, no less—wasn't in the cards for him anymore. He hated that Adam felt knocked for six by Cory's presence, yet running away from a home that he and his family loved didn't seem like the right answer.

His sarcastic Rio de Janeiro comment stopped the flow of conversation. Yup, his little girl could be a closed book all right. He tried again. "I've noticed you haven't done any paintings since you've been in Weeping Willow."

"We've got enough of them, don't we?" She swirled her spoon through her coffee. "The whole basement is cluttered with them."

"Yeah, but what about the *next* one?"

She made brief eye contact, turned away. "There's so much else going on, including my job. I thought I'd give painting a rest for a while."

"Give it a rest? How can you do that? It's who you are, isn't it?" Her slumping posture straightened, as if he'd struck a nerve, so he kept on going. "Look, Willow. I don't understand what you're feeling, and I want to. You're gonna have to paint me a picture."

Maybe it wasn't the right thing to say, but it seemed to work. A smile came to her face, a little like her mother's smile, and she decided she was hungry after all.

†††

Once they were back in the car, somewhere between Vera's Vittles and Langston, Willow started chatting, in small anecdotes at first, about life in New York, how peculiar the subway smelled, especially in the early mornings when the riders were preened up for the workday; how she missed the continuous noise of taxi horns, stuff like that. Leon listened attentively as he steered the wheel, glancing over at her every now and then. Eventually, the topic shifted to the Trudeaus. She wanted to know more about Clarissa, the one Noël called Aunt Clarry.

"I spend a lot of time in her room in the attic," Willow said. "And I find myself thinking about her at night before I fall asleep."

With the abundance of trauma in the Trudeaus' past, Clarissa Montgomery, as far as Leon was concerned, was an unnecessarily disturbing detour, a sidebar he had hoped to avoid. "I heard you hammering up there the other day," he said.

"Yeah. I found that painting of Lily's you told me about, and I hung it up on the brick chimney."

Leon wondered how Willow had managed to sink a nail into brick, but she was an artist and knew the tricks of the trade; she probably strung up a wire or something. She persisted in asking questions about Clarissa.

"Okay, okay. Here's all I know," Leon said. "Clarissa moved to Weeping Willow from New Orleans after Monroe's stillbirth. Jack traveled for his job, and Lily was in no shape to raise all those kids."

She paused. "For how long?"

"Clarissa stayed 'til Bo was grown and the others were in high school."

"That's a long time."

For a moment, Leon thought he was off the hook as far as dishing out any further information. But Willow was too smart for that. "Wait a minute," she said. "It's right there on her tombstone. Clarissa died when she was still young, and she was buried in Weeping Willow, not New Orleans. She didn't just *leave*, she *died* … So how did she die?"

What the hell, she'd worn him down, and he knew she wouldn't drop it. "She killed herself," he said bluntly.

"She *what?*"

He took his eyes off the road to see how the news was hitting her. Thankfully, she looked curious more than upset.

"How did she do it?"

"Gunshot, I guess."

"Whoa." She leaned back in her seat. "Do you know why?"

"Nope."

Nope was a half-truth. It had something to do with Clarissa submitting to Jack Trudeau's advances in order to stop him from forcing himself on Lily—Noël had told him that much. But he wasn't certain, exactly, how that arrangement ended up driving Clarissa to the point of suicide, though who the hell could stand to be touched by a snake like Jack? If Leon were a betting man, he'd lay money down that Jack had gotten Clarissa pregnant, and the poor woman was trapped. That theory was only a hunch, and if he wasn't certain, why say anything at all? "Nope" seemed a good enough answer. He stared straight ahead as he drove.

"There's so much I don't know about Mom's family." Willow sighed. "It's my own fault. I never bothered to ask." From his peripheral vision, he sensed her eyeballs boring into him, that pleading look that always got to him. "But I'm asking now, Dad."

They were a little better than halfway to Langston. "Okay, then," he said. "Ask away. Ask me anything you want. Just remember, the Trudeaus are riddles—they had a hell of a lot of secrets—and I don't know all the answers. Not even about your mom. She told me some of her secrets, but I doubt she told me all of them. Besides, some secrets are better off left that way."

As they approached Langston's city limits, he had managed to give a fairly thorough response to each question she posed. For the time being anyway, his daughter's insatiable need to know seemed satisfied.

✝✝✝

A gritty town even in its prime, Langston, Indiana had deteriorated into one of those dismal, dying steel mill cities that was long past its heyday. Four years since his last visit there, Leon wanted to head straight to the cemetery, but Willow had other ideas. She wanted to take a detour to the old Polish neighborhood where he and his family used to live. "I haven't seen it since you left," she said.

And so he steered the car in the direction of his old home. The streets became increasingly lined with boarded-up businesses and long-neglected houses in sore need of repairs. Finally, they reached the heart of the old neighborhood, once all Polish, now mostly

Mexican, with a handful of Blacks and moldy old Polacks sprinkled into the mix. Leon turned the car onto the narrow street lined with parked cars on either side, Pulaski Street, the street where he'd spent his entire life until Noël Trudeau came along, and it felt, strangely, as if he'd never left. A trick of the brain. Funny how that worked when you found yourself revisiting a place indelibly embedded in your consciousness—half-then, half-now, almost like double vision.

Most of the homes remained in disrepair—shingles falling away, paint chipping, that kind of thing—but many of them actually looked better than they had in a long while, spruced up for a new generation. As they were passing the old brick building that used to be his father's cherished neighborhood bar, Willow cried, "Stop!"

He hit the brakes, pulled over to the curb, and they both examined the old building. Every single window, along with the front door, was boarded up, a shower of graffiti sprayed over the brick. Weeds grew tall between the cracks in the sidewalks. A sign over the door that used to say "The Mazurka Inn" now read, "El Sabor de México," apparently the last business to occupy the space.

"Oh, Dad." Willow turned to look at him, her face filled with emotion. "This brings back so many memories, doesn't it? I can picture Walt cleaning the top of the bar with that old rag of his. Remember his Wall of Fame?—all those old photographs he had framed on the wall?"

"Yup."

She pulled Walt's icon out of her pocket, held it up.

"You still carry that thing around?" He battled his own rising sentiments.

"Yup." She smiled.

Leon drove on. His parents' old brown-brick home was just a

couple blocks down the street. The memories there were a bit more complicated. Great ones, traumatic ones, everything in between. The front porch, their cherished, old gathering spot for friends and neighbors used to seem like a football field, but no more. Its brick, knee-wall railing crumbling, the porch had somehow shrunken into a tiny slab. How could it be? That really got to him. That porch was like a shrine.

As he drove out to the old Polish cemetery to tend the graves of his family, he became aware that he and Willow had reversed roles. He was the one gone mute, uncommunicative, while she kept talking, asking questions, trying to rouse him. He and his daughter were each other's yin and yang, trading parts intuitively, as required. That's the way their relationship had begun, and that's the way it remained.

Leon's man purse full of cleaning and landscaping supplies rested on the back seat. Willow insisted on stopping to buy a couple of small floral bouquets along the way. (In this heat, the flowers would be wilted by tomorrow, but what the hell; it was important to her.) Once they arrived at the sprawling cemetery, Leon scrubbed the piles of bird poop and soot off the two granite stones—one for his parents, one for his brother Ricky—while Willow snipped the overgrown grass around them with hand clippers before placing a bouquet in front of each headstone.

Lost in their own thoughts, they stood and gazed down at the graves. The Ziemny side of the family wasn't as titillating as the Trudeau side, not by a long shot, but Leon was grateful that his daughter had had the chance to experience his parents and Ricky as flesh and blood people, not shadowy riddles from a murky past.

"I wish I'd known Ricky longer," Willow said.

"Me too. I was fifty-five when he died, but even that wasn't long enough. My brother had a helluva big heart."

It was time for the final stop. The old three-story apartment building was set in the center of what used to be the African-American neighborhood, and largely still was, except that now it could only be described as a hopeless slum. The deterioration and devastation were immeasurable. Most of the buildings, some abandoned for decades, hemorrhaged in various stages of desecration and disintegration—half-charred, collapsing on themselves, splattered with obscenities, beyond redemption. Barricades were set up around the old apartment and neighboring buildings, along with chain link fencing to keep people at a distance as the buildings were imploded.

Leon fixated on the apartment, memories of his marriage to Noël popping like flashbulbs. Theckla and Freddie had lived on the second floor; he, Noël, and Adam, still a small child, on the third. He saw the warm yellow light of Noël's candles in the third floor window—God, how she loved candles. He saw the huge Christmas tree that he and little Adam had managed to drag up the dark staircase. The rickety swing in the courtyard out back. He saw the tiny kitchen where Noël had cooked him a Polish feast one unforgettable Christmas Eve. He saw their bedroom.

"Dad? Are you okay?"

He glanced at his watch. In one hour, it would all be rubble.

†††

As her father drove home, Willow stared at his profile. He had become even quieter—she could only imagine the recollections Langston had stirred up for him, good and bad, the way they always seemed to come together when revisiting the past. She, too, had gotten lost in her memories of the Ziemny family, especially

Walt, but for her they had all been good ones, joyous even; the miracle of finding her family after years spent dreaming of them.

"You and I have come a long way, haven't we?" she said.

Leon nodded. "Yup."

"Are you feeling sad?"

"Sad? No, not sad … I guess, I'm feeling … regret."

"Regret?"

"I wish you could have known your mom." Leon swallowed hard, paused before he resumed. The sight of him struggling with his emotions caused tears to well up in her own eyes. "She would've been so proud of you, Willow. I wish to God you could have had it all."

"I *do* have it all." She leaned over to kiss him on the cheek. "I have you."

✝✝✝

By the time they got home, it was around eight-thirty p.m., already dark outside; the summer days were getting shorter. A few minutes later, Adam dropped Booker off, and he came through the front door, bursting with excitement. "Everything's set!" he told them. "The exhumation's going to happen in a little over two weeks—the day after Labor Day!" After he and Leon clinked their sherry glasses—and she a glass of water—to celebrate on the back deck, Willow retired to the attic. They liked to have their man talk, share a second nightcap before bed. Besides, she was much too tired, drained by the emotional day.

When she switched on the light, she noticed that Lily's painting had fallen off the chimney where she'd hung it, even taken a few bricks along with it, leaving a little pile of mortar dust and debris on the wood floor.

Remembering that she had spotted a broom and dust pan standing against the wall on the unfinished side of the attic, she retrieved the items and returned to clean up the mess. Afterward, she examined the gap where the bricks had been, and as she did, another brick jiggled, as if it might have already been loosened before the fall.

"What the heck?" She pulled the loose brick out quite easily. Something small and hard was stuck behind it. She fumbled until she freed the item.

A tiny gold key.

Examining it in her palm, she knew exactly what it was. Yes, it had to be the missing key to the rolltop desk. What a find! Was Clarissa the one who had hidden it there? Was Clarissa the one who knocked the painting off the brick?

Willow moved to the desk, twisted it in the keyhole. It fit like a glove. The rolltop slid open. Inside were several arched pigeon holes, the center section separated by columns, with two long drawers beneath. Every single one of them was empty. Her disappointment surged.

She sat down in the desk chair, thinking. Perhaps it was Dotty and Jerry Richards, or more likely one of their daughters, who had hidden the key behind the loose brick, the way kids do. But why hide a key to an empty desk?

She recalled seeing a rolltop similar to this one, dating back to the 1800s, in a New York antique shop a couple years ago. The owner had told her about secret compartments in some of these old desks, and he had taken the time to show her some tricks as to how to search for them.

She tried a few of them now. No luck.

Frustrated, she racked her brain, determined to remember more of what the guy taught her that day. As she studied the desk, the brainstorm came. Opening one of the step-down drawers below the cubby holes, she felt for a tab along the top of it.

Jackpot! She pressed the tab and, much to her exhilaration, the center section of the cubby holes slid out in one solid block, revealing a secret drawer.

"Okay," she said. "This is it."

Pulling open the drawer, there it was, the hidden treasure! A stack of envelopes of various sizes, along with one large manila envelope, folded to the approximate size of the others, tied together by a black satin ribbon.

Willow took the bundle over to the bed, sat down, and reached for her reading glasses. After untying the tight knot, she shuffled through the envelopes. They appeared to be letters, sent to Clarissa Montgomery at various addresses, mostly in Richmond and other places in Virginia and one (the large envelope) to New Orleans. But the return address was always the same: Lily Trudeau, 1020 Creole Street, Hyssop, Louisiana.

"I don't believe it," Willow whispered.

Wait until she told Leon what she found!—and Booker! They'd be as excited as she was. Gripped suddenly by an odd feeling, she looked around. Clarissa's watchful presence, the presence Willow had sensed up here anyway, seemed to suddenly vanish, and Willow felt alone in the room. Clarissa had gone to some lengths to salvage these letters for someone, someday, to find them. That someday was today, and that someone turned out to be her. But why? She felt chill bumps rising on her skin.

Separating the contents from their envelopes—yes, they *were* letters, all written by Lily!—Willow arranged them sequentially by date so that she could start reading them in chronological order. A quick glance revealed that Lily's handwriting—printing not cursive—was neat, precise, quite lovely. As Willow slipped the empty envelopes inside the large manila one, she heard a sound outside her window. Four quick, successive cracks, like small explosions, coming from the direction of the back deck …

†††

Leon was lying flat against the deck, on his back. His head throbbed. He was suffocating on a thick glob inside his throat, fighting for each breath.

He heard Booker gasping nearby, but he couldn't form any words to ask him if he was okay. What the hell had happened? Willow! he suddenly thought. And then he remembered. Thank God, she'd gone inside the house.

The sound of Booker's panting was getting fainter. Leon heard music—far off in the distance. The two competing sounds came together, Booker's gasps and the music. Leon tried to turn his head, to lift his body from the wetness of blood surrounding him. He saw a full moon in the black sky.

The music was getting louder—loud enough to drown out Booker, loud enough to make out the tune. That old song, that pretty, old song that Noël loved. He struggled to keep his eyes open.

Through half-lids, he saw her … Noël!—his beautiful lost love. There she was! Waiting for him at the jukebox while the song played. He'd been in this place before, the same diner near the Moonstone Inn. Only this wasn't a diner, it was a deck.

He fought to take another excruciating breath, and it hurt like hell. Why was he fighting? It was time to stop fighting. Noël was near enough now for him to see her eyes up close.

And he felt like dancing.

-FOURTEEN-

MIASMA

WILLOW was paralyzed by what she saw. A river of blood was spreading over the back deck, Leon and Booker lying in the midst of it, silent and motionless. Leon was face-up, Booker on his side; their chairs askew. Collapsing to her knees in front of her father, she searched his wrist for a pulse. Nothing. *Nothing!* He was still warm, but he was gone. *No!* A massive hole in his neck still seeped blood, as well as his mouth and one ear. His eyes, like marbles, stared blankly.

No! no! no! no! no! ... it couldn't be! She felt herself dying right along with the father she adored. Without him here to anchor her, she felt herself floating away, away, away. A miasma of utter despair hung over the deck.

Summoning the strength to stand up, she raced over to Booker. Everything became a spinning blur after that. He still had a pulse, but his chest was oozing blood. She tried to sop it up with his jacket before hurrying into the house to get a towel to slow the bleeding and to call 911 from the landline. After racing back outside, she kneeled beside Booker, gently turned him on his back before ripping open his shirt, careful to avoid the wound as she started CPR the way she'd been trained in nursing school, pressing down again and again to the beat of *Staying Alive* for what seemed like hours on end, until her arms burned like fire, until she heard sirens wailing in the distance. Finally the EMTs arrived, taking over Booker's care.

Next came a flurry of others—more EMTs, policemen, faceless neighbors appearing out of nowhere. "How many shots were there?" a policeman asked.

"There were four shots," she heard herself replying. "One right after the next."

Her cheeks felt searing hot, like they'd been branded by an iron, and someone shouted, "She's breaking out in hives!" and an EMT gave her a shot in the arm, telling her it would calm her down. She heard the heavy motor of a firetruck out in front of the house. Was the house on fire too?

More policemen arrived, swarms of them, and she heard them say they were taking Leon to the morgue. The morgue! Her father was being taken to the morgue! Leon would never stand for that! She wanted to tell Leon something, anything except good-bye, but how could she, with all these people gawking?

After that, she felt nothing. Absolutely nothing, as if her soul had short-circuited right then and there in front of this horde of strangers, her disconnected inner wires exposed for all to see. She was dead, yet alive. The miasma hung heavier, hazier in the air. A terrible vapor, a terrible place. She felt as if she were drowning in its black haze.

An ambulance pulled up to the deck. Some police cars were parked on the grass nearby, the others parked in front with the firetruck. Her eyes fastened on the contingent of flashing lights in the darkness—flashing blue, flashing red, round and round—on the grass, in the trees, over the roof. More voices—urging Booker to hang on as they worked on him; an intermittent, "Oh, my God!" from another new arrival in the growing group of gawkers. Somewhere after that, came the sound of her brother's voice. She felt Adam's arms around her, trying to tilt her head away from the sight of Leon's body being lifted on to the gurney. *No! No!* They couldn't just steal her father away like that! Not after she'd come so far to find him! She pushed against Adam's shoulders, but he held her back. Why weren't they taking her too? Why couldn't they see that she was dead too?

She stared at the gurney until she couldn't see it any longer, until the vehicle took him away, took them both away. One, with siren and lights flashing, to the emergency room. The other, sound-less, to the morgue.

†††

Inside Leon's dining room, the northern mockingbird on the wall chirped once as Willow sat with Adam at the table. By then, hours had passed. Calls had been exchanged back and forth on Adam's cell phone and the landline. She was beginning to be func-tional again, a hard thaw from the unrelenting darkness of the miasma. She vacillated between complete numbness and intoler-able pain. Things were still happening in a blur.

Booker had been taken to the hospital in Bedlington, and a policeman called to find out how to reach his family. Willow remembered that his son's name was Cyrus Roberts, that he lived in New Orleans, that he was an attorney, and the officer told her that was enough information to track him down. The next-door neighbors had stopped in several hours ago, an older couple, husband and wife, offering condolences. As the patio doors slid open, Willow had caught sight of yellow tape strung across the backyard as policemen measured things out there, or whatever it was they were doing.

And then, Nick Hardy, her old flame, appeared—*Nick Hardy?*—tapping on the patio door.

Willow couldn't assimilate the sight of him, appearing

incongruously in the midst of her father's murder. He said he was the chief detective in Bedlington, assigned to the case. Maybe it wasn't Nick Hardy, and her mind was playing tricks on her. "Is now a good time for questions?" he asked. Adam told him it was not—that she had been given a shot of Benadryl—and Nick Hardy, if he was real—said he would be back tomorrow at nine a.m. and went away.

Maybe it was all a dream and that's why Nick Hardy had materialized. But if that were true, oh God, why wasn't she waking up? It must have been that shot they gave her. Maybe she was sleep-walking.

Finally, just the two of them, she and Adam sat there in stillness. No more ringing phones. No more intrusions. No more others. Silence, dead silence, except for the bird clock every hour. He pleaded with her to come home with him, spend the night there, but Willow insisted on remaining in her father's house. It was all she had left of him.

"You can't stay here by yourself!" Adam said.

She said nothing. Only one thought brought relief. Was this the time, her time, to kill herself, the way her great-aunt Clarissa had done?

"*Please*, Willow, come home with me!" Adam tried again. "If you won't leave, then I'll stay here with you."

His face was a blur now too, his voice sounded far away. Why was he still talking to her? Couldn't he see she was dead? Her body just needed to catch up, that was all.

Another hour went by. Adam phoned Anne, and put her on speaker. Now it was her turn to try to convince Willow to come home with them, but Willow wanted no part of it. Her brother's wife and child needed him now, and she told him so—or, at least, she thought she did. As for her, she had her own plan. She gazed at the counter where Booker's bottle of sherry, half empty, still stood.

"Try to get some sleep then," Adam said, before reluctantly walking out the door.

†††

The house was stone-cold quiet. Willow stared at the bottle of sherry long and hard; not enough to do the job on its own. She checked the cupboards. After the party the other night, Leon must have tossed out the leftover wine and beer. Or given it to Adam. Booker's half-empty sherry was all there was. She guzzled it straight from the bottle.

God, it tasted good. Numb upon numb.

This was the way Uncle Ricky had died, a recovering alcoholic who had fallen off the wagon one night, too much too fast, and she wondered if the sherry, after all these years of abstinence, might be enough to do her in after all. As she walked through the empty house with the open bottle, she caught a reflection of herself in a mirror. Red marks from the attack of hives were still visible on her cheeks. Uncle Ricky used to break out in hives too, same as she did when overly stressed. She stopped at her father's bedroom door, but couldn't bring herself to go inside. With effort, she climbed the stairs to the attic.

Had Clarissa done the deed up here? If so, how fitting that Willow had selected this room as her own. Leon had no gun that she knew of. If the sherry couldn't handle it, her only means would be her little vials of antidepressants. No one would blame her. Suicide was in her genes.

She sat down on the bed, took another swig of sherry. In her befuddled mind, the Benadryl shot and now the booze, even with all that, she couldn't rid herself of the shattering image of her father lying in his blood, a massive hole in his neck, his eyes gone cold. He died alone, without her. Why didn't she stay on the deck with him? Was Booker dying alone too, in a strange hospital? How was any of this fair? How was life fair?

She took another swig. Alcoholism was also in her genes. And art. Suicide, alcoholism, and art. What an inheritance.

She looked over at Lily's painting, fallen from the wall, now leaning against the fireplace with the hole in the bricks, like the hole in her father's neck, like the hole torn through her soul. She remembered the letters. They were lying on the bed where she had left them. She hadn't read one word yet because of the shots, four shots in a row. Why, oh why, hadn't she remained down there with Leon on the back deck? Maybe then, her body would be dead now too. Save her the trouble of doing it her own way.

She emptied the bottle of sherry, waited. Nothing came, certainly nothing close to death. Looking at the bottles of pills on her nightstand, she reached for one of them, the most potent, and twirled it between her fingers. What was ahead of her now? Her father's funeral, a murder trial, a failed art career, an empty house, an empty life.

She dumped the entire vial into her palm.

As she lifted the capsules to her lips, something stopped her—a jolt from somewhere—not a physical jolt like a yank on the arm, but more like a thought, a shout, maybe a whisper. *You are loved*, it said. Her father had loved her enough to reseed a whole town of willow trees for her. Her mother had loved her enough to surrender her own life for her.

Willow looked down at the capsules in her palm. It was time to do the next right thing, she supposed, and the next right thing was to stay alive. To throw all that love away would be the worst kind of betrayal. She slid the pills back inside the bottle.

Reentering the land of emotions, she was crushed by the unendurable weight of her sorrow. The house was quiet, so dreadfully quiet, no sounds on the floor below like usual, a toilet flushing or someone moving about. Leon was dead. It was no bad dream. She wouldn't wake up, and neither would he.

Splintering into sobs that rocked her body and cut like glass, she cried out Leon's name, only it came out, "Daddy! Daddy! Daddy!"

†††

Time went by. How much time, an hour or a day, Willow couldn't fathom. It was still dark outside, and she was still sitting on the bed in the attic, dazed by grief, liquor, and Benadryl. She felt tired, oh, so tired, though not the kind of weariness that allowed for sleep. Adam had not said the words, but they both knew who was capable of such a savage act. It *had* to be Cory, his own half-brother. Another intolerable ordeal to face.

Oh, God, in heaven, where could she put her thoughts so she wouldn't lose her mind? How and where could she escape?

When Willow was a child of nine or ten in San Diego, she had lived a block away from an art gallery. When things got to be too much, she used to walk there by herself and sit for hours, in front of a different painting each visit, and pretend she had jumped through the frame into whatever scene was depicted. She might be escaping into a narrow Parisian avenue, taking a seat beside a couple at one of the umbrellaed tables outside a café, or climbing up a rickety fire escape in the back alley of a tenement building to play with another lonely child. She learned a lot during those trips, as if she'd actually traveled to those places, spoken with, even been, those people in the paintings. She had lived a hundred lives that way. Later, she became absorbed in the abstracts. When she jumped into those images, she became a shape, a color, a texture, a reason … visible.

Reaching inside her pocket, Willow curled her fingers around Walt's icon. She looked down at Lily's letters beside her on the bed. Something tangible from each grandparent. Clarissa's part was finished, and now it was Lily and Walt's turn to reach out from wherever it was they had gone. Where Leon had gone too.

She wanted to be in that place with them, but she was not. She was alone in the attic of this dreadful house, and these letters, Lily's letters, were as close as she could get for now. The only voice she was able to hear.

Sitting against the bed board, Willow picked up the first letter and began to read.

PART TWO

FIFTEEN

LILY'S MELANCHOLY: 1950

LILY Trudeau paced back and forth in the dark bedroom, the curtains drawn tight. Her husband Jack had just left for work, and she was trying to steady herself, calm herself, before it was time to wake up Bo for first grade (the other three children were still too young for school). She desperately wanted to go back to bed; she was exhausted and sore, probably bruised again, but Jack had forced her to get up, to curl her hair, to put on make-up and a dress he'd laid out for her, including garter belt, hose, and heels. He wanted her "prettied up" after another long, brutal night of relentless, aggressive sex. In Jack's book, this was love.

It was the height of autumn, 1950. Truman was president. Five years ago, shortly after Bo was born, they'd left New Orleans and moved here, to this small place called Hyssop, where Jack operated his own millwork plant. Twenty miles from Baton Rouge, Hyssop possessed a stolen identity. It used to be three-quarters Negro, but now it was one-half white and one-half Negro after Jack and other Jack-type men had barreled into town to grab their share of the Baton Rouge market, snuffing out most of the Negro businesses in the process. As a result of their rapid onslaught, there was no clear line of demarcation between the Negro and white neighborhoods—it was more like a jagged, meandering line—as the white entrepreneurs pushed the Negroes back, family by family, into the shabbiest homes and districts. Why? Lily wondered. Why was it right for these men to cast them aside like that? Hadn't they just fought a World War to defend against bigotry and persecution?

She kept her opinions to herself. There was no one to share them with and, besides, what did her opinions matter?

She had married at seventeen, when Jack was twenty-five. Lily had been a bright student who was able to skip fourth grade and graduate high school a year early. When Jack had come home on leave from the war, both her father and Jack had already decided she should marry him right there and then—who else would have her after the time she'd spent in that sanitarium? hospital?, whatever it was they called it. They'd given her shock treatments there, but they hadn't helped. Her melancholy did not go away.

Glancing at her reflection in the round mirror of the dressing table, she sat down to get a closer look. Yes, she was beautiful— through no credit of her own. She had inherited the shiny raven hair of her father, the translucent, peacock greenish/bluish eyes and delicate pink porcelain complexion of her mother. Lily's beauty was her only worth. In some ways, it had saved her. Without it, she would surely have been shut away in a sanitarium by now, rather than sustaining the lust of an ambitious man like Jack Trudeau. Being beautiful had put her on the front lines of a terrifying world.

Jack relished the fact that the men who worked for him ogled her whenever she had occasion to come into the plant. He loved to overhear their whispers about "what a lucky son of a bitch" he was. He delighted in keeping her pregnant, flaunting his masculine prowess. The very thought of bearing another child sent Lily into panic. So she had learned about womanly rhythms and tried her best to keep him at bay during her peak fertile times, telling him she was on her period. He wouldn't dream of sullying himself during those times.

All four of their children had turned out beautiful too, with the same black hair and peacock eyes. Noël, the only girl, worried her the most. How well Lily knew that a beautiful shell was a woman's prison all its own.

She got up from the dressing table, paced some more. It was six a.m., still dark outside. What to do? Where to go? What to think? Where to put her thoughts? Her anxiety—the anxiety she'd known since her mother died when Lily was eight years old—was overpowering. With trembling hands, she reached into her third dresser drawer, beneath a pile of handkerchiefs, searching for her stash of cigarettes. Gone. All gone. Jack had gotten rid of them—again. She would have to find another hiding place, a safer one, where he would never think of looking. Yesterday, she had discovered a loose floorboard in the corner of the pantry, a prime spot. Jack never set foot in there.

Out of the many doctors Lily had, there was only one who'd been kind, who treated her as if she was a person, not some crazy, dehumanized misfit. He had given her ideas, besides the endless tranquilizers and shock treatments, to help manage her anxiety. Melancholy and anxiety were twins, he told her—the flipside of the same coin—and he encouraged her to write down her thoughts, to get them out on paper, then destroy what she had written. It helped.

From the bottom drawer of her dresser where she kept several boxes of stationery, she took out one box, a fountain pen, and sat down again at the dressing table. Without hesitation, she began writing a letter to the only adult in this world that cared about her, her only sister Clarissa, who shared her childhood wounds.

Dear Clarry,

I miss you! And I miss New Orleans. You and I have gone through so much together, through Mama's death, through Father's wrath, and I hope you're feeling safe and liberated now that you're away at Westhampton, well on your way to being the teacher you've dreamed of becoming. I'm so proud of you to have made it to college! What an achievement!

I miss being able to talk to you in person, the way we used to. Has it really been almost three years since we've seen each other? Maybe someday you can visit again, though I doubt you'd want to remain in Hyssop too long. Jack doesn't seem keen on making a trip to visit New Orleans anytime soon (if that's where you return after Westhampton). Both he and Father want to be the boss, so they're better kept apart.

Remember the pact we made as children? We vowed to never keep secrets from one another. I know we have our phone calls, but it's difficult to talk openly with Jack or the children hovering nearby.

I try to please Jack, like we tried to please Father. Jack is a good provider, and I know I should be grateful. He loves owning his own business and spends ten or more hours there most weekdays. He demands undying loyalty from his employees, and they give it to him. They call him "sir" and do his bidding, I honestly believe his foreman, a dreadful man named Hal Walston, would take a bullet for him.

Maybe it's just because they fear him. I understand that. Like them, I force myself to do whatever Jack asks. Otherwise, I'm afraid he'll toss me out like one of his old suits when he no longer finds me attractive. What would I do without him, Clarry? How could I make my way in this world as a single mother?

I love my children! Please don't think otherwise! But with four of them under the age of six, they need a strong mother with lots of energy, not a feeble one like me. You wouldn't recognize them—they're growing so quickly. You remember Adam as he was when you came to visit—as a peaceful newborn, but he's a restless little creature now. I've read Dr. Spock's <u>Baby and Child Care</u> until I'm blue in the face, but I can't seem to get him through the terrible twos without a daily battle, which he mostly wins.

Bo is my little soldier, bold and brave. He helps me take care of the others on the days I can't seem to get out of bed, and I sometimes fear he's the parent, and I'm another of the children. It's unforgivable for a mother to put a burden like that on a six-year-old child.

Steve is my nature boy; he escapes to his sandbox outside most of the day, scooping the sand into his little plastic pail over and over again, and he never seems to tire of it. Bo keeps an eye on him when I cannot.

And Noël? She's a bit of a mystery. She's a sensitive child and spends far too much time alone. I often find her staring at me with the saddest eyes imaginable, as if she's seeing all the way through, to the marrow of my bones. My biggest worry is that she'll turn out just like me.

I'm a terrible mother, I know I am, but please, please believe me when I tell you I love them with all my heart! I wish I could make this melancholy go away! It feels like a vise that grips me from head to toe, squeezing out every ounce of joy, every crack of light. Jack is tired of my bad days. He gets angry with me when he comes home from the plant and finds the house a mess and no pots on the stove. He shouts at me to snap out of it. I know he's right. He doesn't deserve to come home to a useless wife after putting in a ten-hour day.

Believe me, Clarry, I would give heaven and earth to "snap out" of this dreary mood, or melancholy, or whatever it is you call it. Who would choose to be this way?

Keep studying hard, give yourself a real life. Try not to marry too soon, even if they start calling you an old maid—hold off until you love and love deeply. Please, my sister, wait, wait, wait, until you know marriage is the right thing to do. It is a vow, but if not one of love, it is a vow into slavery. Jack tells me I belong to him—to do with me as he pleases and to do as he says. He thinks that makes it simple for me. He thinks I'm a simpleton; simple-minded.

I try to educate myself—to fill up my holes, to fill up my time. I walk to the library with the children, and we bring home stacks of books. I know there are other worlds out there, beyond Hyssop, beyond this melancholy, and I escape into books— into poetry, art, novels like The Heart is a Lonely Hunter, into worlds I can understand and bring me solace.

Jack doesn't like me to read, and I hide the books. He's jealous of anything that brings me joy or comfort. He obsessively vows his love for me.

Here's the worst part. I honestly believe he does love me—as much as he's able to love. He's haunted by things that happened to him during the war, things that have altered him in ways that made him brutal, in frightening ways he's unable to purge.

What kind of wife feels the way I do? An ungrateful one. That's what my minister told me when I went to him for counseling. "Honor your husband," he admonished. "Be thankful for him and serve him." If the minister thinks I'm ungrateful, God must think so too. Now I'm too ashamed to go back to church.

On the days I can, I keep up a small garden out back—mostly the native flowers, Louisiana phlox, Luna hibiscus, and Virginia willow, because they're easier to grow in this humid and swampy environment, but I also grow red roses. When I'm outside in my little garden, the world seems gentle and safe, like Mommy's garden used to feel to us, even after she was gone. Thank God, you're still in this world!

THE MOURNING AFTER

THE night of Leon's murder or, more accurately, that much-too-early morning, Adam arrived home around three. Anne was waiting for him at the door. She threw her arms around him, sobbing. "How could something so terrible happen in a quiet place like this?" Almost in unison, they said his name: "Cory."

Wide awake and stunned, Adam came to bed only because she implored him to try to get a little rest before they had to face the Herculean task of telling Rocket that Leon was dead. Adam lay flat on his back, staring up at the time beamed on the ceiling, as one minute changed to the next. Anne's eyes were closed, but he sensed she wasn't sleeping either, because her breath was soundless. There wasn't a trace of the moon through the window. He remembered that there had been a full moon earlier, a bright, full moon, shining down on the murder scene with its celestial indifference. Or was it the kind of moon that turned people into lunatics?

Full moon or not, was Cory really capable of committing such an unspeakable act? Adam and Leon had decided it best not to confront him when he had returned from Charlottesville, but in retrospect, their decision had been the wrong one. Fatally wrong. They had no idea Cory would stoop so low as to try to murder Booker—and one of them along with him. Maybe if they had faced him head-on when he got back ... what was the point of rehashing what couldn't be undone?

There was a lot to do today. That detective guy, Nick Something-or other, told them he'd be back at nine a.m. sharp to ask his questions, and Adam had to get dressed and get over to Leon's—now Willow's house—to meet him there. Guilt gnawed at him; he hadn't yet mentioned Cory's name, not to the policemen at the scene and not to Nick. Another error of omission. He would correct that error this morning, difficult as it might be to finger his own brother.

Why was it difficult? What the fuck did it matter what would happen to Cory? Let him rot in hell!

Funeral arrangements had to be made too, and that meant a trip to Green's Funeral Parlor. Adam hated funerals, the sight of a waxy corpse stuffed into a coffin. When it came his turn to go, he hoped Anne would incinerate him on the spot.

The task he most dreaded was the one that had coaxed him back to bed. Today he had to shatter his own child's innocence, rob him forevermore of his vision of this world as a safe and good place. What a sickening thing for a father to have to do.

Just then, Anne moaned softly. She *was* sleeping, he guessed, or maybe she was just drifting in that insulating twilight space before the horror of the events of last night met sunlight.

Adam would miss Leon; he already did. All three of them would. Leon had filled a father-sized void in him, a grandfather-sized void in Rocket. Though Adam had moved here on account of Anne, not Leon, he ended up falling toward Leon gradually, like a tree bends toward the light.

†††

Nick Hardy got out of his car in front of Rose's Drug Store, surveying the miniscule downtown. It looked broken-down. Small and decrepit. He had grown up in Weeping Willow, returning intermittently through the years, but it no longer held any relevance. His parents had died young, in an automobile accident when he was in his mid-twenties. He had no siblings, no relatives, just the house he'd inherited. The first time he left Weeping Willow was to join the U.S. Marines, and they eventually shipped him over to the Persian Gulf during Operation Desert Storm. After that came college at Ohio State and a Master's degree in criminal justice from the University of Missouri in St. Louis. The final time he left Weeping Willow was fourteen years ago, when he was offered a prime position with the Bedlington police department. Near in size to Toledo, Bedlington was a vibrant city, and he'd sold his parents' home and settled into a fourteenth-floor apartment in the heart of it. Nick didn't believe in looking through the rearview mirror. Like Lincoln said, he might be a slow walker, but he never walked backwards.

He'd been awake all night, getting the facts of this case straight, even interviewing some people, and he was tired and hungry. As he headed toward the Turning Point Tavern, he noticed the filmy storefront windows of the downtown shops; they needed a good scrubbing. More than that, they were old and needed to be replaced. There was no real downtown here anymore, just a drug store, a bakery, a bank, and a few odd novelty shops selling outdated wares. Bedlington County covered a big territory, dotted with towns exactly like Weeping Willow—except for all those weeping trees.

A couple of years ago, Nick had been promoted to chief detective of the Homicide Division. Already, the thrill of it was wearing off, and he was getting antsy to move on to someplace larger. A while back, he had put in an application for Denver Homicide, his dream job, his dream location. Still no word. Maybe there never would be.

The year before he left the town of Weeping Willow for good, he had met the girl named Willow. Back then, both of them were restless, contemplating their own paths. She was a student at the Art Institute in Chicago, and she came to visit her father frequently. He was feeling the itch to break out into something larger than himself. In that bubble of time before their transitions seized them, he and Willow Trudeau had managed to forge a connection, and he wasn't easy to connect with. Neither was she. Maybe that was their connection.

They especially connected one night while looking at the Orion Nebula. After gazing through the lens of his high-magnitude telescope at the cloud of gas and dust where stars were formed— *bam!*—it hit them hard when they locked eyes. The next morning, he tried to shake it off.

Falling in love meant exactly what it said: falling. Like spatial disorientation when flying a plane, it made you lose your bearings, your sense of direction as to which way was up and which was down, and he had too much to accomplish for that. A relationship held you back from truer missions. A relationship was a dock, and he was setting sail on the open sea.

When he entered the Turning Point Tavern, all heads tilted in his direction. No surprise there—news in this town traveled faster than the speed of light, especially with something as salacious as their first murder. The waitress came over and poured him a mug of coffee, her eyes puffy red, swollen as ping pong balls. He recognized her, couldn't quite recall her name. Nick knew most of the people here, the older ones anyway, and if not their names, their faces.

"Any news about Leon Ziemny's killer?" Her voice quavered.

"Not yet," he said.

Tears overpowered her, bringing the manager—a guy Nick guessed to be around forty—out from the kitchen. "Why don't you just go on home, Dolly? You're no good to anyone here in this condition. Go get some rest."

Dolly, that was it. Dolly Schmidt. The names were all coming back to him.

Without another word, Dolly put down the pitcher of coffee and left the bar through the front door without the presence of mind to remove her apron. The manager sat down with Nick, introducing himself as Ron-somebody-or-other; Nick didn't quite catch the last name, though he probably should have, just in case. "That poor gal's a mess," Ron said.

"Looks like it. She must've been close to Leon Ziemny."

Ron swatted his hand through the air as if waving away the notion. "Only in her mind. She had it bad for him, but it definitely wasn't mutual ... well, maybe just once." He winked. "If you know what I mean."

Nick took a sip of coffee, flipped open the lined pad he'd stuffed in his pocket. "What'd you say your last name was?"

✝✝✝

At half past six, Adam's phone chimed, the first call of what he guessed would be many.

"Hiya, First Man! Too damn bad about Leon. Is there anything I can do? You need anything?"

That was rich—the killer offering to help. Adam didn't know how to respond, so he said nothing.

"You still there?"

"Yeah, I'm here."

Anne came into the kitchen, put her arms around him from behind.

"I hate to say I told you so, but I warned you about letting that nigger hang around with Leon, didn't I? And you didn't believe me … So is the nigger dead too?"

That was it, Adam thought. Cory was only fishing for information about Booker's condition. "I don't know." He shifted the phone to his other ear as Anne readied the coffeemaker. "How did you find out about it anyway?"

"Everybody knows! The whole town's buzzing."

"Look, Cory, I gotta run. Lots to do today." Adam slammed the phone down on the table.

†††

When Nick Hardy showed up at Willow's door, at nine sharp, Adam was already there, waiting at his sister's kitchen table as she tried to pull herself together in the bathroom. She'd let Adam in ten minutes earlier, looking like holy hell, as if she'd slept in her clothes, or not slept at all, and she wasn't much interested in meeting with Nick or anyone else. She had nearly forgotten about the appointment until he reminder her, and then she made a weird comment, something like, "So he was real." Her major concern was getting to Bedlington to see how Booker was doing. She had called the hospital, she said, but they wouldn't give her any information over the phone, not even to let her know if he was dead or alive.

Through the patio doors, Adam could see the police tape strung around the backyard. Large blood pools stained the deck. He made sure to close the blinds before Willow came out of the bathroom.

While he and Nick (he told Adam to call him "Nick" rather than "Detective Hardy") waited for Willow at the table, Adam tried to size-up the guy, who looked to be around the same age as Willow, though the detective seemed unreadable. He wore his dark hair longer than most police types. His blue eyes showed sympathy, but his demeanor was all cop. His electronic tablet was opened and ready to go when Willow finally emerged. She had combed her hair, yet her shattered appearance, beyond desolation, tore up Adam.

"It's good to see you again, Willow." Nick said. "Sorry about your father."

Willow?, Adam wondered, why not *Miss Trudeau?* Was this guy being *too* casual? She glanced at the detective with what appeared to Adam as familiarity in her eyes. Had they known each other before, or was Nick just referring to the previous evening?

"Tell me what you saw and heard last night." He wasted no time cutting to the chase.

"Didn't I already go through all of that?"

She looked at Adam forlornly, and he shrugged. He wasn't certain how much she had told the police after it happened; she was pretty out of it by the time he'd arrived. "Just tell him again," Adam said as gently as possible. "It's his job to ask these questions."

She lowered her eyes, stared down at the tabletop. "I was up in the attic when I heard the sounds. Four loud cracks."

"What were you doing in the attic?" Nick asked.

"Getting ready for bed, that's what. That's where my bedroom is." Her eyes met his. "Are you interrogating me or something?"

"Of course not." He half-smiled. "Settle down, Willow. I know this is hard."

"Hard? Yes, Nick, it's hard." Her voice was terse. She looked away, in the direction of the patio door—Adam was relieved he had thought to close the blinds. "I'll tell you the whole thing all over again—everything I remember, and I won't leave anything out. I hope you can type fast."

"I flunked typing. But I have a recorder." He tapped his tablet.

Willow recounted her version of events: hearing the sounds from the attic; finding Leon and Booker on the patio; calling 911; giving Booker CPR until the paramedics came.

"You did a good job on that, by the way," Nick commented. "Probably saved his life."

"Then he's still alive?" Her eyes lit up when she looked at him, the first gesture of warmth she'd shown toward the detective, or anyone, since the gunshots.

Nick seemed to notice too. His eyes softened. "Far as I know."

They sure seemed as if they knew each other from somewhere else, Adam thought. He was distracted by the sudden ringtone of *Louie Louie* coming from the direction of the kitchen.

"Leon's phone!" Willow lunged from her chair to grab it off the kitchen counter, as if it might be Leon himself calling. "Yes?" She was nearly breathless. "Oh, hi, Christopher." Her voice deflated, went monotone. "Thank you … Yes, we'll be there later to make arrangements … Oh. That sounds like Leon … I guess that makes it simple for us, doesn't it?"

Returning to the table, she set the phone aside. "Christopher Green wanted us to know that Leon made pre-arrangements for his funeral—he didn't want one."

Without missing a beat, the detective resumed his official business. "By the way, I'm going to need to keep that phone for a while."

A trace of fresh grief darkening her eyes, Willow sat back as Nick reached over to grab Leon's cell. As he slipped it into an evidence bag, he began another round of questions before finally getting to the one Adam was dreading. "Do either of you know anyone who might've done this?"

Willow glanced at Adam.

He knew the responsibility to be forthcoming rested upon his shoulders. "Yeah, we do." He steeled himself to get the words out. "My brother, well, my half-brother, Cory Ketchfield. We think it was him." He cleared his throat. "I mean, we know it was him."

"How do you know that?"

"Because he went down to Charlottesville a week or so ago—closer to two weeks, I guess—to take part in that white nationalist rally that's been all over TV, the one where the woman died. He's never hidden the fact that he was a racist, but I sure didn't know he was a crazy radical! ... I doubt he intended to hurt Leon. I think Booker was his target, and Leon got in the way."

"Did Cory know Booker?"

"Nah. He didn't need to. Booker is Black, that's all he needed to know. He's been bitching to me about Leon letting Booker stay at his house."

Nick nodded as if Cory's racial rantings weren't news to him. "Anyone else you think could've been responsible? Besides Cory?"

It was a stupid question. "In this town, are you kidding?" Adam shook his head. "Not a soul."

"There're other racists here, you know," Nick said. "Maybe not as extreme as your brother, but I've already heard an earful this morning ... How Leon met his doom because he tangled himself up with that N-word bastard ... that kind of stuff."

Willow seemed flabbergasted. "I never heard people here talk like that."

"How long have you lived here?"

She paused as if flustered by the question—or was it by Nick's tone? "Just a few weeks, but I thought people here took care of each other."

"They also watch a lot of television, and play around on Facebook," he said. "They start out innocent enough, sharing pictures of their kids or grandkids, but the next thing you know, they're reposting wild fringe theories because some wacky click bait—I call it 'opinion porn'—has sent them over the deep end. And this whole disinterment thing, well ... it's really got them going bonkers."

"How did they find out about *that*?" she asked.

"Things get around." Nick's eyes were fixed on Willow. "So ... how *did* you know Booker?"

Adam was growing increasingly disturbed by the insinuations of Nick's questions. "I didn't," she said. "I mean, I never met him until I came here and found him staying with my dad."

Nick laughed softly. "Well, that's not how Jeff Miller figures it. He's got his own theories, and he's not shy about sharing them either. He said Booker came to his motel asking specifically for you by name, and then you showed up from New York later that same day. He thinks Booker somehow found out your grandmother is buried with some serious cash—maybe *you're* the one who told him about it—and that Booker coerced you and Leon to do this whole disinterment thing, maybe split whatever's in that casket three ways. But the murder part? Jeff thinks maybe Booker wanted to do away with Leon to keep more of the money for himself, and there was a struggle before the gun went off. Or maybe *you* wanted a bigger split of the cash, and *you're* the shooter."

"Oh, my God!" Willow gasped. "He's really telling people that I'd kill my own father?"

Adam's heart clenched. What a god-awful thing to do to her! On top of losing the father she adored in such a shocking way, making her take the blame for his death was unconscionable. He slung a protective arm across her shoulders. "Where do people come up with this shit? Are they nuts or something?"

"These are crazy times." Nick shrugged. "People make up their own truth nowadays. You repeat it often enough, you get others to believe it too." His eyes shifted back to Willow. "So." He paused momentarily. "You want to let me in on the *real* reason for the disinterment?"

Adam listened as she shared the tale about the buried Bible, the complicated history that had entwined Booker's family with the Trudeaus. "And I don't know the cause of my grandmother's death either, so as long as we're going through all the trouble to open the grave, I thought we could look into that too."

"That's quite a story," Nick said at the conclusion. "Do you trust Booker? I mean, do you think he's being honest with you?"

Willow frowned. "What's that supposed to mean?"

"It means, maybe that Bible has some kind of real monetary value, or maybe something else valuable is hidden inside of the coffin, I don't know. Are you sure he's not just feeding you a line of crap about it being a sentimental family heirloom?"

"I trust Booker like my own family," she said. "My own mother put that Bible inside the casket, and Leon's known about it for years. Besides, I don't even care if it *does* have a lot of value. It still belongs to Booker—it's his murdered brother's Bible."

Nick gazed at her, unfazed. "Did Leon own a gun?"

"Nah." Adam shook his head. "He didn't like guns. Contrary to popular opinion, he thought guns kill people."

"Did he have any enemies?"

"Not a one that I know of," Adam said.

"Either of you know a woman named Dolly Schmidt?"

"The waitress?" Adam raised his eyebrows. "What about her?"

"Apparently, she carried a torch for Leon."

"A torch?"

"It sounds as if they might have had a one-night stand. You know, a woman scorned …" Nick closed his tablet, got up from the table. "I'll be back in touch. Some of my men will be doing more logistical measurements on your back deck a little later. We'll know a lot more after Leon's autopsy."

Adam noticed that Willow flinched slightly at the sound of the word. As he led Nick to the front door, he tried to stifle his indignation. He'd already told this guy about Cory—it was an open and shut case, as far as he was concerned—so why did Nick feel it necessary to go down all these other rabbit holes, at Willow's expense? Adam couldn't contain himself any longer. "What was *that* all about, man!" he blurted out. "Don't you think Willow's been through enough without making her feel like a suspect?"

"Sorry." Nick shrugged. "Like you said, it's my job."

†††

A murder case, in Nick Hardy's assessment, was like a Rubik's cube—you had to twist it around at every angle, every which way, until it all matched up. The solution could be convoluted. While still parked in Willow's driveway, he called in to headquarters to give them two orders. He wanted to get a search warrant for Cory Ketchfield's home. He had already planned to question Cory, mostly because he had discovered from his other interviews that Cory was an instigator who had been fanning the flames of racism in town for quite a while, and Booker's arrival in Weeping Willow was the kerosene. The second order was a bit more unorthodox. "And put a watch on Lily Trudeau's grave."

He had to repeat that one twice. "Yeah, that's right," he said. "I know it's odd, but do it anyway."

He looked back at the house. He had upset an already traumatized Willow. Sometimes he hated his job, but he had to remain impartial and cover all the bases. Maybe he'd overdone the impartiality to hide his old feelings for her. Truth be told, he might have taken the Willow/Booker conspiracy theories more seriously, except that they didn't hold water. After you served in a war, there was no room for delusions, and Nick set his compass by cold, hard facts. As far as he knew right now, the gunshots had been fired from a rifle, not a handgun, and not from close range but from a distance away, maybe as much as two hundred feet. No sign of struggle between Leon and Booker. None of the neighbors had seen anything, but the guy next-door to Leon, Telles Salvo, heard the roar of a loud motor speeding away right after the shots. Not a shred of evidence, other than hearsay, connected Booker Roberts or Willow Trudeau to the crime.

Besides that, Nick *knew* her. Or he used to anyway.

†††

His father let him cry himself out in his arms. After his parents left his room, Rocket sat on the window seat and stared out into the backyard. If he were already a doctor, he could have saved Leon. He knew he could have done it! He imagined himself taking the bullet out of Leon's body, the joy of it when Leon woke up again and came back home.

But he wasn't a doctor yet, and Leon would never be coming home again.

Memories filled his head. He and Leon liked to birdwatch together. The hobby developed kind of slowly, by accident, when they sat together out on Leon's deck on Saturday afternoons and all kinds of birds began to show up at Leon's feeders, colorful birds that Rocket hadn't known existed. Leon bought him a book on bird species, and they would flip through it together whenever they spotted an unusual bird and try to identify it. Leon was an awfully good listener, not such a good talker, but that was okay because good listeners were a lot harder to find.

Rocket wondered what became of people after they were dead. Sure, he had wondered about it before, but then he didn't know anyone who had actually died, which made it seem as if it were something that happened only to other people. He couldn't imagine not seeing Leon ever again or hearing the sound of his voice. The very thought of it pinched his chest with a pain he'd never felt before, way down deep somewhere. Too deep for even a doctor to fix.

His eyes remained stuck on the pitcher's mound in the back-yard that his father had made for him, the one he never played on. He had the urge to go find his father right there and then and ask him ... could they pitch some balls today?

SEVENTEEN

THE BOOK OF RAYMOND

BY the time Willow got to the hospital in Bedlington, her shock over the town's accusations had diminished into a dull, sickly bewilderment. Her hangover nearly gone, she was bludgeoned by another wave of pure, undiluted grief. Leon was dead; the realization sinking in. From experience, she knew that her grief was only in its infancy, its many layers yet to come, that it was impossible to absorb the magnitude of such a profound loss when the permanent wound was still bleeding. Was it really only the day before that she and Leon had visited Langston? In the blink of an eye, yesterday can become a lifetime ago.

Booker was in the ICU, a policeman posted at his door. He'd had emergency surgery, and he was in a coma. His son had been called, the nurse told her, and was expected to arrive later today. Could she see him, *please*, Willow asked—for just for a minute or two? After the policeman made a call to get "the okay from Nick", the nurse allowed her to enter Booker's room.

Even with nearly two full years of nursing training in college, Willow wasn't prepared for what she saw. Booker was attached to an alarming array of tubes, IVs, a ventilator, and a host of other machines that pulsed with the only sounds of life in the room. Worse than that, Booker's skin had a strange, purplish cast to it, his face unrecognizable.

She sat down beside him, laid her hand over his. "Booker, it's me," she said softly. "It's Willow."

Nothing. Not one twitch of movement from him.

She heard the policeman cough from behind her, announcing his entrance. He planted himself in front of the door like a sentry, arms crossed. Despite his intrusion, Willow continued her one-way conversation. "I found something in the attic about your brother. About Raymond."

She'd brought along one of Lily's letters. Coma or not, she was determined to read it aloud to him. It was all she could think of to do. The half-dozen or so letters Willow had already read detailed an escalating pathos as Lily teetered on the brink of an annihilating depression. But then, she had come across this letter, dated February 22, 1953, which seemed to be a turning point for Lily, the catalyst for a major change. Lily had even chosen different stationery on which to write it, not the dour pale gray with the cut-out scalloped borders of the first batch of letters, but on milky cream paper with a Luna hibiscus in full bloom at the top. It was the letter where she detailed her first chance meeting with Raymond Roberts.

After taking her glasses from her purse, Willow began reading aloud.

†††

Oh, Clarry, today has been wonderful from beginning to end! For starters, the weather was unseasonably warm, and it felt like spring had arrived, or at least poked its head out from the cold earth, giving us an early foretaste. Weather aside, it was already a special day to begin with: Noël's seventh birthday. I bought her a doll that she's been eyeing for many months at the department store, and without the slightest hesitation, she named her Amelia Rosalie, as if that name, wherever it came from, has been close to her heart for a long while. Me and the boys gave her a little party with cake and ice cream after Jack left for work. (Yes, he even works on Sundays now.) Afterwards, because the temperatures were soaring into the low-seventies, we couldn't stay cooped up inside the house a minute longer, and we decided to go to the park.

There was a carnival-like atmosphere there, dozens and dozens of people picnicking, playing games, strolling together arm in arm. I soon discovered that there was to be a tent revival of some kind at the far end—the signs called it a Spring Revival Series. Though it's still winter, the promise of spring seemed near on such a warm day.

Among the many people enjoying the sunshine, I spotted a man walking alone, carrying a Bible with half the cover torn off. He brushed passed us with a distracted, reflective expression, oblivious to my presence, or anyone else's. He wore a white linen tunic-shirt that flowed with the breeze as he walked, black trousers, a black wrap around his head, almost like an Egyptian pharaoh might wear.

Instantly, I was drawn to him. I can't describe the pull I felt. There was nothing romantic about it, or curious, or any other familiar emotion I can name, just an overwhelming impulse to keep him in my sight for as long as I could. The radiance in his face drew me in. A peaceful expression, juxtaposed against the intensity of his light coffee eyes—they came together in a way that made him appear as a work of art more than a man, as if a beam of light were shining on him, following him wherever he walked, as I, too, felt compelled to do.

I kept trailing behind him, shuffling the children along with me. If I thought he might turn and notice me, I hid—behind a tree, a post, anything that might conceal me—or else I simply turned my head away for that second. I was afraid that when I looked up again, he'd be lost forever.

Eventually, I followed him into a tent, a large tent packed with folding chairs filled to capacity, the crowd overflowing into standing room only. Everyone under the tent was colored. I led the children inside. A young man surrendered his chair to me, and the children assembled themselves on the ground around the aisle where I sat.

Then I caught sight of him again—all eyes were on him now as he stood at the front podium. He was the pastor!

"I'm going to talk to you today about a big subject," he began. "The biggest, most important subject in all eternity." His voice was instantly compelling, Clarry—a surprising rasp to it, yet coating as honey. "I'm going to talk to you about the core of God's nature." He paused for a moment. "The core of God's nature, my friends, is Love—with a capital L."

"As it says in your program" he continued, "I call today's sermon The Book of Raymond, because God has put this testimony on my heart." His face dimmed as he scanned the crowd. "But you know something? This is the hardest part about being a pastor. Words are inadequate when it comes to God, helplessly small, small as an infant, especially when describing Love with a capital L. The best I can do is ask you to listen with an open heart, and to pray, as Ephesians 3:17-18 prays, 'that you, being rooted and established in love, may have power, together with all the saints, to grasp how wide and long and high and deep is the love of Christ.'

"First, I'll tell you what love is not," he said. "Love is not weak. Love is not a sentimental feeling; not a passing fancy. Love is not an impulse, an illusion. Love is not self-seeking, but neither is it a vow into subservience."

Here, his words grabbed me. I know he was talking to his people, not to someone like me, born into privilege and tormented in my own little prison. He was talking to those who have been suffering for generations under bondage and abuse. However inconsequential my suffering in comparison, I think I understand their pain—if not its depth, then the weight of its ever-presence.

"The Love of God, my friends, is powerful. It is the fundamental force of life, a triad of the intimate relationship between Father, Son, and Spirit—or to put it another way, the love above us, beside us, and within us—or to put it still another way, the love of God, love of others, and love of self. All three are intrinsically connected. All three must be intact for it to be the kind of Love, with a capital L, that comes from God. When even one in the triad is lacking, something's not right. There's work to be done.

"Just listen to what Jesus had to say when asked about the most important Commandments. He said: 'Love the Lord your God with all your heart and with all your soul and with all your mind and with all your strength. The second is this: Love your neighbor as yourself. There is no commandment greater than these.'

"It's all right there, isn't it? All three parts of the triad of Love. John says, 'Whoever claims to love God, yet hates a brother or sister, is a liar.' Jesus tells us to put the needs of others ahead of our own. He wants our love to be the kind of self-sacrificing, tolerant, forgiving love that opens our hearts wider and deeper to the wounds of others, while at the same time, sees them as he sees them—as their better selves. He wants us to see ourselves that way too. We've been told that we have that little angel and devil sitting on either one of our shoulders, but it's not that way; it's not a lateral choice. It's a deeper choice. Jesus bids us to go deeper, into our deepest heart. It's a paradox, isn't it?—by going higher, we go deeper. Jesus wants to transform us, day by day, drop by drop, into our higher, deeper selves; our better selves.

"Think about it. How can we possibly love God if we're at war with one another? If we're at war within ourselves? When we put God first, love falls into order: We love ourselves as God's children, and we love others as our brothers and sisters from the same holy Father. Love is the core of God's being, and as creations in His image, love is the core of our being too, that deepest place where we're able to hear God's still, small voice. Like the circulating blood of the body, love flows from God into our deepest heart, from there into one another, and back to the God who instilled it, in a never-ending chain of supply. The further we move away from love, the further we move away from our authentic selves."

He looked into the faces of the crowd, Clarry, all eyes rapt upon him. I was much too far back to make direct contact. "We live in an exciting time, my friends," he said. "We are children of the Third Phase of creation. The First Phase was God, the Old Testament God, above us. The Second Phase was Jesus, the New Testament God, beside us. And now we're in the Third Phase—the Holy Spirit God, within us. Whether or not we are aware of it, we are being led on a magnificent journey by this divine force. We draw closer to, or further from, this divine force by the choices we make every day, large and small, the choices we make for love, or not.

"Each of us is born on this earth with a particular, unique mission," he continued. "Each of us is on that magnificent journey. As Kierkegaard put it, 'We set sail with sealed orders.'

Sealed from us, but not from God, who arranges our experiences and manifests the people he's put us here to love. He appoints the time in history for our birth. The circumstances. Our parents and siblings. From time to time, we might catch a glimpse of the repeated themes and refrains of our lives, however shadowy. Jung talks about our experiences deepening 'in a spiraling journey of recurring, evolving patterns.' But God transcends psychology, philosophy, even religion. When our souls are anchored in God, who is Love, it puts love at the front and center of our thoughts and actions."

I looked around for the children. Without my noticing, they had moved outside the tent, on the sidelines near the front, where other white children had also gathered to get a closer look at him. I doubt they understood a word of what he was saying, but still they found him fascinating enough to stop their playing or fidgeting.

"And yet, I know you're suffering," he said. "I know your hearts are broken. Our deepest heart is also where we sustain our deepest wounds. Our long history of persecution and suppression has been knitted into your genes. I see the weariness on your faces." He closed his eyes. "I sense it in the repressive air surrounding this tent, even on this spectacularly beautiful day. How much longer? you ask. How much longer must I wait? How much longer can I lift my eyes up to the hills for salvation?"

His eyes reopened, focused on those near the front. "But I also see it in the way you carry yourselves—'strong at the broken places,' as Hemingway wrote. Those who suffer, in fact, are those who know God most intimately. For it is in the midst of suffering that our need for God seems greatest, the spirit of love most visible, the holy light seems brightest."

"Praise God!" called out a woman sitting near me. "Hallelujah!"

a man echoed. A few others stood up, some with their eyes closed in reverence.

"Jesus was the Man of Sorrows," the pastor continued. "Despite the inhumane death he endured for us, he never wavered. Love was his sealed order. His mission on this earth was to teach us how to love."

He paced back and forth behind the podium, his hands clasped behind his back. "So let's think about this a minute. Why do we suffer? Where does it come from?" He moved back to the podium where his open Bible rested. "God doesn't create our suffering. We create our suffering. Hate creates our suffering, and hate wears many faces.

"A brother came up to me the other day, and do you know what he asked? He said, 'Ray, how is it that your God of Love can't put more love on this earth?' And I said to him, 'Brother, how much more love can God provide, when he's already sacrificed his own Son for our salvation? When that Son loved us enough to plead for our forgiveness, even as we nailed him to a cross?'

"If you're like that brother and you want to see more love in this world, open up your own heart and stop fussing about someone else's! That's what each of us has to do—treat others as we want to be treated. The minute we start picking and choosing who's worth loving, it stops being Love."

"God does not create our suffering," he said. "But he uses it, doesn't he? He uses our suffering for glory. He uses our suffering to refine us. 'I shall come out as gold,' says Job.'"

Dozens of others stood up, raised their arms high into the air.

"Did you know, in Old Testament times," he continued, "there was a process for turning mined ore into pure gold? That's the same process God uses to refine us. He uses our sorrows, the sorrows of this earth, tear by tear, to soften and till the soil of our crushed hearts. He uses the waters of this earth, drop by drop, to cleanse us, make us pliable. And he uses the fires of this earth to redeem us, bit by bit, to skim off the dross that collects on our souls."

All around me, people rose from their seats. I leaned over, asked the older gentleman beside me, "Who is this man?" and he handed me a program. Inside was a photo, his name. He was Raymond Roberts, senior pastor of the Hyssop Mt. Zion First Baptist Church. There was also a transcript of his sermon. A short bio said he was the son of Cornelius and Marcella Roberts of Birmingham, Alabama; a brother to Booker; a graduate of Howard University who went on to receive a Masters in Divinity.

✝✝✝

Willow read the last lines slowly, then looked up at Booker, hopeful that the sound of his brother's name might rouse a sign of life, a reaction, recognition, a glimmer. Not a muscle moved. She let Lily's words float through the room for a while. As was her habit, she imagined the images of that Sunday long ago through the lens of art. She pictured Lily and her children walking through Seurat's *Sunday Afternoon in the Park*. She pictured Raymond Roberts' face as a Byzantine painting.

She resumed reading.

✝✝✝

"Here's the prickly thing," Pastor Raymond continued. "God gave us free will, because love cannot be forced. That's not love's way. He gave us the freedom to choose; to choose or to not choose him, to choose or not choose love. Whenever we make the wrong choice, God weeps.

"If some of you out there are having trouble understanding the sheer power of love, then think about its opposite. This world has been broken by sin and hatred. Hate is a forceful thing; I don't have to tell you that. Hate is what keeps us down, keeps us trapped, keeps us oppressed, keeps us in shackles. Hate is what breaks our bones, breaks our hearts. But we can't let it break our spirits. Somehow, some way, we've got to find a way to rise again. 'It is for freedom that Christ has set us free,' says Galatians 5:1. 'Stand firm, then, and do not let yourselves be burdened again by a yoke of slavery.'"

"Hallelujah!" came a collective cry from all four corners of the tent.

"This world has tried everything," Pastor Raymond said. "It's tried war, oppression, exclusion. It's tried money, power, lies. It's tried every form of hate imaginable. None of these things have worked out, but we keep on trying them anyway, these same old tired snares on the wrong side of our nature—our bottom denominator. We try them over and over and over again. War, oppression, exclusion, violence, persecution. You know what this world hasn't tried to settle our differences? Not once, in all our long years of history?"

"Love!" The response was thunderous.

"Yes, my friends, love! Love is the one thing, the only thing, we haven't tried, each and every one of us, all at the same time, to put front and center in thought and action. As strong and despotic as hate might be, God's Love, the kind of love he sewed inside our deepest heart, is stronger. Song of Solomon tells us:

'Love is strong as death, passion as fierce as the grave. Its flashes are flashes of fire, a raging flame. Many waters cannot quench love, neither can floods drown it.'

"Hate, on the other hand, is cowardly and selfish, an easy, skin-deep, ignorant solution that damages its perpetrator far more than its victim. You want to destroy your enemy? Lincoln said, 'I destroy my enemy when I make him my friend.' Historian, Arnold Toynbee told us the same thing: 'Love is the ultimate force that makes for the saving choice of life and good against the damning choice of death and evil. Therefore the first hope in our inventory must be the hope that love is going to have the last word.'

"And it always does, in God's plan. The Man of Sorrows became the Man of Joy. His enduring, unfailing Love keeps our eyes lifted up to the hills, to the joy that transcends this long, harsh winter. It keeps us waiting for the joy of the Second Spring to come, the joy of reunion. It keeps us singing that old Negro spiritual, Go Down, Moses ... 'oh! let my people go!'"

The crowd was electrified now, a palpable, animated energy beneath the umbrella of the tent. Every last one of us was on our feet, including my children! Bo was waving his little cap in the air. Noël was clutching Amelia Rosalie tightly against her chest, her eyes as big and bright as dahlias. Without a cap, Steve was mimicking Bo's waving motion. And Adam's mouth was a perfect little O of surprise.

"Some miracles are happening right now up in Baton Rouge, aren't they?" Pastor Raymond said.

"Yes, they are!" A man raised his clenched fist in the air.

"Our brother, my mentor, the honorable Rev. T.J. Jemison is leading the boycott to do God's work up there."

"Amen!"

"Rev. Jemison just made the appeal to the city council for the right of Negro passengers who pay the same fare to sit down on the bus if seats are available. And it looks as if it might pass."

"Praise Jesus!"

"These are exciting times, my friends. The winds of love, and justice, and liberation are blowing upon us."

†††

Had Booker stirred, ever-so-slightly, or was it Willow's imagination? She looked at his hands, his face, still and silent. Even his chest had no movement despite the rhythmic, hypnotic pulsing of the ventilator. And yet, she could have sworn she sensed movement from the corner of her eye.

The policeman, grown bored by then, was gazing out the window overlooking the parking lot, absent enough that Willow felt there was a modicum of privacy between her and Booker. She continued reading the final part of the letter.

†††

"Love is not a doctrine," Pastor Raymond said. "Love is not a set of rules or laws. Love is not passive. Love is a personal relationship that unites us to God and our brothers and sisters in dynamic action. Together, we rise or fall as one."

He looked suddenly into the eyes of one of the men in the front row, pointing at him. "Jesus promises to never leave you or forsake you, my brother. No matter what you're going through, underneath you are the everlasting arms." He glanced at the man seated beside the first. "Or you. Or you, or you, or you, or you." He looked at each one, seated in various places throughout the tent. And then, somehow, some way, he spotted me, Clarry! We were all still standing, and I'm sure I must've stood out as the only white person, but he gazed directly at me, and I could barely breathe! "And you," he said, his voice growing tender. "You, sister, are loved by God more than you can know. There's nothing you can do, or not do, that can make God love you any less."

Tears flooded my eyes. My knees bowed. Some turned around to look at me, and my cheeks burned hot, probably red as flame. I can't even begin to describe to you the flood of emotions that washed over me. I can only say that it seemed as if I had been released from a suit of armor, like a lifelong paraplegic who can suddenly move her legs!

He shifted his eyes away from mine. "You might ask, so what is love in action? How should we love? ... Forgive, for Love is forgiving. Be patient, for Love is patience. Be compassionate, for Love is compassion. Be merciful, for Love is mercy. Be selfless, for Love puts others first. Seek justice. Respond to someone's need. Be there. Be present. Listen more and deeply, and speak less. Empower, don't control. Encourage, don't tear down. These are just some of the ways Love reveals itself. Love is a giver. So give it, wherever, however, you can. Give it, to whoever you're with. Give it away, give it all away, give and give, until you're empty. Love will fill you up again, for Love is bottomless—a rushing river without end.

"You might think of disciples, like Matthew, Mark, Luke, and John, as biblical folks who belonged to the past. You might think of them as special, anointed people, as saints, but really they're no different from you and me, or at least they started out that way. God's story didn't end with them; it started with them. God's story ain't over! Every life—yours included—is another story in the ongoing book of God's Love. As Mark 4:2 says, 'Jesus taught by using stories, many stories.' Together, our stories comprise the living Gospel of Jesus.

"Brothers and sisters, we are loved with a greater Love than any of us can dream of or even imagine. When we Love, we are in God, and God is in us. When we Love, we transcend. When we Love, we overcome. Dare to love too much—it's impossible! Pascal said, 'When one does not love too much, one does not love enough.'

"So let Love be your only aim, the answer to every question you ask and are asked. When you face any decision, large or small, or you grow confused about God's will for your life, about which way is right and which way is wrong, let Love be your litmus test. Ask yourself, 'Is this what Love would do?' When you follow where Love leads, there you will find God."

✝✝✝

"Who *is* that woman, and why is she in here?" came an angry voice from behind Willow.

When she turned around, she saw a man who looked to be about the same age as she was, storming straight toward her, a look of near rage in his eyes. The policeman raised both arms and stepped in front of him.

"Cyrus?" she asked.

"Yeah, that's me."

The policeman stepped back.

"The question is, who the hell are you, and what the hell are you reading to my father?"

Willow paused for a second, folded the letter back inside her purse, before standing up. She introduced herself as the daughter of the man murdered beside his father, and she went on to explain, in the briefest of terms, about the reason Booker had come to Weeping Willow, about the missing Bible, about the disinterment, about the shooting.

"What in the world was that crazy old man thinking?" Cyrus said when she finished, his rage thawing into a kind of disbelief, or so it seemed, as he stared at his father's motionless body hooked to the daunting menagerie of wires and tubes. "Look where it got him! And for what?"

†††

Willow got into her car for the drive home. Her headache from earlier had returned. Cyrus' angry reaction to her presence in his father's room had stirred up the other whirlwind—the fact that people in Weeping Willow, at least some of them, were blaming her for Leon's death. Her birth into this world had killed her mother, and now there was this.

Her temples throbbed. She felt suddenly sweaty, nauseated. Stopping her Subaru on the side of the road just in time, she leaned out, vomited once, then again.

Relief. The churning in her stomach subsided. She rested her forehead against the steering wheel. *Get yourself together, Willow.*

Before she left Bedlington, she stopped at the Last Oasis liquor store on the outer city limits. Better to buy it here than in Weeping Willow where she had become the talk of the town, an object of intense scrutiny. Imagine that, the invisible girl.

As she walked through the well-stocked aisles of the liquor store, she inhaled the old, familiar scent, the scent of an old friend—the smell of rescue. At the wall of vodka bottles of various sizes and brands, she reached for a couple of bottles of Stolichnaya, Uncle Ricky's favorite—it made it seem less despicable—and paid for them without looking the clerk in the eye.

Back in the car, she convinced herself not to think too much about it, about the fact that she had thrown away nearly eighteen years of sobriety. Who had better reason to fall off the wagon than she did right now? Won't a starving person ingest questionable food, if that's all there is to eat? Whatever would get her through this in one piece seemed within bounds. She could clean herself up later, the same way she'd done it before.

The jarring image recurred in her mind: Leon, lying lifeless on the back deck, his open eyes staring blankly, the bloody hole in his neck. It had really happened. The nightmare was more real than the road ahead. Soon, she would have to pass them again on the way back into Weeping Willow, the trees he had planted for her. How could she bear to look at them?

Cracking her window open a tad, she breathed in the stifling summer air. Would Booker make it? Should she just forget about the exhumation? She imagined bringing Raymond's Bible to his bedside. Maybe that would be the panacea that pulled him out of this, that saved him. The power of his brother's love, the power of Love with a capital L.

Willow understood the power of love, or wanted to. She was born from it. Though her parents were polar opposites, love had been their binding force. Her mother had written to her in her journal about the place where Willow had been conceived, a place on the edge of Lake Michigan called the Moonstone Inn, vacant that late autumn when she and Leon were the only guests. "I felt as if we had fallen through a portal," Noël had written. "A portal into a place where lost dreams come true. And they did come true! I wasn't supposed to be able to conceive another child, but soon *you* will be here." After that stay at the inn, her mother had coined a term. She called them *moonstoners*—herself, Leon, and Willow. "Remember, Willow, we aren't the ones born in the sunlight, but under a difficult moon, our luminance hidden beneath an opaque veil. But when we're cut, we reflect a streak of light."

Willow knew the reason her mother had taken the time to write all of that down for her. It was her way of bracing Willow for birth into a motherless world.

Hold on, she told herself. Wait a little while longer for her own streak of light.

-EIGHTEEN-

CASSEROLES

CAREFUL to keep it level, Joshua Wharton carried the covered dish his wife had made earlier that day, two days after Leon Ziemny's death, a chicken casserole for Willow. That's what people still did here after a death had occurred; they brought a dish of comfort food—homemade, of course—to the bereaved in the hope that some comfort, however slight, might be derived. He knocked on the front door with his knuckles—ringing the doorbell seemed too intrusive under the circumstances—and the girl appeared, looking utterly grief-stricken. A physician recognized the signs of grief beyond a river of tears: dark circles under dazed eyes, sallow skin, the dehydrated look of self-neglect.

"Hello, Willow. I'm Dr. Wharton—*Joshua*, not Aaron."

"Oh, right, I remember." She smiled, or tried to. "My father mentioned you so often. You were a good friend to him. Please, come in."

He stepped inside. He'd been in this house countless times throughout the years, and the thought that Leon was no longer here, but his familiar belongings still were, cloaked him in sadness. "As you can see, I've brought along something for you to eat—it's a chicken casserole. My wife, Melissa, made it for you. It's really quite good, her best dish."

"I'm sure it is. Thank you." She took it from him as he followed her into the kitchen. He expected to find an array of similar platters and plates on her kitchen counter, wrapped in aluminum foil, but there was only one other, besides his, and a round tin. The meager outpouring troubled him. "Would you like a cup of coffee? A cookie?" She opened the tin, held it out to him. "Nancy—Leon's next-door neighbor baked these. I don't even know her last name."

"Oh, you mean the Salvos." He smiled. "Good people." Though he was trying to cut back on sweets, he selected a small butter cookie filled with homemade raspberry jam, to be polite. "No coffee, though."

She sat down at the dining room table, and he sat across from her. A bird clock chirped out the time, startling him, with its three shrill tweets. Joshua folded his hands, looked into Willow's heartbroken face, the face of the girl he had advised her mother to abort, the girl about whom some were now saying such dreadful things—that she should've never come here from New York City and gotten her father mixed up with the Black stranger. Others, like Jeff Miller, were even blaming Willow for her father's death!

He'd first heard of it yesterday, when he went to the grocery to buy the ingredients for Melissa's casserole and bumped into Jeff Miller. "Disinterment? What disinterment?" Joshua had asked. And Jeff replied that Willow was opening her grandmother's grave to retrieve some item from the casket, something valuable, though no one could fathom what it might be. "We would've filed a petition to stop it," Jeff said. "But by the time we heard what they were planning to do, the application was already approved."

All the way home and all night long, Joshua had thought long and hard about it. They were too late to stop the exhumation by contesting it, so someone stopped it another way. If that wasn't atrocious enough, now they were attacking the girl, accusing her of causing her own father's death. What a ghastly, unfortunate thing!

That's when he knew he was going to do it, as sure as he knew his own name. He was going to violate the HIPAA law.

"Willow, I've heard about the exhumation." He gazed into her eyes which reminded him, somewhat, of Noël Trudeau's, though plainer, dimmer. Noël had been a raving beauty, and her mother too. Willow was pleasant enough in her muted way, not unattractive, despite the grief, just plain enough to be easily over-looked. "Given the circumstances," he glanced around the room at Leon's things, "are you still planning for it to occur?"

She shrugged. "It was supposed to be done within thirty days, but now…" her voice trailed off.

"Well, maybe I can help. Maybe there's no longer a need. Your father came to see me three weeks ago to tell me you were interested in knowing the cause of your grandmother's death. Of course, I didn't know about the exhumation—he left that part out—but since then, I've gone through my grandfather's old files, and I can shed some light."

Her eyes intensified.

And so he went ahead and told her, one year before he was legally allowed to disclose it, because he wanted to save the poor girl the torment of the town's wrath, the turmoil of having to open up a grave to find a truth he already knew. He explained that Lily suffered from catatonia and that this catatonia had eventually esca-lated into what they called *malignant* or *lethal*, affecting the body to the point that it interfered with important functions such as blood pressure, heart rate, body temperature, and the kidneys. "It sometimes happens to those who are catatonic for a long period of time," he said.

"So you think my grandmother died of kidney failure?"

"That, and a combination of other body system failures."

He watched her get up from the table, lean against the glass door of the patio; the sight of the blood-stained deck stunned him. "Thank you for telling me that," she said.

Joshua had been hoping the information would bring her some measure of relief, some comfort, like the casserole he'd brought along, but her expression was only sad, so very sad. As dolorous as the trees her father had planted for her, their limbs bending toward the ground.

-Nineteen-

A SHAMAL

EARLY the next morning, a bonanza of homemade food—casseroles, pies, cakes, salads—was spread out on Adam and Anne's kitchen counter. Adam was dipping a spoon into a Pyrex dish of macaroni salad from Jeff and Linda Miller when Nick Hardy called. They'd taken Cory in for questioning late last night, Nick said, after finding a small arsenal of AR-15s, AK-47s, and a stockpile of ammunition in his basement. His computer searches were equally incriminating; hundreds of white nationalist websites, including the Charlottesville rally, and also—according to Nick—"a shitload of racist crap about the Confederate flag."

"I was afraid you'd find something like that," Adam said. He should have been relieved, and part of him was, yet he was also miserable and conflicted for ratting on Cory. And for the injustice of it all—that Cory had to be the one who had been raised by David Ketchfield.

Cory once confessed to him that he'd been petrified of David as a child, scared enough to sometimes pee in his pants at the mere sight of him entering the room; how David went ballistic whenever that happened, until one day he beat Cory into a pile of mush—smashed his head against the wall and gave him a concussion, sprained his arm, knocked out a tooth. "After that, I didn't have a tear, a drop of piss, or anything else left inside of me." Cory had laughed, not the least bit sorry for himself. In his mind, the savage beating from his only parent had been boot camp for becoming a strong man.

Cory might not have felt sorry for himself, but his story haunted Adam. Save for the grace of God and the courage of his mother to hide him away from David, it might've been Adam sitting in that jail. "Well, at least, you've got the right suspect now," he said sadly.

"Maybe and maybe not," Nick replied in his cryptic way. "There are still a few holes."

Adam waited for him to elaborate. When he didn't, he assumed the holes were confidential parts of the case. "So you think there's a chance Cory is innocent?"

"Not so innocent." Nick laughed. "But maybe not guilty of *this* crime... We're keeping him here for now. A couple of his guns were purchased illegally. But I've got some other news too. Somebody tried to dig up Lily's grave last night."

"You're kidding?"

"Wish I was. Nothing serious. They were just kids—four of them, only seventeen years old, and they didn't know what the hell they were doing. As soon as they started digging with their little garden shovels, my guys hauled them into the station."

After Nick hung up, Adam walked out the back door before Anne and Rocket came downstairs for breakfast. He kept on walking until he was far out into the yard, surrounded by a nest of bushes and trees, where he couldn't be seen from any windows in the house, upstairs or down, or by cars passing by on the road. Kneeling down in the grass, he sobbed into his hands.

†††

Lifting a Styrofoam cup to his lips, Nick took a sip of his fifth cup of coffee that Saturday morning. He was back in his office in

Bedlington by then, sitting at his messy desk, mulling over the case. The town of Weeping Willow was like a hornet's nest, one person pitted against the other. Everyone had taken a side. The one commonality was that they were all afraid, and as long as the killer remained at large, they were going to stay that way. Fear was a contagious cancer that spread, if left unchecked, into darker impulses and permanent harm.

The case was far from being solved. As he'd just told Adam, there were major holes in the theory that Cory was the perpetrator. The bullets that killed Leon and wounded Booker didn't match any of his guns. Whoever shot them used a good, old-fashioned hunting rifle. In addition to that, Cory told them he was on his computer at the time of the shooting, and it appeared, from the date stamp on his emails, he was telling the truth.

So if Cory Ketchfield didn't do it, who did? The Rubik's cube seemed to be growing more faces.

Nick spread the pieces of paper around him—the names of people he had already interviewed, both solicited and those who had sought him out, as well as other potential suspects, including—until it could be ruled out one hundred percent—Booker Roberts and Willow Trudeau. Plenty of gossip, yet zero evidence to link either one of them to a crime. Jeff Miller was relentless in his pursuit. "She just shows up from New York City the same day as the Black guy, and you think it's a coincidence?" He had phoned Nick again just yesterday to pose the vexing question, as if Nick were some kind of nincompoop for not figuring out the conspiracy himself.

Nick stared down at Willow's name. He wasn't biased. He would've recused himself from the case in a heartbeat if he didn't instinctively know that Willow was a victim, not a suspect, and victimized twice now because of people like Jeff Miller. The facts bore it out. Still, sometimes surprises happened. Back in the old days, he used to take Willow for rides on his motorcycle. Her eyes had lit up every single time she looked at him, yet she didn't hang on to him during those rides. That was Willow for you, a contradiction.

He glanced at the other pieces of paper surrounding him. Only one similarity seemed to jump out, remote as it might seem. Every interviewee who condemned Willow and Booker also happened to be members of that church on the outskirts of town. Was there a correlation?

Nick sat back in his chair, placed his hands firmly on the arms. They didn't call it a megachurch for nothing. It meant—last Nick checked—over two thousand people, maybe closer to three, belonged to the congregation, the majority from Bedlington. Opened early last year, it seemed to have sprung up out of nowhere, like a dirty-brown mushroom, only it wasn't dirty-brown, it was an alabaster palace. What was the name of it? Some goofy name that didn't give any clue as to the denomination ... Nick couldn't quite recall, so he Googled it.

The Crosswinds of Eden Community Church.

What the hell kind of name was that? Even after clicking onto the website, he couldn't figure out exactly what branch of— Christianity?—it was supposed to represent. He assumed it was non-denominational, which accounted for the vast attendance. Instead of religious dogma, the information on the website focused mainly on its dynamic pastor, Reverend Tommy Brookdale. Nick didn't have to scroll down far to spot the large color headshot of him—white-haired, in a white suit, like a younger Colonel Sanders without a goatee.

He stood up, walked over to the window, peeked between the blinds at the busy street below; another sizzling summer day.

Tomorrow happened to be Sunday. While it was on his mind, he figured it might be a good idea to pay a visit to the Crosswinds of Eden Community Church to see what was cooking there, or frying. He smiled at his own bad joke. Enough years had passed since he had attended a Sunday service that he wasn't sure what constituted proper attire anymore.

Returning to the desk, he Googled that too.

✝✝✝

Dressed casually as the Internet had suggested, Nick was wearing his best blue jeans and favorite button-down shirt as he found an empty, nicely padded seat near the front (single seats were easier to come by) between two families. More like a sports arena, the sanctuary was enormous, with various tiered levels, each of them packed full. Jumbo plasma screens were placed strategically throughout the space, including one of them on either side of the stage. At the center of the stage, the altar, if you could call it that, included a stained-glass depiction of a garden, the Garden of Eden, Nick supposed, given the name of the church, surrounded by several sprays of flowers resembling funeral arrangements. A long row of dozens of American flags topped it off.

He glanced around in every direction at the sea of faces, notably all white, but that was no surprise in this geographic location. They seemed friendly enough, hugging their greetings and chatting to one another, most of them dressed more upscale than Nick (Google didn't know everything after all), especially the women in colorful summer dresses. The petite young mother sitting to his right offered him her hand, introducing herself as Mary Jane Javits, and down there, on the other side of their four small children, she pointed out her husband Elijah, who gave Nick a wave.

"Are you new here?" she asked.

"Yeah, first time. Does it show?"

"A little." She smiled. "Well, welcome. I'm so glad you came. Rev. Tommy is amazing! He's a real fighter."

"A fighter?"

"For God."

The lights dimmed. The lyrics to the opening hymn flashed on every plasma screen. The throng jumped to its feet like one body, clapping and singing as Rev. Tommy Brookdale emerged from the wings of the stage and moved toward the center, dressed in a gold suit. They kept clapping and singing until the lively hymn was over. The screens switched to a display of Psalm 105:15-16 in big black, block letters: "Touch not my anointed ones and do my prophets no harm."

Rev. Tommy raised his arms as he stood at the clear plexiglass podium. "Greetings to all of you, beloved friends, anointed friends, who God watches over and protects from sin and evil, like the good Psalm tells us." He stood back, introduced a female soprano who came out in a sequined black gown to sing a hymn, the lyrics rolling by on the screens. The acoustics were mind-blowing. A male singer, accompanying himself on guitar, performed next, followed by a trio, and rounding it all off, a full choir. The congregation was really into it by then, revved up, on their feet in front of their seats, dancing in place and swinging their arms.

Nick looked down at his watch. Half an hour had gone by before Rev. Tommy returned to center stage to take his place at the podium. Psalm 105:15-16 reappeared on the screens. "Yes, indeed, we need God's protection more than ever, because we live in troubled times, dangerous times. Next weekend we'll celebrate another of our great American holidays, Labor Day. Baseball, hotdogs, apple pie, and Chevrolet, remember that old commercial?"

Those old enough to remember laughed and applauded.

"Yes, my friends, that's the America we love, the America God loves. Morality and righteousness. Simple pleasures. The sight of our great flag waving from every front porch. But I need not tell you that our vision of America, the beautiful, is under siege."

"Yes, it is!" A man shouted. Nick twisted his head around but the man was sitting in a spot too dim to see his face.

"Yes it is, indeed." Rev. Tommy nodded. "We are surrounded by those who want to destroy it. Destroy us. But we won't let them, because we're patriots, true patriots. We're soldiers for God, aren't we? Soldiers who are committed to restoring our cherished vision of America—God's America—the America the beautiful we know and love—to get it back to its original roots, back to the birth of this glorious nation, back to baseball, hotdogs, apple pie, and Chevrolet—all the way!"

The congregation rose to its feet again; more applause.

"But there are enemies who don't share that vision. Enemies who go so far as to mock our flag, like those so-called football players who defile it by squatting down on one knee."

"Fire them!" another male boomed from the far side of the room—this voice Nick recognized as Jeff Miller's.

Rev. Tommy pointed at him, laughed, nodded. "Yes, fire them. Fire them all! Our liberties are under siege from all directions, including our Second Amendment rights, even our religion, especially our religion. They mock us for having religion, don't they? Those New York types look down on us for believing in God."

Rev. Tommy opened his arms as wide as he could stretch them. "Yes, they're coming for us, and they're everywhere! Enemies, opening our sacred borders to dangerous extremists. Even right here in our midst, in that peaceful little town just to our west, the town of Weeping Willow, a beautiful little town for over two hundred years, oh, my, yes, a perfect little town. The kind of town you see on Christmas cards, sprinkled with glittering snow. They even crept into that precious little town and tried to destroy it!"

A murmur went through the crowd. The family ahead of Nick stood up, along with hundreds of others, too riled up to remain seated. Another quote, this one from Psalm 35:1-3 appeared on the jumbo screens: "Contend, O Lord, with those who contend with me; fight against those who fight against me. Take up shield and buckler; arise and come to my aid. Brandish spear and javelin against those who pursue me."

"In-*vaders!*" Rev. Tommy slapped his palm against the podium, then lifted his eyes to the ceiling. "You see, my friends, that's how it starts. Strangers converge on a little town like Weeping Willow, strangers from faraway places, plotting to destroy another peaceful little town with their demonic, un-American values. God loves America, remember that, and we must be his foot soldiers. We must take a stand against sin and evil! We must fight for what's ours! We must not open our doors, or our borders, to these dangerous strangers!"

Everyone was standing now. So as not to make himself conspicuous, Nick stood too. Mary Jane Javits smiled at him.

"And do you know what these strangers came to Weeping Willow to do? They were plotting to desecrate the grave of a good Christian woman, to plunder it with their greed!"

The sound of "boos" rang from all corners of the arena.

"You're right to boo." Rev. Tommy clicked his tongue in disgust. "Imagine that! Even the dead aren't sacred to them! But here's the saving grace—the dark invader was stopped from his evil plans, wasn't he? And so was the fool who took him in, the one who opened his door to these evil invaders. And do you know who stopped them?" He lifted his arms and fired an imaginary rifle. "GOD stopped them!"

The audience exploded—in wild cheers and thunderous applause. The first quote from Psalms 105:15-16 reappeared: "Touch not my anointed ones and do my prophets no harm."

Rev. Tommy was given a hand-microphone. He walked away from the podium, stood at the foot of the stage as a small army of ushers carrying large collection plates pressed forward between the rows. "Fear not, beloved friends, for the Lord hates his enemies, and he will not allow them to touch you, his anointed ones! So fight for the America we love and keep fighting! Give and give generously to God's crusade! Plant your seed in righteousness, and God will assure that you reap your bounty!" The image on the jumbo screens changed to a close-up of Rev. Tommy's impassioned face, right down to the pores on his skin. As the full choir sang a rousing rendition of *God Bless America*, Rev. Tommy exited the stage. Full lighting switched on overhead. The show was over.

"Didn't I tell you he was incredible?" Mary Jane Javits said to Nick before gathering up her purse and program and reaching for the hand of the child beside her. "I sure hope we see you again."

✝✝✝

As people filed out of the arena, Nick remained in his padded seat, stupefied. What had just happened here? He might be lapsed in his church attendance, but the service reminded him of an old quote by Jonathan Swift: "We have just enough religion to make us hate, but not enough to make us love one another." No subtlety about it. Rev. Tommy was inciting his adoring congregation to terror and rage as surely as if he'd lit a grenade and tossed it into their hair.

Elbow on his knee, he rested his chin in his palm, thinking. He had caught a sermon or two while channel surfing TV, and those other super-sized churches didn't seem to be muddying up religion like this one did, playing on people's worst fears. The way Nick saw it, everyone had their own opinions, emotions, beliefs—the trouble was, each of us was a flawed human being who saw things through his own flawed lens. That's why Nick tried hard to steer clear of those blinders when it came to values. That's why he surrounded himself with like-minded individuals—EMTs, fire fighters, other cops—who were centered, grounded by a shared sense of honorable mission. That's why he became a homicide detective. He'd learned the hard way, by fighting a war, that violence never solved a thing, or if it did, it only opened up a larger problem somewhere else.

He shifted in his seat, stared at the altar decked in flags.

And yet, someone had to stop the bullies, hold them accountable. Nick had built his career on that. That was where things got dicey—when emotions got so out of hand that the real bullies became unrecognizable. The most abominable sin, in Nick's estimation, was a dirty cop—or a dirty anyone in a position of moral authority—who manipulated truth to suit his own ends. Truth was truth. Facts were facts. That's where the line had to be drawn. The facts had to be followed, wherever they led. Otherwise, without even realizing it, *we* became the bullies, the self-righteous judges.

He looked around the vast space; a small group remained in one of the higher tiers, talking and gesturing excitedly among themselves, arms flailing.

This whole thing reminded him of a *shamal*, the northwesterly wind blowing over the Kuwait desert that he experienced during the Gulf War. A shamal was the worst kind of wind, kicking up a blinding dust and sandstorm that could be dangerous if inhaled into the lungs as it often included droplets of poisons—acids, chemicals, metals—the same as blinding hatred. Sometimes those winds blew slowly. He and his fellow troops were advised to move in the opposite direction whenever a shamal was headed their way.

How slowly had *this* shamal been blowing? Since last year? Last month? It didn't matter—the congregation was already spinning in its cyclone.

The arena was now empty; Nick was the last one left. He got up from his seat, walked through the mall-like lobby, exited through the golden arched doors, into fresh air. Inside his car, he sat for another long minute before turning the key. Rev. Tommy might cut a charismatic figure in his gold suit, but Nick assessed him to be a classic snake oil salesman, a provocateur, messing with valuables beyond money—though he was raking in plenty of that too, as evidenced by the overflowing collection plates. This guy was messing with people's minds and hearts, twisting their earnest faith into pipe bombs, until one of them—(which one? That was Nick's to figure out)—had been provoked to murder Booker Roberts and killed Leon Ziemny in the process.

He thought about Mary Jane Javits and her husband Elijah. Sweet young couple with a sweet young family, who came there for prayer, not provocation, and he wanted to punch his fist through the windshield over the way Brookdale was manipulating them. Insidiously, like a predator. Inch by inch. Sunday by Sunday. Not to mention, what the golden guru had already done to poor dead Leon, to Booker, to Willow, without getting his own hands dirty. Real harm was being done to real people.

Still absorbed in thought, Nick started the car and drove through the parking lot toward the main road. Emotions were unreliable. Opinions weren't fact. No matter our feelings or views, we had to trust in the common ground that united us as human beings, didn't we? We had to plant ourselves on that firm foundation, choose that solid place, again and again—the Absolutes we knew to be true, that couldn't be doubted, weren't open for conjecture. Things like our shared humanity, decency, mutual respect, integrity, truth. *Truth!* What about the God's honest truth? Couldn't we, at least, be on the same page when it came to that?

He glanced at the alabaster building in his rear view mirror. If not, we'd end up being swept away into a shamal, a toxic temple of our own lies.

TWENTY

WENDING THROUGH UNKNOWN COUNTRY

THE next morning, a little past ten, Willow was curled up on her bed in the attic, sipping a glass of vodka, her hair uncombed, her teeth unbrushed. Her world was shrinking. She was afraid of the town, afraid of the rest of the house, and so she had been camping upstairs in the attic, daring to go down below only for food and other essentials.

She couldn't face seeing Leon's things, still in the places he'd left them. She couldn't bring herself to enter the sanctity of his bedroom, where he'd hung two portraits of her mother, painted by Uncle Ricky, on opposite walls. The sight of her mother's face, in the very room she had lain in wait for Willow's birth and written a diary for her, always made Willow weepy, but now there was a deeper layer. Now there was the lack of her father too, the tangible lack of him—his watches on the dresser, ticking off the time that had run out, the clothes she had seen him wearing less than a week ago, hanging in his closet, likely still carrying his scent. In the other room sat his desk. Nick had confiscated Leon's cell phone and his computer, Booker's phone too, yet the more personal items remained, like his White Sox bobblehead. On the kitchen counter was the start of a grocery list; the sight of Leon's handwriting, for some reason, struck her as most personal of all. *Mayonaise*, he'd scribbled, misspelled, with only one n.

To avoid all that, she holed up in the attic.

Her cellphone rang on the nightstand. Nick again. He had called her yesterday, Sunday, pressing her to leave the house and move in with Adam and Anne for a while, and she'd told him she would think about it. "Don't think so much, Willow!" he snapped. "Just do it!"—said with an audacious familiarity that belied the passage of time between them.

What was his urgency? The attic was her refuge—her place to hide, her place to drink—but how could he know that? Now he was calling to tell her he had some bad news. Bad news? What else, after losing Leon, could be so bad? What else could be taken away?

The latest bad news was that Cory was going to be released from jail later that morning. Nick couldn't make anything stick; there was nothing he could hold him for. Hearing the self-recrimination in Nick's voice, she remained silent, though her heart twisted with tenderness for him. "I really think you should move in with your brother for a while," he repeated. "Just to be safe."

"From Cory?"

"From anyone. There are some wild ideas floating around out there about you."

"So you've said." Hearing it again caused a fresh squeeze of torment.

"Don't be so stubborn! Just go to Adam's house."

The same as before, she told him she would consider it. And then, she hung up. Willow had other things to occupy her mind today. Other things to do, other things to get settled. She had been neglecting her job, for one, but couldn't seem to come up with one word to write about Neo-Impressionism. Who cared about Neo-Impressionism anyway? Combing her hair was perhaps an easier start before she worked her way up to bigger things, like driving to Bedlington to visit Booker. No change with him; he was still in a coma.

The medical examiner hadn't yet released Leon's body, but Christopher Green called yesterday to say it would happen soon, maybe in the next day or two, and so Willow spent a good portion of the next hour trying to find a priest who might say a word over her father's grave. The Rite of Committal, they called it; she'd picked up a thing or two about Catholic sacraments during time spent with Walt. Though Leon had not been a practicing Catholic for years, it was in his blood, and she wanted to honor that, for his sake and for Walt's too.

There were no Catholic churches in Weeping Willow, but there was one relatively small Presbyterian Church and two small Methodist churches, all of them, she learned, in danger of closing; apparently, the megachurch's massive attendance had siphoned regulars away. Maybe Christopher Green knew of a Catholic priest. She punched his number on speed dial.

A few days ago, she and Adam had visited with Christopher Green to firm up her father's arrangements and, at that time, he provided them a copy of Leon's will, which Leon had included in his pre-arrangement packet. Unorthodox as it might be to leave your will at the funeral home, it was typical of Leon's practicality. They discovered he had amassed a sizeable amount of money over the years, the majority left to Willow, the rest going into a trust fund for Rocket's education. Adam and Anne weren't hurting for money—Adam had made sound investments before retiring and Anne's late father had left her a hefty inheritance—but Leon wanted Rocket to have every opportunity for a crack at the top medical school.

Besides the priest, Willow had another matter to discuss with

Christopher Green. As soon as he answered, she informed him that she no longer wanted to exhume her grandmother's body for cause of death.

"You're canceling the disinterment?"

"No. I still want to get the Bible. I just don't want to exhume the body."

"Okay, that simplifies things," he said. The disinterment had already been scheduled to take place in one week, before dawn, to ensure as much privacy as possible. He assured her that the site would be screened beneath a tent, with ample security present. "I'll make sure everything's done respectfully," he added.

"I'm sure you will."

"And all the officials are set to be there—health and safety, environmental. Nick Hardy will be there too."

"Nick? Why Nick?"

"We needed police presence, and he volunteered—since he has a vested interest in the case." Willow reiterated that she didn't intend to be anywhere near the coffin when it was opened. "You can stand as safe a distance away as you feel comfortable," Christopher said.

Lastly, they discussed the Catholic priest. As it turned out, he did know someone, his own priest, Father Sean Mahoney from St. Luke's Church in Bedlington, and he promised to give him a call. "Before we hang up—." Christopher paused. "I think I owe you a big apology."

"For what?"

"I'm sort of the one who spilled the beans to Cory about the disinterment. He was here for a plumbing job that day, and you know Cory—talk, talk, talk, talk—he's always such a friendly guy that he sucks me into his gossip, and the next thing you know,

I kind of let it slip. Anyway, I heard that he was arrested and all and—"

"Don't worry about it," she said. "Cory's being released today. Nick says he's not the one who did it."

"What a relief. I mean—I know it's probably not for you, with the killer still out there."

After she hung up the phone, Willow braced herself to make the trip downstairs to fix some lunch. Food had zilch appeal to her since Leon's death; it never did have much allure, but now she had to force herself to eat, the same as when she was young.

She creeped down the attic stairs and into the kitchen. The house was dark, the drapes tightly drawn, including the closed blinds on the glass sliding doors, so she didn't have to look at the bloodstains. Carrying the next in the series of Lily's unread letters, she rested it on the counter. Willow had become obsessed with the letters. They seemed her only link to the world where her precious lost father had gone.

She scoured the cabinets for something easy to prepare. A can of tuna. Couldn't get much easier than that. She wondered why it was there when Leon hated tuna, hated fish of any kind. She twisted the can around until she found the "use by" date, and it was still good. Booker was probably the one who bought it. After she cranked the lid off with a can opener, the thought of Nick Hardy crossed her mind, his sudden intrusion in her life during this most-terrible of times.

She had met Nick in her late twenties, magnetically attracted to him as a force of nature. He was a rugged and restless individualist, strong-willed and sure of himself, an uncharted landscape. He was no game player, and he'd made it clear that his independence was his lifeblood. Nothing or no one could pin him down; not a place, not a job, not a woman. He had dreams of moving out west, landing a detective job in some big city. Forewarned, she should have known not to blight his unmapped landscape with her footprints, yet, like a fool, she'd hoped anyway. If her heart had been broken, (and, holy God, it had been), it was her own doing.

Grabbing a fork, she sat down at the table, pushed Lily's letter aside as she speared a chuck of tuna straight from the can. The memories were gelling into focus, the way memories do when dwelled upon—the little dive in Bedlington where she and Nick used to go for late dinners, the motorcycle rides, the night they gazed through his telescope at the Orion Nebula. Their relationship never quite came into focus, as if they were separated by a veil, except in that moment when the telescope was fine-tuned.

Illusive as their relationship had been, its pull seemed innate, instinctive. Like her, Nick once disclosed his own doubts of being worthy of love. But his worth was more than clear to her. She saw through to his core—his underlying decency, his needle-straight moral compass, his bright, razor-sharp mind, his calling. Nick Hardy had a Maltese cross tattooed over his heart, the cross of defenders and firefighters.

And over her own heart, she carried his memory like a closed locket.

Silly, sentimental thought. She stabbed another piece of tuna. But how were you supposed to describe those kinds of feelings? How did scientists describe them? A rush of chemical changes in the brain? A rogue molecule in our DNA that deceived us into believing one person was different from the rest? Or *was* it deceit? Maybe our DNA was simply more honest than we were.

Unlike her emotion-ruled mother and grandmother, Willow had her pragmatic side, the side she got from Leon, so she understood it in Nick, admired the way he navigated the snares of this world, such as marriage, like landmines. The last time she saw him—before this calamity, that is—was when he was headed for his new police job in Bedlington, she for New York City, and they had wished each other a wistful *Bon voyage*. Well, wistful on her part anyway.

The bird clock sang two times. The tuna can was empty.

Behind the closed drapes, the windows had eyes; the town was staring. Willow reached for the letter, got up from her chair, grabbed the bottle of vodka from the kitchen cabinet, and returned to her fortress in the attic.

†††

March 15, 1953

Dear Clarry,

There I was in the park today, at this Sunday's revival, when a group of colored women pulled me aside and warned me not to return. "Why?" I implored them. "Have my children not been well behaved?"

No, they said, it wasn't the children that concerned them. It was me. It looked wrong, they said, for a white woman to keep coming back week after week without a husband. It was inviting trouble, and their distress over my presence was robbing them of their own joy from the revival.

I meant no harm, I explained, dumbfounded. I tried to tell them how much the revivals mean to me, how much they're helping me. But they remained unmoved.

Crushed, embarrassed, and on the verge of tears, I told them they could rest assured—I would not be returning.

My heart is broken, Clarry. Pastor Raymond's sermons were like water to my soul. Even my children noticed the difference in me. I can't understand why my attendance at a public gathering, a spiritual gathering no less, presents any sort of problem. I realize, of course, that white and colored are not supposed to mix, but I'll never understand why. I find the Negroes' spirituality to be richer, fuller, more natural than my own church, where they recite prayers verbatim through pinched lips. Maybe I'm wrong to feel that way, but I do.

Why is it that I can't seem to think, to do, anything right? I fit in absolutely nowhere.

†††

March 27, 1953
Dear Clarry,

Jack told me that he called you to let you know I've been in the hospital again, this time in Baton Rouge. I just arrived home today. As usual, they put me in the ward for "crazy" people. I hate that word, but that's how everyone sees us—damaged beyond repair.

It was a very small ward, only seven beds, and I bonded with a young man there, another patient, just nineteen years old, named Robbie. He's not crazy. He's a sensitive, kind boy with his whole life ahead of him, and I tried to convince him that he didn't deserve to be there. He's a homosexual, and they were giving him shock treatments to stop it; the same awful treatments they give to me, to all of us, like we're wild animals that need to be electrocuted into deadness. They make us take off our shoes and wait. My turn usually follows Robbie's. I can see him lying unconscious on the table after his "treatment," a rubber heel in his mouth to prevent him from biting his own tongue as he convulses.

As terrible as the hospital was, it's far worse to be putting my children through this latest agony. Only Adam seemed happy to see me when I came home—he ran to me and threw his little arms around my legs. Bo and Steve treat me like I'm made out of china, and Noël just stares at me with those beautiful, sad eyes, as if I'm totally lost.

But here is my good news, Clarry. I'm not lost any more. I was found!

God works in mysterious ways, as they say, and I had a surprise visitor while I was in the psychiatric ward. Pastor Raymond Roberts came to visit me. Well, that's not exactly how it happened. Bible in hand, he was on his way to visit another patient when he spotted me sitting alone in the day room. "Mrs. Trudeau?" He arched his eyebrows, backed up slowly, then entered the room where I was sitting.

"Please, call me Lily." I touched my ratted hair. "I must look a fright."

"Do I look frightened?" He grinned.

No, he didn't look frightened, but neither would he look directly at me. He kept glancing around as if to assure that no one was scrutinizing him for stopping to speak with me. He remained standing. "I suspected you suffer from melancholia," he said.

"How could you possibly have known?" I asked.

"I saw it in your eyes … the same look I sometimes see in myself when I look in a mirror. I've battled melancholy for most of my life."

"You?" I was stunned. "But, why? You have so many gifts!"

"We all have our gifts, Mrs. Trudeau."

"Lily." I corrected him again.

"Can I tell you something shocking?" He paused for a moment, still standing a distance away, and I nodded. "I'm a Negro."

I laughed. It had been so long since I heard my own laughter that I barely recognized the sound. "Yes," I said. "You certainly are."

"I thought, maybe, you didn't notice." His smile dissipated. "Most white people see Negroes quite differently from themselves."

"Most people occupy themselves with petty things to avoid their own truth."

He seemed to consider this. "Maybe so," he said. "But I can honestly say that you are the most open minded person I've ever met."

"What brings you here?" It seemed a logical question for me to ask, particularly since he'd brought up the subject of race. Hospitals for Blacks and Whites remained segregated places.

"I'm here to visit someone," he replied.

"Cedric?"

He said nothing, but his silence confirmed it. Cedric is a Negro gentleman, a decorated veteran from WWII, who'd been admitted two days before, yet to appear at our daily group meetings—probably because they banned him from fraternizing with the rest of us. "How is it that Cedric was allowed to come here, to this hospital, I mean?"

His eyes again examined the hallway outside the door, still empty of human traffic. "There are no wards like this for Negroes," he said. "Luckily, Cedric has friends who have some influence, particularly since things seem to be changing some-what in Baton Rouge, thanks to Rev. Jemison."

"Yes. You've mentioned him at the revivals." I patted the chair beside my own. "Please, sit down, Pastor Roberts."

He remained standing, his eyes pensive. "It's hard to use your gifts when you're being held down all the time," he said. "Sometimes, you get weary. I think that melancholia is really hopelessness that becomes too big a load to carry for too long a time. At least, that's how it was for me." He lifted his Bible with half the front cover torn away. "See this? This is my most precious possession. This book is what saves me, over and over again." He explained that it had belonged to his great-great grandfather back when he was a slave. "Only the love of Christ can save us from that kind of hopelessness. He can save you too."

"I don't know that I'm worth saving," I said. "I feel as if I exist in some parallel realm from other people, outside of God's love—and everyone else's. I'm an alien in this world, Pastor Roberts. I don't even know how to be a person!"

"We're all aliens here." A sad smile crossed his lips. "All of us, just visitors, refugees. As Fra Giovanni put it, 'we're pilgrims together, wending through unknown country, home.'"

What beautiful words, I thought, yet meaningless from my perspective. "Home? Where's that? What's that?"

"Home is where we feel loved. Our unhappiness and dysfunction in this world begins from feeling unloved." He sat down beside me. "We all have a home in God, Lily." For the first time since he arrived, he looked into my eyes. In them I saw an acceptance I'd never quite seen in another human's eyes before. He allowed me to feel, I dare say, God's acceptance too. "Why did you stop coming to the revivals?" he asked.

"Yes, the revivals. They really were revivals for me."

"Was it something the women said to you?"

I didn't reply.

"You must understand, they're very protective of me. They see danger where I see opportunity. God's word is for everyone."

Our conversation went on for quite a while after that. I didn't know I had that many words inside of me. Turns out, each of us had recently celebrated our twenty-seventh birthday. He spoke of his family, his calling to become a pastor, of his little brother, Booker, spirited and devoted to him. We talked about my children, and eventually he asked about Jack. "You'll probably think me terrible to say this," I said, "my own pastor thought as much. But I'm afraid of my husband. Terrified, sometimes. I know that I should submit to him, that's what the Bible says, and that's what my pastor says."

"And the Bible also says, 'you did not receive a spirit that makes you a slave,'" he said. "Bondage is not marriage."

I took this statement in with a degree of relief. "And yet," I paused briefly. "You preach that Jesus wants us to put others' needs ahead of our own. Maybe I should just do whatever my husband—"

"Yes, Jesus does want us to put others' needs ahead of ours," he interrupted. "But out of love. Not out of fear or force. We can only give of ourselves from fullness, not emptiness. Jesus never asks us to bow to abuse or degradation." His eyes darted away from mine. "Not that that necessarily describes your situation."

"Pretty close …" Tears sprang into my eyes. I stopped myself from elaborating.

"God understands your suffering. Jesus was the Man of Sorrows, the Savior of the Lost. As long as he's here with you—and he promises to never forsake you—you can't be lost."

When he stood up to leave, I asked if he might—if it wouldn't be too much trouble, that is—consider stopping by when he visits Cedric again. "Rest now," was all he said.

That night, I slept well, perfectly well, and when I awoke, I felt lighter, clearer-headed than I've been for a long, long while. The doctors were falling all over each other, patting themselves on their backs. They thought their shock treatments had made the difference.

To my surprise, Pastor Ray came to see me again, two days later. This time, he pulled a little book out of his pocket. I glanced at the cover: <u>God Calling</u>, by A.J. Russell. "I came across this book a while back," he said. "I find it to be a powerful testimony of how deeply we're loved. Maybe you will too."

The book came into being, he explained, when two women, besieged by tragedy, poverty, and misfortune, humbly prayed together in silence every day and waited for God's voice. They did this because they believed God is a living God who still speaks, and they believed Jesus when he said, "Where two are gathered in my name, there I am, in the midst of them." The women called themselves the "two listeners", he said. "They wrote down everything their hearts heard, and this book was the result." He smiled at me. "You and I are gathered in his name. So let's see where God leads us."

Every day, I read this book, Clarry, and it fills me with surges of hope, as if God is sitting here with me, the God I've been yearning to know, Pastor Raymond's God—the God of Love, who sees us as our best selves, no matter our brokenness.

On the day I was to be released, I did something bold. I asked
Pastor Roberts if he would consider counseling me. "I'm
making good progress," I told him. "I truly believe that, with
your spiritual guidance, I'll find the strength to lift myself out
of this melancholia, once and for all, and be a proper mother
to my children." We could meet privately at his church, I went
on to say. That way, I would not cause him any public embar-
rassment or rouse up anyone's anger, colored or white. I would
be very careful. I would bring Noël with me for every single
session. I would mail a suitable, anonymous donation to his
church—using cash, so the money could not be traced back to
me. This was, I told him, my last, best chance.

He hedged around, not saying anything for a long while. But
then he warned me—

✝✝✝

Willow's cellphone rang. Fumbling to grab it, she knocked her
glass over in the process, vodka dripping onto the hardwood floor.

"Yes?" Her voice came out strangely hoarse.

"I saw your light on." The unrecognizable male voice said.
"How's about a little bedtime company?"

"Who is this?"

"Oh, come on. Take a wild guess."

Willow's heart was throbbing.

"It's Cory, baby!"

Cory! She panicked, disconnected the call. Cory was out there,
watching her house! With trembling hands, she punched in Adam's
number on speed dial. She had to check on him right away—she
feared Cory was on another rampage and might have hurt Adam
or his family, shot them even, and she was next in line. It took

several rings, her terror mounting at the sound of each one, before Adam answered. "Yeah?"

Are you okay?" she said.

"Huh?" He sounded groggy, confused. "Willow?"

"Yes! Are you all right?"

"What time is it?" She heard the sounds of him fumbling around. "It's three in the morning!"

Three in the morning! She had no idea.

"Are *you* all right, Willow?"

She had let her imagination run amuck. She should have looked at the time before phoning. "Cory just called me," she replied, embarrassed.

"Cory? How the hell did he get your number?" Adam seemed fully awake now.

"I don't know."

"What did he want?"

"To get together, I guess."

"To get together? In the middle of the night? Jesus!"

"It just freaked me out, because it's so late," she said. Though, of course, she hadn't realized *how* late. "Nick has been after me to stay with you and Anne for a while. Do you think I could come over?"

"Nick, shit, *I'm* the one who's been after you to stay with us! Get out of that house right now, and come straight over! Come right now! We can go back for your things later. I'll be waiting up for you."

"Okay … only …" She paused. She might have thought she'd dreamed the whole thing about Cory if she hadn't still been wide awake, reading Lily's letters, when his call came in. "Only, I can't drive. Do you think, maybe, you could come and get me?"

"Of course, I can! I'm getting dressed right now ... but why can't you drive?"

"Because ..." She was in bad shape and knew she couldn't hide it. Dizzy, disoriented, she wrestled with herself to get the next words out. "Because I'm ... kind of ... drunk."

†††

By the time Willow came out of the house rolling a packed suitcase behind her, she was surprised to find Nick standing beside her brother's idling truck in the driveway, leaning against the door on the driver's side, engaged in conversation with Adam.

Willow stopped short at the sight of him. "Nick? What are you doing here?"

"He called to let me know about Cory right after you did," Adam said.

She was floored. "How did *you* know that Cory called me?"

"I didn't know he called you," Nick said. "But I've been watching your house all night, and I saw him pull up. As soon as he spotted me, he high-tailed it out of here."

Twenty-One

THE SAVING POWER OF LOVE

SOMEWHERE inside a foggy dream, he had heard the girl's voice, reading to him. He heard the sound of his brother's name and the words of his sermon, spoken by the girl, but he couldn't make contact with whatever world she was in—all he could do was listen. It was the same with the music playing right now. He heard the singer, the instruments—a tinny sound, as if coming from inside a little box. It was a singer he should know, but the sound was too small, too far away to remember the name. He heard his son's voice, the doctor's voice, other voices; he heard them all, in sound waves, through the ether of the universe, but he couldn't make contact with any of them.

Later, he heard another voice, close to his ear, this one female. She remained with him for days, weeks, who knows how long? A voice unknown to him. "Sleep," she said, sweetly. "You're safe, in a secret place where no one can harm you." Her presence was calming. "I know it seems lonely in this in-between place, in this pocket of air," she told him. "Like you, I heard their voices, distant as rolling thunder. I could hear them, yet I couldn't reach them. But I wasn't alone, and neither are you. The arms are always holding you."

He tried to twist his head to see her, but his eyes were blind. He tried to move his leg, his arm, a toe. He could not break through.

"Then I discovered it was them, not me, who were living in a pocket of air," she said, "the people on the other side of this bubble. They lived under water, while I was somewhere larger, and they swirled around me, day after day, in their own little pockets of air. Their voices were like fish breathing, their mouths flapping. Sometimes, trying to connect, I'd imitate them. I think they were trapped in that watery world. I think the glass between us was time."

She remained with him, this unknown voice, hour after hour, reassuring him that all was well. But her voice was growing fainter, and he could hear both sounds simultaneously, her voice and the little box with the music trapped inside. He recognized the singer now. It was Smokey Robinson, one of his favorites. And then she said to him, talking over Smokey, "It's time to swim."

He kicked his legs, flailed his arms. He pushed, pushed, pushed against the glass.

"Pop!" The music was shut off. Now there was only one thing he heard: His son's voice. "Can you hear me, Pop?"

†††

On the drive over to Adam's house, Willow tried to assemble her thoughts into some coherence, but they were jumping around like popping corn. Her mouth felt dry, dehydrated from fear and liquor. Sometimes—and this was one of those times—life felt like a polyptych, a painting in sections or panels—but all she had was this one incomprehensible piece. She desperately wanted to see the pattern, the whole picture of where she was right now, to make some sense of it.

"Anne wants us to take out a restraining order on Cory," Adam said.

"For what?" The couple blocks of downtown shops rolled by her window. "For calling me in the middle of the night?" That sounded like a coherent question, didn't it? And she hadn't slurred her words, had she?

"He wasn't just calling you! He was fucking *there*, Willow, right outside your door! What was he planning to do?" He rubbed his forehead. "Thank God, Nick was there to stop him!"

Even in her jumbled state, she could see the extent of her brother's agitation. She hated herself for doing this to him, adding to his stress. Like Nick, he'd been after her to leave Leon's house and stay with him and Anne, and she should've listened to them. Adam held so much inside; he always had; bearing his burdens internally for the sake of those he loved, which somehow included even Cory, who was out of jail now. They'd just have to find a way to live with him, she supposed.

She hated living in this town. Only a few weeks ago, it had seemed the epitome of hiddenness and security. No longer. It was a web of fear and hatred. Fear and hatred, hatred and fear—they went together like ham and beans, two foods she detested, so the simile seemed apropos. Why were her thoughts jumping around like popping corn?

Why, indeed. It was because she was in that wretched place between drunk and sober.

The two-lane country road had grown completely dark, the houses few and far between. Adam turned on the high-beams—the bright shaft of light made the shadows of passing terrain seem sinister. "Did you and Nick have a thing or something?" His question came out of the blue.

A *thing?* That was a good name for it, actually. "Kind of," she said. "But that was a long time ago."

"He's not married, you know."

Did he tell her that, she wondered, for encouragement or as a warning?

†††

By the time Adam pulled the truck into the driveway, the kitchen window glowing in golden light, Willow was beginning to feel a sense of relief. Despite the alarming circumstances that had brought it about, her arrival seemed another homecoming, of sorts. Rocket and Anne were waiting by the table for them when they came through the back door, Rocket gushing about how much fun it was going to be to have her staying in the upstairs room across the hall from his own. "We'll be like roommates!" he said. Anne served them oven-baked cherry pie she had taken out from the freezer, with gobs of whipped cream sliding off the warm crust, and Willow was not only hungry for a change, but ravenous. No one mentioned Leon's death. No one mentioned Cory. No one mentioned the accusations of the town. No one mentioned that she had been drinking. It was nothing but acceptance, whipped cream, cherry pies ... homecoming.

After that, reality set in. Before Anne ushered Rocket back to bed, Willow caught her knowing glance at Adam, their signal that it was high time for him to have this conversation alone with his sister. Anne gave him a kiss on the cheek, hugged Willow, and she and Rocket left the kitchen.

As soon as the sound of their footsteps on the stairs subsided, Willow felt the change in atmosphere. Her eyes flitted away from Adam's. She could almost hear the gears of his brain grinding to figure out a way to open the conversation. His fingers played with the salt shaker, twirling it round and round.

"Leon used to do that," she said.

"Do what?"

"Play with the salt shaker like that."

"He did?" He stopped the movement. "I can't believe he's gone. God, I miss him! He helped me through a lot of shit since I moved here."

"Like what?"

"Oh, you know. Just the usual shit." She observed him with a keener eye. Deep lines creased the skin around his eyes. One of his fists was clenched. "You were lucky to have a father like that," he said.

"Don't I know it." Her gaze drifted away, toward the window. It was still pitch black outside. She felt nearly sober now; the pie had helped. But the anxiety—and flood of grief—that made her drink in the first place were beginning to mount again. "I'm sorry," she said.

"For what?"

"That Leon wasn't your father too." She observed the sadness in his face after she said it. "You never put it in so many words, but I know it's been really hard for you … to have Cory living here … reminding you of your own father."

"Yeah, well." He pulled at his collar, a familiar gesture when he was trying to put the kibosh on a subject—mainly himself. "In retrospect, Uncle Steve doesn't seem too bad in comparison, does he?" He laughed, a quick, uneasy sound.

It was an irony Willow had also considered. "I guess, after all is said and done, he and Aunt Betsy did the best they could when it came to us."

"Considering we wrecked their lives—as they so often

reminded us. Or, at least, Aunt Betsy did." He began twirling the salt shaker again. "She sure could be blunt, couldn't she? But Uncle Steve—there was an innocence about him. He was like a little kid, hiding in the basement whenever something bad happened."

She couldn't recall the two of them ever discussing Uncle Steve and Aunt Betsy since they'd left San Diego. Holding their California memories under water seemed the best way to keep them buried. Now everything was bobbing on the surface.

"Yeah, but you're right," he said. "They did the best they could … Have you told Uncle Steve about Leon?"

"No, I didn't." She shook her head. "Oops."

With everything else going on, it had slipped her mind. Her mouth felt as if it were stuffed with cotton balls. Her head was beginning to pound again. She was dying for a gulp of vodka as she braced herself to ask him a question, *the* question, the one she'd never had the nerve to ask him outright. Rising from the table, she poured a tall glass of water from the tap, returned to the table. "Can I ask you something?"

He gave her a nod, albeit a tentative one.

"Did you resent me? You must have."

"Resent you? For what?"

"For killing Mama."

"Stop it," he said.

"But it's true. You know my birth killed her. You knew that *she* knew it would kill her. You knew I was the one who took Mama away from us."

"Yeah, I knew all that." He clawed at his collar. "But she sacrificed her life for me too. She left everything she knew to run away to Langston and hide me from my deranged father."

"That's not the same thing."

"Sure, it is. Leon and I had this same conversation once. She sacrificed herself for him too. She left him because she wanted him to have a better life."

Willow didn't hear him now, she couldn't hear him—her tortured thoughts were like fermented poison, and she was desperate to release them. "I screwed it all up, Adam! I'm the one who insisted on doing the exhumation with Booker, even though I knew Leon was uncomfortable about it. I'm the one who didn't stay out on the deck with them that night! Maybe the people in this town are right! I killed our mother, and maybe I killed my father too!"

"Jesus, I said stop it!"

"Oh, God!" She erupted in a torrent of tears. "Oh, God! Oh, God! Oh, God!"

Adam fell to his knees beside her chair. "Listen to me, Willow." He grabbed her shoulders. "You didn't kill Mama, and you didn't kill Leon! Don't ever say that again! Mama knew you *had* to be born, that you'd be the one to save Leon and his whole family. Leon told me that he couldn't imagine life without you. And neither can I!" Tears were spilling down his own cheeks. "Here's the God's honest truth. I never resented you, not even close! You and I are refugees from the same camp. We didn't have the same father, but thank God, we had the same mother. You were all I had left in this world after she died. I needed you then, and I need you now! I hate the crazy things the people in town are saying about you, but fuck them! Just fuck them, Willow, okay? *We* know the truth, and that's all that matters. It'll be okay. Really, it's going to be okay! We're in this together. We've always been in this together."

She threw her arms around him, engulfed in sobs. Adam's healing words, his succor, felt like a million shades of redemption.

He could have resented her because of her birth, but he didn't. He could have lectured her about drinking, but instead, he chose this—to just love her, when she needed it the most.

This was a letting-go moment for her, a turning point, a sobering into a deeper place that no longer hurt. Oh, how she loved her brother! He was here for her, always had been, always would be, and in some intangible way, so was Leon, their mother, and all those who had come before them. Pastor Raymond said that love goes on, and here it was, right now, in the goldenrod glow of Adam and Anne's kitchen. The saving power of unconditional love.

✝✝✝

Three days later, on the first day of September, Adam stood in front of Leon's coffin, along with Willow and Christopher Green, waiting for the Catholic priest to arrive for the graveside service. They had been waiting for nearly an hour. Their gazes kept being drawn back, over and over again, to the shiny surface of the casket, especially Willow's; she couldn't take her eyes off it. Adam scanned his mother's tombstone, the neatly dug hole in the ground beside it, the blooming rose bushes on either side. It gave him comfort to think, finally, they were together again on this gravesite that Leon had groomed so devotedly over the years.

All of a sudden, Willow decided she wanted to see Leon's body. She asked Christopher to open the coffin.

Christopher shifted his weight on the grass, from one foot to the other. Leon didn't look like himself, he told her, nothing like himself. The gunshot had left him discolored, swollen. "We tried the best we could to fix him up, but I'm warning you, it'll be a terrible shock."

She glanced up at the sky, back at the coffin. "Better not, then," she said. "I want to remember him the way he was. The way he is now."

The waiting went on. Adam looked at his watch to assure the second hand was still moving. Christopher interlocked his fingers and cracked his knuckles for the umpteenth time. Willow's eyes drifted to the awaiting grave. Adam was relieved he hadn't dragged Anne and Rocket along. Dealing with Leon's death was difficult enough for his son without forcing him to stare at Leon's coffin and the open hole in the ground for this makeshift, awkward ceremony. They'd have their own private ceremony later on today—just the four of them—in their front yard by the wishing well. Anne had insisted on it. Rocket wanted be the one to choose the reading.

It was early morning, not even eight yet, the hot sun beaming overhead, reflecting off the surface of the casket. Christopher, dressed in a suit and tie, same as Adam, was sweating profusely, and he was beginning to stink. Or maybe it was him. No wonder Leon didn't want a funeral. Rituals were mind-numbing, stiff and unnatural, like wearing a frickin' suit and tie in ninety-degree humidity. The awkwardness of it all seemed almost comical, in an excruciating sort of way. He could almost hear Leon shouting from inside the coffin, "Let's get this goddamned show on the road!"

After an eternity of another twenty minutes or so of knuckle-cracking, throat-clearing, and glazed eyes, a black Buick pulled up. Adam watched the solitary figure of Father Mahoney, dressed in full black regalia and white collar, doddering toward them ever-so-slowly, another eternity, as he maneuvered through the rows of tombstones.

Up close, he was an impersonal man with a milky, unwrinkled face, despite advanced age. As he offered condolences, his features remained unchanged; not unkind, just detached. "It's so good of you to come," Willow said, as she slipped him an envelope—compensation for his effort.

He opened his book and began to read.

"To you, O Lord, we commend the soul of Leon, your servant. In the sight of this world, he is now dead. In your sight, may he live forever. Forgive whatever sins he committed through human weakness and in your goodness, grant him everlasting peace. Through Christ our Lord. Amen."

Father Mahoney sprinkled the top of the coffin with his wand of incense, gave the sign of the cross. And that was that.

†††

Later that day, the afternoon shadows growing longer over the grass, Adam walked out to the backyard, to the pitcher's mound, pacing back and forth, deciding whether or not he should go through with it. He punched a couple digits on his cellphone, disconnected it. He tried again, three digits that time before he hung up. Finally, he entered the full number. It took only two rings before there was an answer.

"Uncle Steve?" He cleared his throat. "It's Adam."

"Adam!" He could hear the surprise in his uncle's voice, followed by dead silence.

It was Adam's turn again. His nervous stomach was doing flip-flops. What *had* he called Uncle Steve for? The pause seemed endless. The words weren't really all that important, he guessed, only the connection. "I just called to say ... *hello*."

-TWENTY-TWO-

MEMORABILIA

WELL, what do you know? Adam had called. After all this time.

Steve was moved, so moved he considered taking a trip to Weeping Willow to visit Adam and his sister, but he knew he couldn't bring himself to do it. There was too much baggage in that town—the old house, the old dreams, the old memories of growing up alongside his three siblings, all of them long dead, as well as his parents, and Aunt Clarissa who had been like a surrogate mother until she went and killed herself. It was too much, too painful, a bulging door Steve had nailed shut. Still, Adam had finally reached out to him after all these years, and he had to do *something* to reciprocate. Another idea came to mind. He could ship Adam's old belongings to him, the ones Betsy had packed up and put into storage.

When he first mentioned the idea to Betsy, she was resistant. "He hasn't been in touch with us for thirty-five years!" she said. "Now he makes one little call. So what?"

"But it was a good call. He sounded sorry."

"Did he *say* he was sorry?"

"Not in so many words. But he *called*, didn't he? What do you want him to say?"

"How about, 'Thank you for raising us'?"

"Come on, Bets. Let it go. Let's look forward, not back."

She eventually relented, and the two of them took a drive down to the storage locker so that she could point out the exact box. Betsy was the one who had put it there. She was the packrat, not him. He couldn't even remember what all she had stowed away. It had been so long since they had been to the storage unit that he wondered why they kept paying for it, holding on to old junk they never needed or missed.

Awash in the brightness of the San Diego sunlight, a maze of storage buildings eventually appeared, row upon row of identical units with identical red garage doors. As they hunted to locate their own space in the labyrinth, Steve made a lame joke about being glad he wasn't drunk or he'd never find it, but Betsy didn't even smile. Eventually, he found the right unit number, and stopped the car.

Sliding open the garage door, he was overwhelmed by the jumble of items, crammed in any which way. The box was one of the first things Betsy had ever stored in there, way in back, which meant they had to sort through the old hammock frame, water skis, lawn mowers, an assortment of dinosaur TV sets and video tape recorders that weighed a ton, a variety of useless rubbish, until they finally made their way to the back wall.

"That's it!" Betsy said. And there it was, sitting on the floor, a large J.C. Penney box marked "Adam" with a thick, black marker.

They decided to take it directly to the UPS Store on the way home. Before they did that though, Steve squatted on the concrete drive just outside the storage unit and opened it, despite Betsy's protests. As he rifled through Adam's baseball memorabilia, his posters, his old baseball, his childhood treasures, a flood of unexpected memories flashed through his mind. He remembered how lost Adam had seemed when he first came to California. How he didn't talk much. How he picked at his food. How he stayed in his room alone most of the time. But, man oh man, how he loved this stuff, especially that old baseball. Steve used to watch him through the window, tossing that ball by himself in the backyard, again and again, without a soul there to bat it. Later, when Willow was old enough, she would try to bat, or at least retrieve the balls for him. Afterward, they would huddle together and talk back there, like co-conspirators. "Sullen children." That was how Betsy used to describe them as she watched them from behind the drapes. Sullen children who never took to the California way of life, or to them, for that matter.

Among Adam's belongings was another box, unopened, still tied in brown paper and wrapped with string. It was addressed to Adam, the return address from Mobile, Alabama. "Shit, Betsy, what's *this?*"

She glanced at it quickly, turned away. "What does it look like?" she said. "It's a package that came for him. After he left us."

Steve turned the box over in his hands, examined it. "It has to be from Theckla Chavis." But it wasn't the return address he remembered for her old apartment. The package had been sent from a nursing home, postmarked July 1982. His heart twisted. "We never gave it to him?"

"He wasn't around, remember?"

"We could've sent it to him!"

"Where?" She diverted her eyes. "He was at that minor league camp out east, and he didn't even bother to give us the address."

Steve struggled to understand. "But he gave us his address eventually."

"When he finally got around to it!" She paced in circles on the driveway as if trapped, her face growing red. Was she livid, defensive, or something else? "I figured we'd give it to him when he came to visit, and you know how *that* went."

"But he loved Theckla!" Steve clung to the package.

"You mean, like he should've loved us?"

"Betsy!" Usually he caved in long before they got this far in a disagreement—he couldn't bear to argue or to see her upset. This time was different.

"What?" She glared at him. "Why are you looking at me like that? Like I'm some kind of a monster!" She shook her finger in front of his nose. "That Theckla woman stirred up trouble for us—and him. Don't you remember how he wanted to live with her instead of us? He kept writing to her, calling her in secret, like we kidnapped him or something!" She sat down on the curb, broke into tears.

Steve wasn't certain what to do next. He looked down at the box in his arms, then at his wife. He was angry. He seldom got angry, with her or anyone else, and he wasn't even certain it was anger he was feeling right then, only that whatever it was he was feeling was uncomfortable, unsettling, close to unbearable.

The unopened package in his arms, he sat down on the curb beside Betsy. He considered just tossing it. Making it go away. Or opening it. But what did it matter what was inside? Theckla didn't have a pot to pee in. What else could it be but some sentimental parting gift that would make Adam feel guilty for not visiting her in the nursing home before she died?

"You don't think it killed me to have Adam treat us that way?" Betsy continued to sob. "You don't think it broke my heart that he just cut us off? How can I *get over* something like that?"

They'd had this conversation before, many times, and there wasn't much else to say. Steve didn't feel like saying the usual things, about how much they'd given up for Willow and Adam, or how ungrateful the two of them were. He looked down at the package in his arms. "Did you ever open it?"

"Of course not! I'm not that much of a monster!" A new wave of tears engulfed her.

Steve got up from the curb, placed the package back inside the bigger J.C. Penney box with Adam's other things. He opened the back door of the car and slid it onto the seat.

Betsy stood up, wiping her cheeks dry with the back of her hand. "You mean, you're still gonna send it to him?"

He didn't reply.

They drove to the UPS Store in silence. Betsy remained in the car while he went inside. The woman behind the counter taped up the J.C. Penney box to seal it shut, printed the label, asked if he wanted to ship it by air or by ground. Efficient and impersonal, all of it. Steve handed her the money.

He thought it would be nice to send Adam a surprise delivery filled with his happiest childhood keepsakes, something to seal the newfound truce between them. But now there was this unopened package, and his act of magnanimous kindness had become an act of unforgivable neglect. *Bingo!* he could hear Adam saying in his mind. *You finally get it.*

The blood of incriminating emotion rushed into his face, the same way it had flooded into Betsy's at the storage unit. Staring at the box, still sitting on the scale on top of the counter, he knew it was now or never.

On second thought, maybe Betsy was right. Why send it to Adam now? Opening up the past didn't make sense. What was the point? It was better to stay where they were; keep their same old justifications for doing what they did or didn't do.

In one fluid movement, Steve snatched the package off the scale without even asking for his money back, and left the store.

-TWENTY-THREE-

FIGHT OR FLIGHT

WHEN Willow arrived at Bedlington Memorial Hospital the next day, a Saturday, she discovered that Booker had been moved from intensive-care and was now settled in a private room in the cardiology unit on the top floor. A policeman remained at his door. Entering the room, she found Booker sitting up in bed, still hooked to a tangle of tubes, IVs, and machinery, no longer requiring a ventilator. It seemed a miracle to see him alive and alert, almost as if Leon could be resurrected too. The small television suspended from the ceiling was switched on, but he didn't seem to be interested; he was staring, brows furrowed, at the white wall.

"Willow!" His eyes enlivened when he noticed her standing in the doorway. "I was hoping you'd visit me."

She walked to his bed, leaned over the oxygen tubing in his nose, and gently kissed his forehead. "It's so wonderful to see you awake! When did you come out of the coma?"

"Oh, time's still fuzzy … I think it was a few days ago."

"I call here every single day, and they didn't let me know."

"No, they wouldn't, would they? Not with all their privacy rules."

She pulled over the high-backed vinyl chair from beneath the window and sat down beside the bed. "How do you feel?"

"Like a truck ran over me. But better than yesterday." Booker's grin quickly dissolved, his forehead again creasing with deeply rutted lines. "I can't even begin to tell you how sorry I am about your pop. Leon was a friend, a real friend. After he warned me about that white supremacist, I had no idea I was putting him— *any* of you—in danger too. Maybe I should have, but I didn't." He began to weep.

"Shhh." Willow placed her hand over his, careful not to disturb any of the IVs poking from his bruised skin. "You're not to blame, Booker. It's not your fault."

She took a tissue from the small box on his bed tray, tried to wipe his tears. Grief did that to you—how well she knew; it made you reexamine the "would'ves" and "should'ves" until you lost your bearings. She understood his guilt; it was more than survivor's guilt. In their shared single-minded passion to retrieve the Bible, she and Booker were compadres in this mess. "None of us could see this coming," she said.

"Maybe *we* couldn't, but Leon could." His eyes drifted toward the ceiling. "He smelled trouble early on. I've been lying here thinking about it. Remember that day in the kitchen, when we were filling out the application for the exhumation—the way he started clanking those pots and pans? I wish I would've listened to those pots and pans."

She smiled sadly. That was Leon, banging things around when he was getting impatient, the Leon she missed so fervently. "He couldn't possibly have known the horror of what was coming," she said. "What he knew was the way people gossiped around town, and he didn't want them knowing our business. I've been doing a lot of thinking too. And I came to the conclusion that he's with my mother now, the place he always wanted to be. Your brother said that God promises a second spring, the spring of reunion. I'm guessing Leon wouldn't want to come back here again on a bet."

"He loved your mama, that's for sure." Booker's gaze deepened as he turned to look at her. "... You say that Raymond talked about a second spring? I thought I heard you reading to me when I was in a coma. I heard your voice, like you were under water, but I heard you just the same—half real, half from somewhere else. I thought my mind made the whole thing up until you said that just now. What I don't understand is, what *was* it you were reading?"

She explained to him about the stack of Lily's letters she found in the attic just before the shots were fired. He shut his eyes, his lips silently moving as he absorbed the news. Was he praying? "I haven't finished reading them all yet," she added, "but I brought another one along with me today, if you'd like to read it."

"Oh, my ... Oh, my ..." Booker's lids fluttered open. "There's nothing in this world I'd like more ... Do you think you might read it to me? It still hurts too much to move around, to lift up my arms." He tried to shift his weight on the mattress, but could only manage it slightly. "One thing I can tell you is that your pop died the way he wanted to. He and I talked about it, about how we'd want to die if we could choose, and he said he wanted to go fast, before he knew what hit him. That's the way it happened all right. We were just sitting out there on the deck, and he was telling me about your trip to Langston. That's the last thing I remember." He glanced at the IV on his arm, at the equipment surrounding him. "We choose the way we want to live. Maybe we choose the way we want to die too."

Willow stared out the window. She never asked Leon how he wanted to die. His father had been just the opposite—Walt had hoped to die at his own pace, in his own bed, and sure enough, he died in slow motion, the way Alzheimer's takes you. To Walt, sudden death—without time to reflect back on life—was anathema.

The sunlight streamed into the room. Across the street from the hospital was some kind of factory, its parking lot loaded with cars, and for some reason she was reminded of Cyrus. She turned her head, scanned the room for visible signs of his presence, for personal objects he might have left behind while stepping out for a time, maybe to the cafeteria for lunch. "Is Cyrus still here?"

"He had to go to New Orleans for a couple days and finish up some business. He'll be back toward the end of the week. He's still mad as hell at me for coming up here in the first place. I wake up from the coma, and first thing, he starts lecturing me." He chuckled.

"That's our job as children."

"Children who think they know better than their parents. How does it get turned around that way?" Booker attempted to shift his position again, wincing slightly.

"You know," Willow began when she thought he was comfortable, "I haven't stopped it—the exhumation, I mean." She searched his face for a knee-jerk reaction.

An unmistakable brightness came to his eyes. "You haven't?" An instant later, he contracted his brows. "Maybe Cyrus *does* know more than his old man. Maybe we should reconsider it."

"He wants you to reconsider it?"

"He thinks it's too dangerous—not to mention, ludicrous."

Willow leaned forward in her chair. "Do *you* want to stop it?"

His enlivened expression at the first mention of the disinterment, juxtaposed against his deflated silence now, told her all she needed to know; what she'd suspected all along. She glanced at the policeman standing outside the open door. "I think you're safe as long as you're in here," she said. "It's still arranged for the date you set before you got shot—this Tuesday."

"This Tuesday? I thought it was scheduled for the Tuesday after Labor Day?"

Willow nodded. "Monday *is* Labor Day."

"It is?" Booker sighed. "I guess I lost track of time."

"They're going to do it in the middle of the night, at two a.m. They want to get it done before dawn. For privacy's sake."

He lifted his hand with effort, as if made of iron, up to his dry lips; his eyes glazed on the ceiling. "I kept telling myself I was doing this whole thing for Cyrus. I told your daddy that I wanted to die in peace, and finding that Bible again after all these years would give me that kind of peace. But maybe I was doing it for myself all along. Am I wrong, Willow? Is it putting you in more danger if we go through with it?"

"The danger's passed." Willow tried to say it convincingly, though she wasn't totally certain. She only knew—from what she'd heard from Christopher Green and mostly from Nick—that the townsfolk seemed to assume the exhumation had been called off after the shooting. Thrown off the scent of it, there seemed no imminent threat. Or so she hoped, anyway. "You were right, Booker. Your brother's Bible wasn't meant to be stuck in the ground. My grandmother certainly wouldn't have wanted that. Even Leon didn't want that—believe me, he could be a lot more direct than rattling pots and pans when he wanted to be. You said it yourself when you found out about Cory. We can't let fear stop us from doing the right thing."

"My accomplice." He grinned. "My sweet accomplice."

"I promise I'll call you right away, after it happens."

"Thank you, Willow, again and again, for all you're doing for me. You have no idea how much it means."

"Oh, I think I do." She smiled. "I'll bring your luggage next time, so you can have all your things."

"Would you mind bringing my car keys too? Cyrus asked if you could leave it in your driveway, and he'll pick it up next time he comes. All these loose ends. That detective guy, Nick Hardy, brought me back my phone the other day. Nice fella." Resettling his head against the pillow, he closed his eyes. "Now, read to me, girl."

✝✝✝

April 28, 1953
Dear Clarry,

I know it's been a while since I've written. It's time to confess my deepest secret.

For the past several Monday afternoons, Ray has been counseling me in his church. I've been very careful. I pretend I'm going to the five and dime, and I take Noël along with me, while Bo watches the other children. The five and dime is just two blocks beyond the Mt. Zion First Baptist Church, and we cut through the back parking lot on the way. I make certain that no living soul is around before I knock on the back door of the sanctuary, where Ray is waiting on the other side. He locks it as soon as we enter. After our sessions, I continue on to the five and dime, just to make sure the clerk sees us there. I make it a point to buy something, an item or two as additional proof to show Jack and others I was really there, should I need it.

Isn't all this a ridiculous charade to go through just for counseling sessions?

Ray and I remain in the sanctuary with Noël the entire time. The church is quite plain, with dark paneling on the walls, a simple gold cross hanging over the altar. On the east wall, there's a striking stained-glass window in hues of purples and blues, depicting a Negro Jesus praying by the rock at Gethsemane. When the afternoon sun streams through that window, it casts a magical rainbow light. Noël sits in a pew by herself near the back, playing with Amelia Rosalie, the doll she never lets out of her sight, while Ray and I sit together in the first pew, or on the altar steps, or I sometimes sit beside him on the piano seat as he plays hymns. We always sit far enough away from Noël and talk softly, so she doesn't overhear.

I feel such a difference! I feel as if these counseling sessions are unpeeling my ugly, outer skin, like an onion, layer by layer, slowly revealing the real Lily that lies underneath. Sometimes I wake up in the mornings with a startle of joy. Ray often talks about the second spring that God promises, the spring of reunion to come, and sometimes it seems already near.

We talk about so many things. Mainly, he focuses on my feelings of despair. He gives me Bible passages to read at home, and then we discuss them. "To be a sensitive person is to suffer," he said. "When you're ruled by your emotions, you're forever in a stormy place, a ship tossed at sea." Like that kind doctor I once had, he encouraged me to consider funneling my emotions into something creative—art or music or writing. Though I already garden, and write these letters to you, of course, I decided to try oil painting. To my amazement, though I'm such an amateur, it's been an enormous release.

Ray believes that the key to getting a handle on emotions is to try to transcend them, especially the "fight or flight" impulse, our natural human response to fears, threats, or attacks. He calls this impulse a mechanism of this world, necessary in some situations—like if a tiger is about to attack us—but it's not helpful in other realms. He believes that if we consciously choose to neither flee nor fight in most situations, then we open ourselves to go deeper, into our higher nature. "Think about it," he said. "If we don't fight, and we don't run away, what are our other choices? To remain? To face it? To listen? To forgive? To enter into the discomfort of the moment and fully bear its suffering? … To Love?" He pointed to the stained glass of Jesus kneeling beside the rock. "When Christ knew he'd be captured and crucified, he didn't run and he didn't fight. Beyond fight or flight is … transcendence."

When he talks like that, Clarry, his eyes become bright and clear, as if he's backlit by some radiant force, and I know that he is. He believes there's a very thin veil between this life and the next, between past and future. "This is a messy world," he said. "We live in an in-between place. But we must still continue to plant our seeds, without seeing the harvest."

He's told me about the writings of a psychologist named Abraham Maslow who created a framework to describe our basic human needs and motivation, a five-tiered, triangular hierarchy, where we can't ascend to a higher level until the lower needs are met. At the base of this pyramid are our survival needs, such as food, water, and sleep; then our safety and security needs; then love and belonging needs; then esteem needs; until we reach the top of the pyramid, self-actualization. According to Maslow, the longer the need is denied, the greater the motivation to fulfill it. "Here's the one place I differ from Maslow," he said. "I think the need to love and be loved is the bedrock of all of them. More integral, more urgent, than even survival. We'll starve for love, jump into a raging fire, endure unimaginable suffering for love. We'll even give up our own lives, willingly, for love."

He reads philosophers and poets as well as theologians. He's written numerous essays, discourses and shares them with me. I tell him he must get them published. "Published?" He laughed.

"It's dangerous for men who look like me to think too much."
And so he stuffs them back inside his Bible.

Ray tells me I'm very intelligent, that my self-education through
library books has served me well. He tells me that I have a beautiful mind, open to ideas and knowledge and tempered by a
loving heart, the kind of mind that should be able to soar, not
stunted by shock treatments and tranquilizers.

Here is where the story changes, Clarry, as all stories eventually
do.

Yesterday, when he was speaking to me, we began to laugh
together about something or other, and a moment came, one
of those rare moments when he allows his eyes to linger on
mine, and I felt something switch. Suddenly, he was no longer a
pastor, my counselor, but a man, raw and real. I was consumed
with a love for him so overpowering that I became terrified! And
I thought about those women at the revival and felt a crushing
guilt. Had they seen this coming long before I did?

"I must go!" I cried. "I won't be coming back!" I rushed down
the altar steps toward Noël, gathered her and Amelia Rosalie
quickly, pushed her along. When I glanced up at him, he was
standing there in the same spot at the altar, dismayed.

My heart thick in my throat, I hurried to the back door,
slammed it shut behind us, tried to catch my breath again. I
forced myself to make the trip to the five and dime. A half-
block away, in between the church and the five and dime, we
always see old Mrs. Peabody sitting on her front porch with a
ball of yarn and whatever it is she's knitting, and today was no
different, except that today she seemed to give me a flicker of a
look, for a brief second, as if she was on to my secret. It must
have been my nerves playing tricks on me, because she waved

and smiled after that, like usual, as Noël and I passed by. Surely, if she suspected something, she would've talked by now.

†††

Willow enjoyed staying in Adam's guest room, a very pleasant room. Anne had a knack for decorating. The flowered curtains were sewn from a lovely fabric, a taupe background with large, salmon-colored flowers and leaves of olive green, a subtle, soothing combination. The bedspread was the same design, as well as the cushion on the window seat; the walls a soft beige, allowing for plenty of light when the drapes were open. In the corner nearest the window stood Willow's easel with a blank canvas on it. Adam had taken it upon himself to bring them over from Leon's house, just in case she felt like painting again.

This was the evening of Labor Day, and she was lounging on top of the bed, still dressed in jeans and a t-shirt, her hair pulled back in a ponytail. No nightgown tonight. In a few hours, she'd be leaving for the exhumation.

She was just about to read the next of Lily's letters when there was a knock on the door. After his teeth were brushed and his pajamas donned, it had become Rocket's habit to come to her room and the two of them would have their "just before bed" talks, the time of day when both seemed apt to share whatever was on their minds. She laid the letter on the nightstand, placing her reading glasses on top. "Come in, Doc," she said.

Rocket rushed in—quick to settle down in his usual spot, the window seat, swinging his legs, back and forth.

"Don't get too comfortable there." She smiled. "You've got a big day coming up."

"I know."

Tomorrow began a new school semester. Rocket was going to be a sixth grader, the highest class in the elementary school. "I can't wait," he said. "But I'm kinda scared too."

Willow nodded. "I can understand that. It's a big deal, being in sixth grade. You're the top dog."

"Yeah, I guess." He shrugged. "Sometimes I can't wait to grow up. And sometimes ... not so much. Is that normal?"

"I hope so," she said. "I still feel the same way." She could see it in Rocket already. He was a Trudeau, through and through—a *moonstoner*, her mother might say—a born thinker whom Willow feared might inherit their melancholy. "But you know something? I have a feeling it'll be the start of a wonderful time in your life."

"You think so?"

She did think so. Beginnings and endings, as T.S. Eliot wrote in "The Four Quartets," were one and the same; a continuous circle. However it was equivalent in their separate worlds, she and Rocket always seemed to be on roughly the same wavelength at any given time, and this night was no exception. As he would soon lie dreaming of what sixth grade would hold, she would be standing on the far end of a graveyard, waiting, wondering, what would come next?

After Rocket left for bed, she began reading Lily's next letter.

†††

May 4, 1953
Dear Clarry,

Last night, as Jack snored at my side, I was tossing, turning, my heart flaming. My dear sister, I am so deeply in love with Raymond Roberts! In spite of the pain of it, the intense joy of falling in love must be the closest we come to heaven on this earth. The whole world seems vibrant and meaningful to me.

Everything feels connected. Even the cracks on the sidewalk seem to sing.

I dare imagine a world where I am the pastor's wife, standing steadfastly at his side in his holy mission as we greet his parishioners, one by one, on Sunday mornings. I dare imagine sharing springtime with him, just one springtime would be all I'd ask, where we could picnic openly in the park, laugh freely. Yet I know it's another world I'm imagining, far away from this one.

Ray has been the pathway to all that is lasting and good, beyond this place of suffering. He has put me on the vessel that sails beyond, and I cannot turn back, nor can I go forward. He's right about us living in an in-between place. As he puts it, we're <u>on</u> earth, but we're <u>in</u> heaven. My body is still here, my heart already beyond.

It makes me wonder, what is true marriage? Is it a snare?—saying vows in our own ignorance and trapped in them once we know better? Is it clinging to someone, anyone, for fear no one else will have us? Or is it a blessing from God, reserved for one person who unlocks our deepest heart?

The only thing I know for certain is that I can't leave it the way I left it last week and have Ray thinking he's done something wrong, something to offend me. I owe him that much, don't I? I owe him the truth.

And so, I awakened this morning as two Lilys. There is this new Lily, sitting at her dressing table, her heart filled with indescribable joy as she puts on her best red dress, a red comb in her hair; and then there is the other Lily, anguished, fearful, guilty for the act she has already committed in her dreams; and they merge together as Noël and I walk hand-in-hand toward his house—the Lily driven by fear and the new Lily, moving beyond. I hear

Ray's voice in my head: "It's step-by-step that we go forward, trusting in each new moment of each new day, not in yesterday, not in tomorrow, but in *right now*—where God is."

It is a Monday afternoon, the same time my counseling session would have taken place. Ray lives in the rectory behind the back of the church, an alley in between. When we finally reach our destination, no one is around to see us. We go to the back door, closest to the alley. I knock. It takes a long while until he answers, and I almost leave, but I don't. I stand firm. The new Lily has subsumed the other.

At last, he opens the door, his eyes widening in surprise, or is it shock? Or fear? Or relief? I see all these emotions on his face, and many more. "Please," I say. "It's urgent that I speak with you."

With Noël still gripping my hand, he pulls me inside, motions us into his front room, small and stark, but there's a soft sofa in it, where I settle Noël and her doll. I look around for privacy, but the kitchen has no door. I notice the staircase. "Can we talk up there?" I ask.

He stiffens, yet nods.

From my purse, I retrieve Noël 's coloring book and crayons, spread them on the coffee table in front of her, and make her promise to remain downstairs while the two of us talk. "Just like in church," I tell her.

After I follow Ray up the staircase, he stops in front of a closed door. We stand face-to-face in the hallway. Without saying a word, I can see in his eyes that he already knows my truth. He knows it, because it's also his truth. We are beyond words. He and I have reached the *tetelestai* of our union, that transcendent place beyond fight or flight.

TWENTY-FOUR

THE MIRROR UNDIMMED

THE night of the exhumation had arrived, the full team assembled in the dark, some of them already working to clear the topsoil with a backhoe. Adam had opted out of attending; he thought the whole thing too morbid. But for Willow, retrieving the Bible for Booker was the one way, the only way, to find meaning in everything that had happened. Against Adam's advice, as well as Christopher Green's, she insisted on being there, standing alone off in the distance, in front of her mother's and father's graves.

Assorted vehicles surrounded the scene, blocking it from her view. A tent was set up over the grave, with a big, bright light shining down. Somewhere inside the tent, Nick was standing in the mix with the others. He had told her he would come out and give her a high sign when the coffin was opened—if the Bible was undamaged, he'd raise his right arm; if it was beyond salvageable, his left.

Willow watched and waited, glancing at her phone then and again for the time of day. The Garden of Resurrection was built in a location that afforded an unobstructed view of the night sky. A bright half-moon was shining overhead, dozens of stars twinkled in various intensities of light, and Willow tried to count them to distract herself from the disturbing noises coming from the tent as they worked to unearth the grave. She spoke intermittently to her father and mother, as she waited. "Mama, what will they find?" she asked. "Was this *really* the right thing to do, Dad?" The night grew cold; she hugged her sweater around her body.

The excavation seemed to go on endlessly, long enough for her to drift into a state of complete detachment from the whole affair, long enough for it to seem surreal, like she was sleep-walking through a half-dream, half-nightmare. Christopher Green had briefed her in detail—too much detail—beforehand. He told her it was impossible to know exactly what they might find—what state of decomposition Lily's body might be in. She could be mummified or destroyed by bacteria. He painted a gruesome picture of various stages of disintegration and decay. But at the end, he added a hopeful note. It was a good thing, he said, that Lily had been buried in a metal coffin, bronze to be exact, and also in a concrete vault; Booker's Cadillac would yield every opportunity for the best outcome.

As dawn was breaking, she heard sudden, increased commotion, their voices rising in baffling sounds of exclamation, surprise, almost celebration. Surely that meant they had found it! She waited for a sign from Nick. More hubbub inside the tent. At last, he emerged, raised his left arm.

The Bible was unsalvageable.

No! She couldn't assimilate it. *No!* How could this be? The realization was crushing, overwhelming. All of it, all of it—there had been so much to fight through for this moment—and now, all of it, including her father's death, *especially* her father's death, had been in vain. *No!*

Nick began walking toward her with an unusually brisk gait. "You aren't going to believe this," he said, when he reached her, "but your grandmother's body is completely intact, almost like she was just buried."

Willow was stuck in stunned disbelief. She couldn't process what he was saying. "Christopher says it's been known to happen if it's airtight enough," he continued. "It's rare, real rare, but I guess it happens." He sank his hands into the pockets of his jeans.

"I don't get it," she said. "If it's that airtight, where's the Bible? Was there any sign of it?"

Nick shook his head. "Not one shred."

Willow clawed at her hair in confusion, glanced down at her phone. *No Bible?* She knew she had to call Booker and tell him. Even given the wee hour, she had promised she would call as soon as she knew, but how could she bear to tell him? She was disappointed beyond belief, yes, but Booker would be devastated. "I want to see her," she said.

"What?"

"I want to see my grandmother's body."

Nick gave her a doubting look. "Are you sure that's a good idea?"

"I need to see her! ...*Please*, Nick." Fighting back tears, she felt suddenly like a helpless child. She couldn't seem to move. Her legs had become boulders.

Taking her hand, Nick guided her over to the group. The walk toward the tent seemed like miles, and she gripped his fingers all the way. The men were standing around the coffin, gawking into it with disbelief. At the sight of Willow, they parted, stepped aside, stood back, staring at her as if she were an actress in some B-horror film as she approached the open casket under the garish spotlight. Her heart, a glob of jelly, pulsed in erratic rhythm. Her body had gone wobbly.

She forced herself to do it. She forced herself to look down into the coffin, into the shockingly lovely face of her grandmother, Lily Trudeau, eerily untouched after forty-nine years in the ground. Her features seemed muted, as if covered by a gray veil, but she was lying peacefully in a red dress, a red comb in her black hair, dressed exactly like her last letter had described, appearing so similar to how Willow imagined her own mother might look. She was overwhelmed by the sense that Lily had been waiting for her, for this very moment. As her secrets were being unearthed by her letters, so was her body also unearthed, preserved in some uncanny way that transcended time—and now that she was fully revealed, she could turn to dust. Finally, her soul could be free.

The men, the tent, the night, faded away. Willow's mind was whirling, and she could scarcely breathe. She could not take her eyes away from Lily's face, younger than her own. Willow was struck with the realization that she was glimpsing something unfathomable, something impossible to behold: In gazing at her grandmother, she was gazing into a mirror undimmed, an un-seeable place between a past—existing long before Willow was born—and an eternity, far beyond her grasp.

Her legs felt boneless, like soggy noodles, until they finally gave way beneath her.

Twenty-Five

THE FAVOR

AS the first rays of light cracked over the horizon, the crew was finishing up, flattening the fresh mound of dirt that re-covered Lily Trudeau's grave. Christopher Green spotted an older woman he recognized, one of his former clients, visiting her family plot. She watched them intently. Here goes, he thought; the dominoes would soon fall. This woman would tell someone, who would tell another, who would tell another after that, and soon the whole town would find out the exhumation had taken place in the dead of night in the Garden of Resurrection.

After The Trudeau gravesite was completely cleaned up a half-hour or so later, Christopher had a splitting headache, and so he stopped at Rose's Drug Store to pick up a bottle of aspirin. "When you disturb a dead body in their grave, they can't be resurrected, you know." Phil Rose admonished him once he reached the cash register. "And you better watch your own step too. Didn't you ever hear of the 'curse of the pharaohs'? Those people who opened up King Tut's tomb died long before their time."

Too wired to go home to sleep, Christopher went straight back to the funeral home and sequestered himself in his office. Images of the night played through his mind, from the grinding sounds of the backhoe, to the unbearable quiet before the lid was opened, the exclamations of amazement afterward, to the sight of Nick Hardy catching Willow just in time as she fainted.

Ensconced inside the security of his dark office, Christopher racked his brain for an answer. How could Lily Trudeau's body remain virtually unsullied without one remnant of the Bible? True, it was paper, and paper deconstructed easily, yet the environment was airtight. He just couldn't understand it.

Too bad his father wasn't around. He knew more about that kind of thing than Christopher did. On impulse, he grabbed his cell phone and punched his dad's number.

✝✝✝

Like his father before him, Ben Green was a round man; a round torso, a round belly, a round face, a round profile, like a beach ball with legs. In every family photo, the Green men looked alike in their shared roundness, except when it came to Christopher, with his basketball-player physique. When Ben was younger, particularly in high school, it had been tough for him—you know the way kids can be—they called him Porky Pig, as if being round meant that he didn't have any feelings. Now that he was in his seventies, it didn't matter anymore. He was no longer a round peg in a square world; this retirement community was brimming with men and women as round as he was. His wife, Sybil, used to be round too, but she had thinned out over the years and become birdlike. They had a good marriage, he supposed. Sybil had stuck by him after his stroke, taken over the reins and never relinquished them.

Ben and Sybil were having breakfast on their veranda when Christopher called. Ben thought that he sounded kind of hyper, especially for this time of day, his words coming out rapidly, disjointed, as he explained the bizarre reason for his call. He'd had to excavate a grave, something Ben never had to do in his entire career. When he got to the part about the Bible and mentioned the name *Lily Trudeau*, Ben felt his heart accelerate. He told Sybil they had a bad connection, got up from the patio table, and went inside the house. Once he was out of Sybil's earshot he said to his son, "why didn't you call me about this sooner?"

"I guess I didn't think of it. Why would I?"

"Because I could've saved you a hell of a lot of trouble!"

"What do you mean?"

Ben was about to explain when he heard another phone ring on Christopher's end.

"Hang on, Dad. I have to take this call. I'll be quick."

Ben sat down on the sofa, beads of perspiration gathering around his temples and the back of his blunted neck. That was another characteristic of the Green men; they seemed to have no neck at all, as if there were chin, then shoulders, nothing in between. He wiped the perspiration with the back of his hand, the hidden memories rising to the surface. Memories of Noël Trudeau, the girl he'd adored from afar, back in high school. Noël hadn't exactly been popular—mostly because her mother was that crazy woman, and you know how kids can be—but she was undoubtedly the most beautiful girl Ben had ever seen—raven hair, bluegreen eyes, luminous skin. Ben remembered how he couldn't stand to watch the way that big bully, David Ketchfield, bossed her around like he owned her. Later, the whole school had found out the thug had gotten her pregnant, forcing Noël to drop out of senior year, shamed and humiliated.

But Noël had always been so nice to Ben, so sweet—they'd sat next to each other in English class—and she would take the time to talk to him, to ask him about his day when other girls wouldn't give him so much as a frown.

His son came back on the line. "Okay, I'm here," Christopher said. "What was it you were saying?"

"I was saying, you should've called me before you went through all that. Lily Trudeau's daughter, Noël, *did* put the Bible in the coffin. But after she went to church for the funeral, she changed her mind."

"Changed her mind?"

"Yeah, that's what I said. She changed her mind."

The memory was in full-bloom. The way Noël had clutched Ben's arm and pulled him aside after her mother's gravesite service, whispering close against his ear, *could you please do me a favor?* He would have done just about anything for Noël Trudeau—robbed a bank, stood on his head, howled at the moon—but all he could do was what he could. Later, after his father realized all the fringe benefits Ben had thrown in for Noël's sake, he read Ben the riot act—for knocking off the cost to open the grave, for giving Lily the largest room in the funeral parlor for her wake, for upgrading the coffin from copper to bronze. For putting in a concrete vault at half the cost to make it as airtight as possible, because Noël couldn't bear to think of her mother rotting away in the ground. Ben had done what he could. As he laid Lily out on the slab in the back room of the funeral parlor, he'd given her an extra dose of embalming fluid to keep her firm, taken meticulous care to make sure she looked as beautiful as possible. He'd done it all for Noël. And then there was the final favor.

"After the graveside service," Ben said, "Noël asked me to take the Bible out of the coffin before it was lowered into the ground. She wanted it back." And that's the way it had happened. When the mourners had left the gravesite, Ben had completed that final favor for Noël Trudeau. He'd opened the lid, removed the beat-up

Bible with the cover half torn off, and tucked it away in the bottom drawer of his file cabinet.

"Well, holy crap of all craps!" Christopher said, along with a flurry of other assorted, off-color interjections of astonishment. "Did you open up the Bible and look at it before you gave it back?"

"Why would I have done that? I know what the Bible says!"

Christopher seemed to be swearing under his breath, maybe just mumbling, but Ben was too lost in the memory to be listening. On second thought, Ben *had* opened the Bible because of the papers stuffed inside. Lots of papers. But they all seemed to be ramblings about God from what he could tell at a quick glance, so he'd stuck them back where he found them. Noël had told him she would come to pick up the Bible, and the thought of it had thrilled him. Another chance, probably his last, to see her.

He'd waited three long days before she finally came, but come she did. He led her into his office, closed the door behind them. She was such a wreck, totally distraught, and she started to weep. Ben dared himself to step forward, to try to comfort her. And then that loveliest of girls, Noël Trudeau, curled her arms around his round body as she sobbed. It was as close to paradise as Ben would ever get on this side of the grave.

"Dad? Are you still there?"

"Yeah." Sweat streamed down Ben's temples, the memory slowly receding. "I'm here." And here he was. He looked around the small pastel room of their condo, heard Sybil shuffling about on the veranda.

"That was nearly fifty years ago!" Christopher said. "How in the world did you ever remember a thing like that?"

†††

Christopher stared at the dark screen of his phone, tucked in the palm of his hand. Live and learn. He should have called his father right away—he really *could* have saved them a ton of time and headaches.

He could hear Mrs. Nichols entering through the back door to begin her work day. Other than that, the funeral home was quiet; no viewings today. He remained at his desk, debating whether or not he should tell Willow the truth about the missing Bible. Something held him back. The time didn't seem right. Besides that, he felt vaguely responsible for not contacting his father sooner— another thing that was making him feel guilty. He rarely called his father. Like almost never.

But none of those were the real reasons. Willow was a New Yorker, and New Yorkers liked to sue. That was the crux of it. Though it wasn't his fault, not by any stretch of the imagination, you never knew about people. Whether it was at Noël's request or not, was it ethical for his father to have taken the Bible out of the coffin without any family being present? Noël was dead and couldn't corroborate the story. What if Willow—or that old Black dude—decided to turn on him? What if that Bible had real money in it, or some other valuables, and they accused the Greens of stealing it and then charging an arm and a leg to open the grave, knowing full well the Bible was never in there to begin with? (Booker's attorney had been the one on the other line, notifying him that he'd already sent full payment.)

Just keep your big trap shut, Christopher. That was what he told himself. That was his best bet.

What difference did it make anyway? No matter what he did or didn't tell Willow, the Bible would still be missing, and the powers-that-be obviously wanted it to remain that way. Why tempt fate? Silence was golden, as they say, and his silence might be just the ticket to appease any curse the pharaohs had in mind.

-TWENTY-SIX-

RUMINATIONS

NICK sat in his unmarked car, ruminating.

While he'd been surveilling Willow's house that night Cory had phoned her, he had seen something unusual that prompted him to return for another stakeout the following evening—and he'd seen the same baffling thing. The next day, he had done more research, probed around town a little more, and the picture began to congeal.

Still a long shot, it was time to put meat on the bones of his hunch. Tonight, he wouldn't just park and watch. This time, he went up to the door and knocked ...

✝✝✝

Early that Saturday morning, Willow remained holed up in her bedroom at Adam's place. Only four days since the disinterment, word of it had spread throughout town, and Nick had advised them to lie low until the outrage subsided.

She was nearing the end of Lily's letters; the final four, all relatively brief. Oh, how she would miss them! The letters had been her saving grace, her personal companions, and when she was finished reading them, it would seem like the line to that other place, the place where Leon had disappeared, was disconnected.

Dear Clarry,

It's a lovely June day, the first day of summer. I spent the afternoon out back standing at my easel, looking out over the garden
as I tried to capture one of my red roses on canvas. Jack came
out of the house, glanced at my painting, and settled himself
on the porch step, staring at me as he sometimes does. The urge
seized me to put a flame to my rose. And he asked me, 'Why did
you have to go and spoil it?'

Jack doesn't think it's art if it doesn't mimic reality. His world
is black and white, cut and dry, either/or. I painted it that way
because it's my reality.

Joy and terror consume me. Terror, that I might be pregnant.
Joy, because I might be pregnant with Ray's child—and then
the terror closes in again. After that one and only time with
Ray, I force myself to endure Jack's nightly torture so he'll think
this child is his. But I know the futility of it. If it turns out I'm
carrying Ray's child, soon Jack, and everyone else in Hyssop,
will learn the truth.

And when that happens … God help us all.

What a terrifying predicament! Willow rested the letter on her
lap, ruminating. The blank canvas on her own easel stared at her
from across the room.

Four days ago, as soon as she revived from fainting in front of
Lily's coffin and awakened in Nick Hardy's arms, she had walked
away from the grave and called Booker. After she informed him the
Bible wasn't there, his voice sounded older, weaker, so profoundly
disappointed, and she feared it would impede his recovery.

She arose from the bed, stared out the window overlooking
Adam's yard. The morning sun was high, covering the room in

a blanket of brightness. Lily had been a passionate woman, the same as Noël; they'd both loved and been loved deeply. Willow's thoughts drifted to Nick. The walk across the cemetery toward Lily's open coffin remained a bit of a blur, yet she remembered how he had held her hand all the way there, steadying her. Did he still have feelings for her, however obscure, or was he simply being a good detective? She already knew she still had feelings for him. When he was close to her, she felt as if she were surrounded by mountains. In his sermon, Pastor Raymond had said, "From time to time, we might catch a glimpse of the repeated refrains in our lives, however shadowy." Nick Hardy was one of those refrains.

The two of them hadn't had one personal, let alone inti-mate, conversation since he had resurfaced in her life, but that was nothing new. It was the same way between them years ago; holding things in, leaving things unsaid, undone, letting their body language, their shared gazes, do the talking. Or was it that way? Was Nick even the man she thought he was? Every person came with their own universe—their own dreams, experiences, their own broken pieces—and we only see a slice of them at any given time.

A knock on the door snapped her musings. "Can I come in, Aunt Willow?" Rocket bounded into the room, took his usual place on the window seat while she resettled on top of the bed with Lily's letters.

"What's up, Doc?" she asked.

"Nothin' much. Who are all those letters from?"

"How did you know they were letters?"

"I just guessed 'cause you dropped a bunch of envelopes on the floor."

"I did?" She looked down at the hardwood floor where the manila envelope had fallen open, spilling out its contents of the empty envelopes she had stuffed inside. Rocket leapt from the window seat and stooped to pick them up. "These are letters I found from your great-grandmother," she said.

"Oh." He didn't seem terribly interested.

"I found them in the attic. At Leon's house." The mention of Leon's name caused the features of his young face to sag. "I know, honey." She kissed the top of his head. Rocket brought up Leon's name nearly every night during their private talks before bedtime, and together they were processing his feelings of grief. "Where's your dad going? I saw him get in his truck a while ago."

"For a drive, I guess."

"A drive?" Not a good sign, Willow thought, to go nowhere in particular all by himself on a Saturday morning. "Is he okay?"

Rocket shrugged as he assembled the envelopes into a tidy stack. "How come these letters were never sent?"

"What? Of course, they were."

"No, they weren't. There's no postmark on any of them."

"Oh, sure there is. Let me see." Willow took the envelopes from his hand. Sure enough, he was right. There were various addresses to Clarissa, the same return address from Lily, a postage stamp on each, but no postmark. How come she hadn't noticed that before? Then again, she hadn't looked at the actual envelopes since that awful night just before Leon died, when she had first found the letters and separated them from their envelopes. The large manila envelope, on the other hand, had a variety of cancelled stamps, nearly two dollars' worth. A round postmark in red ink was dated August 17, 1953, the day of Raymond Roberts' murder.

Willow was floored. Apparently, Lily had not mailed any of these letters to Clarissa except at the very end, in one big batch. Perhaps she began writing them as a cathartic exercise, as her doctor had suggested. Yet she hadn't destroyed them. Why not? Did Lily consider the letters her insurance policy? ... her confession? ... her testimony?, if need be, never intending to share them unless the threat of personal injury forced her to do so? That must be why she'd written them the way she did—journal-like, documenting conversations and events.

"You know what?" Willow ruffled Rocket's black hair. "You're a smart kid."

†††

Adam was driving absentmindedly, ruminating. He had no idea where he was going until he caught himself heading due east through back country roads. He was sick and tired of living this way.

Every night, Nick had stationed a policeman in front of their home. The cop was subtle enough, parked behind bushes and trees after Rocket went to bed, often in an unmarked car. For Anne, it was a comforting thing; the cop's presence made her feel safe enough to fall asleep, leaving Adam alone to toss and tumble beside her. *He* should be the one making certain they felt safe.

Things seemed to be escalating. Cory was on the loose. If Cory wasn't the one who had fired the shots—(Adam still wasn't convinced that he wasn't)—then the killer was still out there. Nick had told them that someone had strung a noose around one of the trees near downtown, not a droopy branch of a weeping willow, but on one of the prominent oaks that had been there forever. As long as Booker remained in the hospital with a cop posted at his door, Adam assumed he would remain safe, and as soon as he recovered enough to be released, his son was planning to whisk him straight back to New Orleans. That left only Willow as their prime target. Or what if they decided to go after Anne or Rocket?

A quick glance at the clock on the dashboard startled him. He'd been driving for almost two hours and was nearing the Pennsylvania border. He had to get back! What was he thinking to have driven this far? Eyeing a safe place to turn the truck around, he dialed up Anne to assure her he was on his way home. Instead of back roads, this time he entered the ramp to the toll road.

His brain was spinning like their old washing machine shifting into rinse cycle, bumping and jerking from present to past. Life was complicated. Too complicated. Willow had found all those letters in the attic—she showed each one to Adam after she finished reading them—and he'd read them. Quickly, yes, but he'd read them, just the same. To Willow, they were a comfort, a distraction from all the crap that was happening. But Adam found them disturbing. Another senseless drama that had torn two families apart.

Adam had been able to spend the first nine years of life with his mother; she was complicated too. Before she died, she had long talks with him, conversations she had to *force* him to have, because he was too afraid to have them—those conversations meant he was saying goodbye to her. Each time after he left her bedside, Aunt Theckla tried to comfort him. She wanted to pray with him, but he wanted no part of that either. Why should he want to talk to a God who was going to take away his mother? He hated the prospect of going to live with Uncle Steve and Aunt Betsy in California after she died. He and his mother had visited them once before, right after Uncle Adam's funeral, but they had come back sooner than planned. California was too sprawled out, and his mother had found it hollow and unreal. When his mother died, Willow would be all the family Adam had left in this world—if she didn't go and die at birth, that is.

The sight of the green road sign jarred his thoughts back to the present. The sign informed him he was still sixty miles away from town. *Damn it.* Half the Saturday would be gone by the time he got home. He stepped on the gas.

One of the things he remembered most about his mother was that she cried a lot. She thought he didn't see or hear, but he always saw and heard. He had tried to do the right things, to be a good boy, but no matter what he said or did, it wasn't enough to make her feel happy.

Some of his earliest memories, surprisingly vivid, were of Freddie Chavis. Whenever his mother cried, Freddie would come upstairs from the apartment below to spend time with him, give him every ounce of his attention, just the two of them, while Theckla tended to Noël. He spent hours and hours with Freddie, building balsa wood airplanes, watching cartoons and game shows on TV, but mostly, Freddie would take him out back to a fenced-in patch of grass behind the apartment building and demonstrate his super-duper pitch. Adam couldn't get the hang of it. He was way too little to pitch with any speed or accuracy, his hand too small to curl around the baseball, let alone hurl it the way Freddie showed him. Besides that, he felt too sad, knowing his mother was inside the apartment crying her eyes out.

But Freddie wouldn't give up. "See this ball here?" he would say. "Think of it as your troubles. That's the way I always thought of it. I wanted to play in the major leagues when I was young. I was good enough to make the leagues too, only I couldn't. No one that looked like me could do it, until Jackie Robinson came along. But *you* can do it. You can do anything you want to. So try again, boy. Take this ball in your hand, twist it round and round, and then toss it, as hard and fast as you can. Toss it far away, and all your troubles will fly away too, right along with it."

And it had worked! When Adam pitched that ball, with Freddie's help, it was pure magic.

He would never forget the feel of Freddie's big, wrinkled hand over his own, guiding his fingers to grip and twist the ball just so, to get the most velocity. He memorized the feel as best he could, as if he were blind, so that he could try to master it on his own when he was older and Freddie was no longer there. The super-duper pitch was a cure-all for whatever ailed him, a private code between them that no one else could understand.

Adam wished Rocket liked baseball; he knew his son was still grieving Leon. He wished Rocket wanted to learn how to pitch, or even to bat (maybe he could show him how to bat away his troubles)—any position would be just fine. But Rocket didn't have the slightest interest in that mound out back. He never played on it. Not even once.

Twenty-Seven

WATERFALL

ROCKET had left Willow's room less than an hour ago, and Adam still wasn't home from his drive. Willow could hear faint sounds of Anne baking downstairs—the running Mixmaster, the banging of cake pans (reminding her of Leon). She decided to go downstairs to the kitchen to keep her company.

It was impossible not to like Anne. Three years older than Willow, she looked much younger, her fresh, delicate face dotted with freckles. When Anne first met Adam, she was a waitress for the upscale Stadium Club at Comiskey Park, and for her it was love at first sight. "I made it my mission to marry him!" she later confessed. It took a while before Adam caught up with her—he used to call Willow in San Diego too late at night, forgetting the time difference, with his 'Should I's? or Shouldn't I's?'—but once he decided he should, he never second-guessed himself. Anne was the calm, solid presence that kept him grounded. Exactly who he needed.

"Is everything okay with Adam?" Willow asked as she took a seat at the table.

"Oh …" Anne stopped the Mixmaster. "I think he just wanted time to be alone. I try to give him the space he needs when he gets that way." She wiped her hands on the towel hanging on her shoulder before joining Willow at the table. "But I always start baking when I'm worried."

Willow smiled. "My grandmother Mary used to do that." That

was where their similarity ended. Gentle Anne was the antithesis of iron-willed Mary Ziemny.

Willow thought about vodka, but she was losing the craving. Like Adam, Anne hadn't mentioned a word about her drinking. Though Willow had fallen off the sobriety wagon for only a few days, she knew she could beat it—she was already beating it and hadn't had one drop since coming to Adam's house. She didn't need a program or sponsor; all she ever needed was a reason. Adam's and Anne's unconditional acceptance was more potent than a thousand interventions, and Rocket was reason enough.

"Cory has gotten Adam so twisted in knots on so many levels," Anne said. "And he hates that the town is torn apart."

"Maybe we should move away from here?"

"I don't think we need to do anything that drastic." Anne said. "I was born and raised in a small town, and I understand them. Every time a new person comes to town, it's like adding a new horse to a fenced pasture. All the other horses have to rearrange themselves, jockey for position, figure out who they are all over again, until they adjust to the newcomer … Right now, the people here are terrified. Once they catch the person who killed Leon, things will settle down again."

"I hope so," Willow replied with grim skepticism. "But don't the other horses sometimes terrorize the interloper till he finds a new pasture?"

†††

After Willow returned upstairs to her room, she reached for Lily's final three letters. Since the trio seemed to go together, each written a week apart, she read them back-to-back.

August 2, 1953

Dear Clarry,

It's been three months now since I've written to you, three months
since I went to Ray's home, and the doctor has confirmed it. I'm
pregnant. I told Jack right away, and he reveled in the news.

I'm certain the child is Ray's. Don't ask me how I know. I just
do. I can feel the difference.

A Summer Revival in the park—a series of three on consecutive
Sundays—was my only opportunity to tell Ray. I attended the
first one today, and here is what happened.

I dared not enter the tent. Instead, I stood on the grass, not far
from where the children played with their toys on the blanket
under the cypress tree. Every seat in the tent was taken, the
spectators overflowing on to the grass on every side, including
a fair amount of white people standing at a distance. At one
point, Ray looked over, spotted me. I was too anxious to absorb
even one word of his sermon.

When it was over, I waited. I waited for a clearing of the
crowd surrounding him. I waited until the white people had
completely dispersed.

Ray walked out of the tent, giving me a quick glance before
heading over to the blanket where my children played. He sat
down with them, cross-legged, and batted Bo's paddle ball,
much to their delight. Slowly, I approached. "Good morning,
Pastor Roberts," I said. "Miracles are everywhere." I knew I had
to talk in code, formally, the way we always did under public
scrutiny. My stomach is still small, the bump undetectable
under my waistless dress, so I pressed my hands against it so he
could see the form of my profile. "Here, too."

He looked up at me, aghast, handed the paddle ball back to

Bo. As he stood up, I saw tears forming in his eyes, and I forced myself to turn my head away. When I did, I saw Mrs. Peabody, watching us with interest from across the grass, though too far away to be within earshot. Even so, I pulled at the blanket, ushered the children away. Without making any further contact with Ray, we hurried from the park.

Such an abrupt farewell to the one who has changed my entire life.

✝✝✝

August 9, 1953
Dear Clarry:

Something alarming has happened. Two mornings after last Sunday's revival, Jack came to the breakfast table, unfolded his napkin on his lap the way he always does, and then asked, "How is it that you know Mrs. Peabody?"

A jolt surged through me. "I don't." I strained to sound unconcerned. "Noël and I wave to her on the way to the five and dime, that's all. She's always out on her porch." I watched him butter his toast. "Why do you ask? Is she not well?"

He stopped all movement except to raise his eyes to meet mine. "She's been telling people she saw you in the park last Sunday." His gaze tore through me like a missile.

I'm frightened, Clarry, deathly frightened! Even if Mrs. Peabody suspected something, the only thing she could possibly know— and even that's a longshot—is that Noël and I stopped into the Mt. Zion First Baptist Church on those Monday afternoons. She would have no way of knowing about the other encounter.

Ray's house is not even remotely visible from her home. But my being in his church is sin enough for this town.

I knew I had to go to the second revival today. I had to warn him! I know what you're thinking—you're wondering if your sister has gone completely mad, and maybe I have.

I took the children, spread the blanket the same as the Sunday before, but this time, I sat there with them. I had written him a note, explaining my fears and begging him to leave Hyssop right away. After the sermon was finished, I asked Bo to take my note to him in the tent—to make absolutely certain he didn't drop it or give it to anyone else along the way. I told him to tell Pastor Ray that it was a prayer request. My Bo is a smart boy, reliable and obedient, painstakingly accurate as to detail. I watched from the sidelines. I watched Bo hand him the note.

Ray slipped it into his pocket.

It is done. Ray has been warned. Hopefully he is, right now, planning his escape to safety. All I can do now is wait and pray.

August 16, 1953
Dear Clarry,

A few days after the second revival, I was startled to receive a call from Ray after Jack had left for work. I was aghast to realize that he was still in town, still in danger. He was taking quite a chance to phone—sometimes there's a party line listening in, but I heard no tell-tale crackling. He spoke quickly, hanging up before I had a chance to reply. "The last revival is on Sunday, Mrs. Trudeau," he said, talking in code. "If you plan to attend, maybe you could bring that bag you carry, and I'll be happy to drop the answer to your prayer requests into it, along with several months of suggested Bible readings."

I did exactly as he said. Without stuffing the blanket into it, I took the straw bag to the final revival today. The group was the largest yet with plenty of white people on the sidelines—Ray is attracting quite a following—and I felt we were inconspicuous, dwarfed by the size of the mixed gathering. I stood with the children, who sat on the grass under the cypress tree as Ray preached his sermon.

His face looked absolutely radiant, Clarry, as if an angel was shining over him, and my heart splintered into a million pieces. A horrible foreboding struck me. I had the feeling that I was watching him give the final sermon of his life.

When he finished, we waited nearby. We waited just outside the tent, near one of the stakes at the front, the empty bag dangling open on my arm. The crowd still plentiful, he passed by as he exited the tent, released an item into my open bag, heavy enough to force my arm downward, but we did not so much as glance at one another in the crush of the group.

I didn't open the bag until I got home. Ray had given me his Bible! His Bible! I was overcome with panic, with dread! He might as well have given me a copy of his final will and testament! Inside, he had stuck a note, like a bookmark protruding from the gilded pages. I've included it in this letter.

Oh, my dear God in heaven, what have I done? I cannot sleep. I cannot eat. I hear the rumblings of a crumbling earth beneath our feet! I don't know what will become of Ray! I don't know what will become of our baby! I don't know what will become of me! Jack will not learn the full truth until after the baby is born, but when he does, he'll go mad with rage!

Regardless of what happens to me, you will, no doubt, hear stories, terrible stories. I'm sending you these letters, Clarry, because I want you to know the truth. I want you to know that it was all because of love. I had no other choice. *We* had no other choice. And for making that choice, Ray and I are now standing on the precipice of death.

But what about my children? What will become of my precious children? Please promise me, Clarry, that you will look after them if something happens to me! Their welfare is my deepest sorrow, my only regret. My children—and maybe even their children too—will bear the weight of this cross in some shape or form as long as they live.

✝✝✝

Lily's final, desperate letter fell on to Willow's lap. She could feel her grandmother's helplessness, her sorrow, the horror of her impending doom.

The sound of Adam's truck rumbling up the driveway brought a rush of much-needed relief. Willow got up from the bed, looked out the window to make certain it was him. She smiled as Anne dashed outside to greet him. They looked so happy.

Returning to the bed, Willow picked up the letter again, reread Lily's parting words: *My children—and maybe even their children too—will bear the weight of this cross in some shape or form as long as they live.* That meant Lily's five children. That also meant her only grandchildren, Willow, Adam, and Amy, Uncle Steve's daughter.

Lily had been right. In one way or another, however directly or indirectly, her sorrow had been woven into their genes. Who could guess the wounds that tore through the heart of a family, passed from one generation to the next, right along with eye color, food allergies, quirky traits and mannerisms? Like it or not, aware of it or not, we picked up our parents' load and carried it from there. Lily had tried to reach across time by writing these letters.

In the shimmer of that second, Willow felt the transcendent power of love—similar to the way she'd felt it in Adam's kitchen that night, and when that whisper came out of nowhere the night Leon died and saved her from suicide. If they shared Lily's wound, a wound deep enough to span across the generations, might they also have the ability to heal it? By understanding Lily's suffering, might they be able to heal themselves in the process? In time for Rocket?—and all those yet to be born.

Finally, Willow unfolded the page Lily had tucked inside her last letter, written in the distinctive penmanship of Pastor Raymond Roberts. Willow's heart ticked up a beat. Handwriting told so much about a person, so intensely intimate that she felt the power of his charisma from the unique way he formed his letters. It was dated August 16, 1953, the day before his death, the same date as Lily's final letter. Lily had mailed the entire batch of letters to her sister the following day, only hours before his murder.

Willow read his note, read it again; once more.

There it all was; not another sermon *about* love, but the way Raymond Roberts had *lived* it, right to the end. First thing tomorrow, she would take the note to Booker. It was all he had left of his brother.

But for now, she was driven by the need, a nearly urgent need, to go over to the blank canvas that sat on the easel. Her grandmother had left them her letters. Her mother had written her a diary. Willow wasn't a writer. She was an artist—whether anyone valued her paintings was of small significance. Her story, her pilgrimage, her Book of Willow as she knew it, was hidden within the paints, in the colors, in the thickness or thinness of brushstrokes, there to reveal. The soul left scant evidence of its own existence, yet all forms of art were its secretions, its physical remains.

Her emotions pouring out, the images began to form on the canvas; a blur of sharp, geometric shapes of various sizes, reminiscent of the Russian painter Wassily Kandinski, in graduated shades of purples, violets, blues, and blacks, images of her own healing from the inside out, the sharpness of the shapes slowly rounding, softening, as they cascaded downward into the bluest of the blues, in connecting circles of engulfing waves … like a waterfall.

-TWENTY-EIGHT-

ANKLE BRACELETS

WHEN Dolly Schmidt had turned sixteen back in 1959, she received a pretty gold chain from her parents to fasten around her ankle, quite the rage back then. Her grandmother had gifted her a diamond brooch in the shape of a crown. What was a sixteen-year-old to do with an old diamond brooch? She kept it anyway, of course—it was worth a lot of money—and it sat in her jewelry box with the tiny, spinning ballerina on top until just last year.

Also when she'd turned sweet-sixteen, Dolly had entered a pageant. She wasn't the prettiest among the girls, but she was pretty enough, and perky, really perky, and she could play the clarinet like a pro. All these attributes added up to her winning the coveted title of Miss Daisy.

Dolly was a go-getter, and she aimed high. It was no surprise when, three years later, she was chosen for marriage by the most impressive man she knew, the hot-shot heir of his father's electronic parts company. They moved away to Philadelphia to open a subsidiary there.

In the early years of their marriage, he treated her royally, showered her with the finest clothes, jewelry, trinkets, and they were a team, a real team—she was perky and a go-getter and she knew how to throw the right kind of parties for his business associates. Later, when she got thick around the middle and her face sagged into her neck, he lost interest. He was CEO of the whole shebang by then, and she thought he was working all the time, when actually he'd been filling his free time with a bevy of women half her age and size.

Dolly understood the way the world worked. A woman's looks had a shelf life, and when she lost her youthful sparkle, she was nothing, no one. She had served her purpose, resigning herself to her fate as a wife in-name-only. And then one of his dalliances became serious enough for him to ask her for a divorce. Not ask— there was no asking about it. He notified her of his intentions as if their marriage were a merger gone wrong, a contract to be voided, which it was—she had signed a pre-nup (what did she know at age nineteen?). There being no children between them, another of her failures, she received the grand total sum of zero. It was all there, ironclad, in black and white.

Dolly had rattled around for years after that. She became a secretary, but without any training, that didn't work out too well. Waitressing suited her much better. She moved to Weeping Willow in 1993, the only divorced person in town until Leon Ziemny showed up years later. The people there were nice to her, felt sorry for her. They took good care of her, in their own good way, including her when and where they could, though she stuck out like another species in her singleness, a bystander at social events.

Now there was church, the Crosswinds of Eden Community Church, Rev. Tommy, and the others who embraced her like family. Since she had little money for the collection plate, she gave in other ways. She gifted the church with her only possession of value, her grandmother's brooch. She volunteered to work in the church office two afternoons a week, on her days off, alongside Telles Salvo, who kept the books for Rev. Tommy. Telles wasn't as quiet as he used to be. The church staff celebrated her last birthday by taking her to a restaurant in Bedlington, and she ended the evening by getting a small tattoo. Next to the ankle bracelets that she still liked to wear, on her right ankle, she now sported a pretty daisy tattoo, small and tasteful, not like Cory Ketchfield's flamboyant creations all over his body, but just enough to show that she was still a go-getter, no matter what her ex-husband or anyone else might think. Including Leon Ziemny, who had taken advantage of her one night, taken everything she had left to give, then blamed it on too much liquor the next morning. Afterward, he acted as if it had never happened, as if she were nothing, no one.

When she saw Nick Hardy heading up her walk that morning, she wasn't surprised. It was only a matter of time before he came here, asking his questions. She let him inside even before he knocked.

She *wanted* to confess; she had wanted to tell someone her whole story for a long time. Nick was a good listener, with his striking blue eyes, intent upon her every word. She told him about being Miss Daisy, about her ex-husband, about settling in Weeping Willow, about her friends in church and her work with Rev. Tommy, about Leon. She pointed out her daisy tattoo, and he took the time to admire it. She let him ask his questions, every last one of them. She was disappointed, deflated, when it came time for him to leave.

"If you need to know anything else," she called out to him as he walked to his car, "just give me a call. Okay, sugar?"

†††

Nick had enough to go on, enough to prepare to make an arrest. He went back to his headquarters in Bedlington to assure that the warrant was in order. He didn't want any slip-ups. By the next morning, it was all wrapped up. He called Willow and Adam to tell them he was on his way over, that they had apprehended Leon's assassin. "I'll tell you everything when I get there."

A second warrant of arrest was also issued, and he checked on that one too, before he left. They had searched that mammoth place with a warrant, and after a review of the books, they arrested him at his lavish estate in Bedlington, set on sprawling acreage, with a garage full of assorted vehicles, a house full of fine furnishings. "God wants me to have these things!" he protested, eyes blazing like a lunatic's.

The murder mystery was solved. That Rev. Tommy Brookdale was also being indicted for embezzling church funds, was—as far as Nick was concerned—icing on the cupcake.

Twenty-Nine

THE ROAD TO EMMAUS

"**WHY** does Nick have to be so cryptic?" Adam expected no answer. Anne and Willow were sitting on either side of him at the table, Anne drumming her fingers, Willow biting her thumbnail, awaiting Nick's arrival. Rocket, thank heavens, had just been picked up by the school bus, exempted from the big reveal. "Why didn't he just tell us who murdered Leon over the phone?"

"Honey, that's not the way." Anne caressed his hand. "We'll have so many questions. It's better he tell us all together."

"I suppose you're right."

When they finally heard the sound of tires crunching over the gravel driveway, Adam shot up from his chair, moved to the window. Nick had been there enough times to know to come to the back door, but, still, Adam waited for him, trying to read his body language as he strolled up the walk, which was futile because Nick Hardy was unreadable, so damned cryptic. He swung open the screen door, the days still hot enough for screens, and Nick entered the kitchen, nodding at Adam and Anne before his eyes settled on Willow.

"Please, sit down," Anne said, and he did. She already had the matching mugs in place on the table, along with cream and sugar. She poured hot coffee from the carafe, set it down in front of them.

"I'll get right to the point." Nick turned to Adam as he took a sip. "We took Telles Salvo into custody this morning, and I'm one-hundred-ten percent certain we got the right man."

"*Telles Salvo?*" Adam was dismayed, and from the look on her face, so was Anne. Telles Salvo didn't make a stitch of sense to him. Telles was a nice guy, kind of shy, didn't look you in the eye when he talked, probably in his sixties, maybe a little younger.

"You mean Dad's neighbor?" Willow asked.

"Yeah." Nick sat back in his chair. "Sometimes the most obvious person seems too obvious. Ballistics told us the shot was fired in the proximity of his back shed, not exactly from there, but somewhere in between the shed and Leon's backyard. Of course, I interviewed Telles and all your neighbors right after it happened—he was the one who told me he heard a truck driving away—but all their stories were pretty much the same and nothing stood out. Besides, I couldn't figure out a motive for any of them. Telles has lived next-door to Leon for years, hasn't he?"

Adam nodded, still flabbergasted. "Ever since Leon moved here." So Telles Salvo turned out to be the killer. He couldn't fathom it.

"That long?" Willow said. "How come I didn't even know his name until after Leon died? He was awfully quiet, wasn't he?"

"Exactly." Nick gave them a second longer to absorb the news, took another guzzle of coffee before he continued. "But then, that night I was watching your house, Willow, I saw the light go on in his shed at one a.m. and it stayed on for hours. I thought to myself, 'What kind of guy plays in his workshop all night?' So I watched the house the next night; same damn thing. After that, I did some asking around, and I found out some very interesting facts about Mr. Salvo."

"Such as?" Adam asked.

"Such as, he worked part time for that pastor nut at the

megachurch, kept his books for him. I found out that Telles had been making some pretty disparaging remarks about Booker—I guess it really pissed him off to have a Black man staying right next door to him. When I went to his door to check it out, his wife was there alone, pretty close to frantic. Turns out, she'd been worried sick about Telles for a while now. He was a regular at the holy church of delusions, and Nancy said she didn't recognize him anymore, that he'd completely changed, become addicted to his computer when he wasn't at church. He was on his computer so much that she didn't want the thing in the house anymore, so he hooked it up in the shed. When we confiscated it, we found a pretty abysmal search record, plenty of white nationalist websites and other kooky places. Last, but definitely not least, Nancy showed us where he hid his rifle in the shed. And the bullets were a perfect match." He refocused on Willow. "So there you have it."

Adam remained too dumbfounded to ask many questions. Anne inquired about Nancy, how was she doing?, how difficult this must be for her, that kind of thing. Willow asked mostly about the church. "I don't get it," she said. "I thought half the town went to that church. That's a lot of good people. What's wrong with it?"

"Tommy Brookdale is what's wrong with it," Nick said. "He's a con man. He played on their worst fears. He sucked them in slowly, the way predators do. Whatever he did or said, no matter how outrageous, they went along with him because they thought he was some kind of anointed messenger. Gradually, the messenger became their messiah, and the church became a cult. He kept leading them closer and closer to the edge until some of them, like Telles, fell off."

"And Cory," Adam said.

Nick nodded. "Yeah, Cory, too. Though Cory's more hard

core. I think he had those beliefs long before Brookdale came along to stoke them."

In agreement with that assessment, Adam said nothing. He still couldn't wrap his mind around it. *Telles Salvo? Really?* After Nick had emptied the coffeepot practically all by himself, Anne got up to clear the dishes.

As Nick headed for the back door, he turned around. "Hey, Willow," he said. "How about a motorcycle ride later this afternoon?"

Looking from one to the other, Adam couldn't help but notice the chemistry between them. And he smiled.

†††

Willow was delighted to see Booker sitting up in bed, eating his lunch when she arrived later that morning. He appeared more like the way he was before the shooting. A policeman was no longer posted at his door. As he unwrapped the cellophane from his Jell-O cup, he looked up. "There's my sweet girl," he said. Yet she couldn't miss the discouragement in his eyes. Before, when she'd come to visit, there was always a glint of hope as he awaited the latest news on the recovery of his brother's Bible.

She pushed the vinyl chair over to the side of his bed. "Have you heard the good news?"

"What good news?"

"They caught the man who shot you."

"Yeah, I heard all about it. Nick Hardy came to see me first thing this morning." He sighed.

"Well, at least they got him." He seemed to take it in with an air of almost indifference. As he'd explained to them before, men like Telles Salvo were a reality he'd sadly grown accustomed to.

"Any word when you might be released?" she asked.

"Not yet. I'm hoping it'll be soon. I'm doing therapy now, and I feel good, stronger every day. Cyrus is anxious to get me home."

"Is he back in town?"

"He's coming in tomorrow. He has an appointment with my doctor to talk about my release. That boy can be pretty persuasive when he wants to be. He's lining up therapy for me in New Orleans." Booker finished his Jell-O, pushed the tray aside, most of the other food uneaten.

"I finished reading Lily's last letter," she said. "And enclosed in that letter, there was another letter … written by your brother."

Booker's body froze. "You found an actual letter from Ray?"

She nodded. "He wrote it the day before he died."

He sank back against the pillow. He closed his eyes for such a long time that she was afraid he was experiencing a medical event and nearly pressed the red button for the nurse. "Okay," he said, his lids opening. "Let's hear it."

"You sure?"

"I'm sure. I'm all buckled up."

August 16, 1953
Dear Lily,

Ever since you told me about our child, I've thought of nothing else. I've been racking my brain to find a way to take you away. I've even tried to come to you, but every time I do, there are eyes everywhere; the town is loaded with spies. And so I must put this in God's hands.

You and I are on the road to Emmaus, soon to see His face.

I have a confession to make. The first time I saw you

sitting under the tent, I sensed how much you were hurting, enough to not even give a second thought, in these perilous times, to being the only white face among a tent full of Negroes. I wondered what could've happened to you to bring you to that daring place with your broken heart wide open. And I knew it was God who put you in my path. All my preaching about Love, I guess He figured it was time for me to experience its fullness first-hand. You opened my heart to springtime.

Last night, I dreamt of my own death, a dream too vivid to be anything less than a premonition. I saw them tearing my flesh apart with their bare hands, limb by limb, but I wasn't there. I tell you this not to frighten you, but to comfort you when it comes to pass. As our little book, <u>God Calling</u>, puts it, "How could they know my spirit was free, unbroken, unharmed? … risen above these Earth furies and hates, into the Secret Place of the Father?" No matter what they do to my body, hold on to the words of our dying Christ, "Forgive them, Father, for they know not what they do."

Now that day is here, the day they will come for me, but I don't despair of it. I'm not going to flee, and I'm not going to fight. What else is worth dying for, if not Love?

Please try not to be afraid. It will be the same for you. Together, we will transcend. Remember, Jesus' promise: "You will be sorrowful, but your sorrow will turn to joy, a joy no one will take from you." Joy is the child of sorrow, the truth that lies beyond it, as is our precious child.

Where do our best dreams go, Lily? They must go somewhere because it is God who has written those dreams on our deepest hearts. I believe those dreams wait for us to catch up. They wait for us in the second spring.

Until then, I've been given another vision that God will hide you and our baby away in a safe place, in the 'Secret Place of the Father', and hold you there, where nothing, no one, can harm you.

Trust in that, Lily. Trust and wait. Wait … for the joy will come.

†††

When Willow finished reading the letter, she looked up at Booker. He remained motionless, in the exact same position the entire time it was read. "Booker?" she asked softly, "are you all right?"

"Yes," he said. "You know what I'm thinking? I'm realizing that you and me, we're family. The Trudeaus and the Roberts are kin. What relation would you have been to me, if things had turned out different, if we were able to know your Uncle Monroe?"

She smiled.

"I don't know exactly," he said, "but how about I just call you my niece? My grand-niece. You want to know something else? I think Lily came to me when I was in a coma. I can't really remember what she said, but I remember the sense of her being here with me, comforting me. You think that's possible?"

"I believe it is."

"Yes, I believe that, too … what we see, hear, smell, taste, and touch with our physical senses are just a part of the picture. But we dismiss our spiritual senses, and those synchronicities we sometimes experience. My brother talked a lot about fight or flight, didn't he? About transcending them." He pressed the button on his bed remote to raise his head higher. "I've been thinking about that too. We're hardwired for fight or flight. They come in pretty handy when we're in stressful situations."

He thought for a moment, grinned suddenly, surprisingly, the first grin Willow had seen on his face in a long while. "I had a dog and cat once," he said. "Like fire and ice, those two were. The dog was always after that cat, and the way that ended up was that the cat lived his whole life hiding under the bed. When he died, I got another cat, same dog. When the dog chased after that one, the new cat stopped dead in his tracks, looked the dog square in the eyes, and the dog didn't know what to do about it. They never had a problem after that. In fact, they curled up together to sleep. *That's* transcendence."

She laughed.

"But I have a much more significant example," he said. "The civil rights movement back in the sixties. You don't think we were afraid on those marches? You don't think we were angry? But we didn't run, we didn't fight back. No, ma'am, we dug deeper. We kept right on marching. Transcendence is when fear becomes courage, and anger becomes justice."

The sunlight streamed through the window, into his eyes. "Should I draw the shade?" Willow asked.

"No. That sun feels awfully good."

"I'm trying to think of an example of fight or flight in my life," she said. "The first one that comes to mind is Leon. When his father—my grandfather Walt—was diagnosed with Alzheimer's, I watched Leon run away from it, from him. Then I watched him do battle with Walt, night after night. And then one day, like your cat, he stopped running or fighting, and I watched him become the most loving caregiver in the world."

Booker bowed his head. "I'm sorry, Willow ... so very sorry that your father's gone."

"Gone? He's not gone." She glanced around the room. "He's somewhere, maybe even right here, but he's definitely not gone ...

Raymond's got me thinking too. He saw things so differently, from such a unique perspective. We saw Raymond's savage murder, but he saw his spirit rising into freedom. We call Lily's vacancy 'catatonia', but your brother saw it as God's way of hiding her away in a safe place. We saw their stillborn baby, but he saw ..."

Booker was silent for a long while. "Your daddy loved music, didn't he?"

Surprised by the sudden shift in topic, she nodded. "Oh, yeah." A flurry of memories came to mind as she pictured Leon under his headphones, the way he came alive when he listened to his oldies, especially Eric Burdon and the Animals, the way he disappeared into the sound.

"Music is another one of those transcendent things," Booker said. "The universal language, beyond words. You know, I've been wanting to do something in your pop's honor. What do you think he would say if I set up a scholarship at the Loyola College of Music and Media in New Orleans in his memory?"

The thought of it. Music from a new generation being released into the Cloud because of Leon. What *would* he say? Willow knew exactly what he'd say—*holy shit!* Her father, even as a memory, would always have that way of making her laugh and cry at the same time.

†††

Willow sat on the bench of the picnic table in Adam's backyard, waiting for Nick to arrive. She had to admit it; she had butterflies in her stomach. How silly for a woman her age. It had been eons, maybe since him, since she had felt that light-headed rush of excitement over another person's anticipated appearance.

Was he feeling the same way? Was this some kind of beginning?

Was the timing finally right? Is that what she really wanted? As she sat there, musing, she felt a little like Lily on the day she went to Pastor Ray's house, as if there were two Willows battling inside her—the self that weighed her down, kept her stuck in pain and fear, and her deeper self that saw things from a higher perspective.

Well, she would have to wait and see how the afternoon unfolded. At any rate, a ride on the back of a Harley-Davidson seemed exactly what she needed right now, a blast of life at its best—the wind rushing against her face, the visceral at-oneness with nature, the thrill of speed, the thrill of *him*. She had been holding herself back, but not today. In a week would come the first day of fall, the feeling of autumn already in the air. Finally, she was ready to squeeze the last gasp of vitality from summer.

After he pulled up and dismounted the shiny black Goliath piece of machinery, he slowly sauntered over, his signature, self-assured way of walking, and sat down beside her, backwards, his legs facing away from the picnic table.

"I have something to tell you," she said.

"Me too."

Summoning the courage to confess her feelings, she told him to go first.

Quickly, he shared his news. He'd been promoted to a plum position with the Denver Homicide Unit and was leaving town tomorrow. She needn't worry about the case, he said; he'd left it in good hands, with a good man, a Sgt. Timothy Olson. He handed her his card.

How wonderful. How deserving he was. He was a great detective, the best, and he'd been waiting for this dream job as long as she'd known him. She said all these things to him as she stuffed the card in the pocket of her jeans, her heart quietly breaking. Beginnings and endings were one and the same.

"Now what was it you were going to tell me?" he asked.

Willow paused, scrambling for an improvised reply. "I wanted to say thank you, of course ... for everything you did."

"C'mon, Willow. Why *wouldn't* I do it?" He steadied his elbows back against the table. The sunlight hit his eyes, blue as the Pacific Ocean. "Hard to believe how time flies," he said. "Remember that old bar we used to go to? The one with the foosball table?"

"And the Christmas lights." She smiled.

"Christmas lights? I don't remember those. All I remember is ... those were good times."

They were more than good times, she thought. They were star-filled nights, perfect nights for where they were in life at that time. Him, drinking his gin and tonics, sailing into that hazy, euphoric place of lowered inhibitions; and her, sipping colas instead of alcohol, drinking in every detail—the glow of colored Christmas lights strung over the bar, the cozy dark wood walls and beamed ceiling, Nick Hardy's blue eyes, and the sight and scent of spring-time and all things young. She was fully present in those moments, aware of their rarity, even as she was living them.

"Yes," she said. "Those were perfect times."

"Perfect?" His eyes intensified as he asked. Hers too, or they must have, because she felt herself falling inside his gaze, and leaned into his kiss. "What will you do next?" His voice was soft.

She fought to recapture her bearings. "Heal, I guess."

"And you think you're going to be able to do that here?"

"I think it's the *only* place I can do it."

He gave a half-shrug, glanced upward. "It's a perfect day for a motorcycle ride."

She stood up from the bench. "Fall is almost here," she said. "Before we know it, it'll be winter."

"Maybe it'll be a mild winter, who knows?" He entwined his

fingers through hers as they walked toward the motorcycle. "After that, it's spring again."

He didn't wear a helmet. Neither did she. In anticipation of the ride, she had braided her hair, but as she climbed onto the seat behind him, she regretted the braid—the wind whooshing through her hair had been one of the best parts. As he kicked up the Harley with a roar, she unplaited her hair, and off they went, wending through the curvy back country roads, deserted this time of day, except for the two of them. Revving the engine up faster, faster, he thrusted them into the landscape until they blurred into it, disappeared into it, and yet she pulsed with life. What if they crashed now? Would that be such a bad way to die? It would be the perfect way, if she were ready.

She wasn't ready, not quite yet.

She held on to the sides. Like the last time, she wanted to hang on to him, but she didn't. Back then, it was to prove to him that she wasn't afraid; that she could be as fearless as he was. Now it was because she knew he wasn't hers to hang on to. Nick Hardy was a wild, beautiful bird, his independence his *élan vital*. His wings were already outspread for the next journey.

Somewhere amid the rush of at-oneness with nature and Nick, Willow became aware that her deeper self had overridden the self that weighed her down. A good thing, she realized; the invisible Willow was the authentic one after all. As the motorcycle slowed, she rested her cheek against his back, savoring the moment before it was no more. In this wild bird, she had found a searching, untethered spirit equivalent to her own, which was also, paradoxically, what kept them apart.

A bittersweet conundrum; a double-edged sword. That she would always love this man for exactly who he was, for that and that alone, without conditions, without diminishing his *élan vital*, without blocking his light with her shadow. The same way an artist loves a sunset, a seascape, and all things inherently beautiful on their own; without painting herself in the picture at all.

-THIRTY-

THE NEIGHBORLY THINGS TO DO

BY the next morning, before it even hit the news, it seemed everyone in Weeping Willow had already heard the news of the double arrests. That became apparent to Adam as he and Anne made their weekly trip to the grocery store. While choosing avocados, they were approached by Dr. Joshua Wharton. "Thank God, you and your sister can start getting back to some semblance of normal," he said. "If there's anything I can do, just call." But at the check-out lane, two customers refused to wait in the same line with them, one of them being Dolly Schmidt, though she didn't move a foot until she'd given Adam an earful. "Your sister from New York City and that—that *man*—did this to Telles!" She wagged her finger in Adam's face. "It's all their fault! Rev. Tommy was trying to save us, and you had him arrested like a criminal!"

"Now, wait one minute," he had started to say, but Anne took him by the forearm, gently led him away to the check-out line on the far end of the store.

Adam thought it would be over once an arrest was made. How wrong he'd been. On the drive home, he contemplated the long, difficult road ahead of them, especially for Willow. Nick told them the megachurch was closed for the time being; its parishioners would be scattered like lost, livid sheep. Eventually, the trials for both men would be starting—blasted all over the local news, and they'd be forced to relive Leon's murder over and over again. But for now, Adam had to put all that on a back burner. For now, there was only one person he needed to see.

†††

Adam found Cory in the garage, unshaven and unkempt, his burgeoning torso squeezed into a sleeveless muscle undershirt, his mass of tattoos in full glory. He was pulling tools off a pegboard, tossing them into an open cardboard box. On the garage floor sat an array of boxes, a dozen or so.

"Going somewhere?" Adam asked.

Cory didn't bother to look at him, kept right on packing. "There's nothing here for me anymore," he said. "The people here are wussies, just like you. You're the chief wussy."

"What's that supposed to mean?"

"It means what I said. You're a fancy has-been pitcher who got used up too early, and so you sit on the sidelines like a wussy."

Adam let the insult go. He wasn't standing on the sidelines—he saw himself more as an umpire. "So where are you planning to go?"

"Back to Texas. Back to where people are strong and loyal." He turned around, stared him down with narrowed eyes. "You think I don't know that *you're* the one who ratted on me? Turned me in to the cops? How else would they have known I went to Charlottesville? You're the only one who knew that!"

"And you're the one who marched with those white suprema-cists … aren't you?"

"Hell, yes, I marched with them!" His eyes were flaming, his bloated cheeks flushing pink. He came closer, stopped several inches away from Adam's face. "You gotta fight, and you gotta keep fighting! You gotta show 'em who America belongs to! You gotta keep 'em in their place, not lay down dead like a fucking wussy!"

"Get a grip, man!" Adam stepped back.

"How can I get a grip? You even went after Rev. Tommy and the church!"

"Brookdale is a whack job!"

"Oh yeah?" Cory moved forward again. They were eyeball to eyeball. "How would you know?"

Adam felt his hot breath on his face. "Because I heard about the kinds of things Brookdale was preaching! Since when is 'hate your neighbor' the new Commandment?"

"Did you ever hear of an eye for an eye?"

"Did you ever hear of turn the other cheek?"

Cory assessed him from head to toe. "You just don't get it, do you? You think you're so superior. But you're dumb. Thick as a brick, if you think opening up your arms to all kinds of degenerates is the way to go."

"Degenerates?"

"Yeah, degenerates. Like niggers ... like Muslims ... like illegals ... you name it! We've got to fight to keep what's *ours*! Fight for our rights! Fight for our religion! Fight for our liberties!"

"What about *their* liberties?"

"Are you a Commie or something?" Cory paced in circles, clenching and unclenching his fists. "Not only are you dumb, you're a hypocrite. You think you're so self-righteous, opening up your arms to every degenerate that comes along, but you go ahead and thumb your nose at people like me. You mock our church and our pastor. You blame us for taking liberties away from the degenerates, but you want to take away *our* liberties! How does that make *you* any better?"

"Excuse me for thumbing my nose at Telles Salvo for murdering Leon!"

"I warned you about that, didn't I? I warned you that nigger would bring Leon down!"

"Brookdale was stealing *your* money!"

"Says who—you? Rev. Tommy is a fucking genius, and if he wants my money, he can have it!"

"He's a genius all right! He taps into people's ugliest wounds and harvests their pus like venom!"

"Rev. Tommy has our backs! These charges are fake!"

"Your Rev. Tommy is as guilty as Telles. Guiltier! He's the one who whipped up Telles!"

"You should be whipped up too! Not sticking your head in the sand like a wussy!"

"Telles used to be a quiet, decent guy! What the hell happened to him?"

Cory's face was crimson red now, heart attack red. Maybe his own face was too. Cory raised his fists.

"Go ahead, hit me!" Adam stood firm, without flinching. They were at a stand-off, and Adam knew it. They might as well have been living on two separate planets, howling into the cosmos. Nothing could make either of them change their minds. Adam didn't know what had happened to Telles, that might be true, but he sure as hell knew what had happened to Cory. David Ketchfield, that's what, the father who had beaten the piss—and everything else that mattered—out of him.

Pastor Ray's words from Lily's letters were thumping around his brain ("beyond fight or flight is transcendence" … "when we start picking and choosing who's worth loving, it stops being love" … "ask yourself, 'is this what Love would do?'"). But how was

Adam supposed to love this person standing in front of him? He
didn't know the words to say, not one. All he could think of to do
was throw his arms around Cory and hang on to that big, burly,
lost man for all he was worth.

For a second, maybe five, Cory remained completely still.

†††

Ever since Leon had come to see him that day, the last time
he'd seen him alive, Joshua Wharton had been reading about the
Trudeaus in his basement, sorting through their old medical files,
one by one. He found the files compelling in a way only a physician would. A physician could read beyond the dry medical lingo
to unravel pieces of a person's hidden story, at least in a town the
size of Weeping Willow, where he'd come to know the inner man
or woman almost as well as their physical body.

He reached the final file; the slim, flat file of Monroe Trudeau.
Only two pages long. He sat down in his usual chair.

His grandfather's notes stunned him for two reasons, the first
being they were surprisingly brief and surprisingly unmedical, just
one long, handwritten paragraph. There were the usual statistics,
of course—Harley was too disciplined to abandon his training
completely—like the fact that Monroe weighed only four pounds,
one ounce, that he was thirteen inches long, and that his stillbirth
occurred at seven minutes past ten p.m. on Christmas Eve, 1953.
But it was the second reason that stunned the bejeebers out of
Joshua, the final stat that Harley had recorded. In his tidy, unas-
suming handwriting, he had made the startling notation: Monroe
Trudeau was a Negro.

Jolted, Joshua went on to read the rambling paragraph, more
a confession than case notes:

I tried to make him cry," Harley wrote. "I tried to do everything I medically could to wake that baby up, to rouse it, but his little eyes were sealed as if they were never meant to be open to this world. His mother howled in grief when she saw he was dead, and she christened him on the spot, the first word I've ever heard her speak. She named him Monroe, before slipping right back into her catatonia. I cleaned the infant up in the bathroom, dressed him in the white satin gown that someone had laid out for him, all the while wondering what to do. Jack Trudeau and his children were waiting in the living room. Jack didn't seem to have a clue that his child might be of a different race. He was Lily's caregiver, the only functioning parent, and I knew I had only seconds to make a life-altering decision. When I came out of the bathroom, I saw that Noël had snuck into the room. In her innocence, she regarded her dead brother as if his skin color was no surprise. She knew she wasn't allowed in the room where her mother had given birth, so I made a pact with her that neither of us would tell a soul. There was no going back. I covered the little corpse in a blanket, head and all, and carried him to the front door in the living room where Jack and his sons waited. I told Jack the infant was born dead, that he had a horrible deformity—that his head had been crushed in the birth canal—and it was best not to look. I told Jack his job was to tend to Lily, that it had been an extremely difficult birth, and off he went without pressing to see the child. I carried the baby over to Ralph Green's house a few blocks down the street. It was snowing outside, a frigid Christmas Eve. I could hear carolers off in the distance. Ralph knew the right thing to do; he didn't hesitate. He drove me over to the funeral parlor, the life-less bundle in my arms, and he found a small pine coffin in his back room. We laid Monroe inside, dressed in his white satin, and closed the lid on that tiny, sleeping angel. Ralph nailed the coffin shut on all sides. Afterward, he and I swore to God and all things holy that we'd never breathe a word of this to anyone, and we shook on it. And then, he took a bottle of scotch from his desk drawer, and we had ourselves a few stiff belts.

When he finished reading, Joshua debated whether or not to trash Harley's notes. The Trudeaus, except for Noël, (what a secret for a child to hold inside!), likely never knew the truth, so why risk them ever finding out? As Ben Franklin said, "Three may keep a secret, if two of them are dead." He held the slim file on his lap. He couldn't bring himself to destroy it. These records were treasures, and they were safe down here in the dark. Who would even want to read a medical file that was sixty-four years old? Even Aaron, his own son and another physician, didn't have the slightest interest in perusing them.

Joshua stood up, gazed at the stack of boxes, piled long and high. He supposed he'd have to consider getting rid of them one day before he died and could no longer be their guardian. He put the file down, on top of the box, and began heading for the stairs. It was nearly lunch time.

On the third step, he stopped, turned around, came back down. Grabbing a matchbook from a nearby shelf, he struck a single match, held it to a corner of Monroe Trudeau's file, and dropped it on the concrete floor. He watched the flames rise, curl the folder, shrivel it to ash. He watched until the little fire burned itself out.

†††

His grandfather stayed on Joshua's mind throughout the day, the way he and Ralph Green had pulled together to protect Lily and her children, gone beyond the pale to do it too, overstepping their professional boundaries to save that poor family further heartache. The way neighbors used to look out for neighbors. No need for the Salvation Army, food pantries, or adult protective services. It was just the right thing to do.

Harley would be appalled, he thought, by what was happening in Weeping Willow now. He used to tell Joshua and his other grandchildren that he moved here from New York City because this town felt to him like a spoke of humanity—spread out, quiet, covered with weeping willows, and that was the kind of place he'd been searching for. In summertime, the Whartons and other neighbors would take vacations to larger places, to the hubs of humanity, to the edges of the United States, to big cities and state capitals, exhilarated by the rush of people, the pace, the sights, before returning home again. Back then, neither place was bad or good, right or wrong, red or blue, as they now called them. They were only sparse or dense, calm or noisy, horizontal or vertical.

Not that "back then" was so ideal. Far from it.

Two years after Monroe Trudeau's stillbirth, Emmett Till was tortured and murdered in Mississippi at the age of fourteen. As long as hatred had no expiration date, every day would know its own devils.

THIRTY-ONE

LINKS IN THE CHAIN

WHEN Adam arrived home from Cory's house, he noticed an unfamiliar sedan parked in the driveway, a small Hertz sticker stuck on the driver's side window. *Now* what? Grateful that it was a weekday and Rocket was at school, he rushed for the back door and yanked it open, then stood frozen in the doorway. Alongside Anne and Willow at the table, there sat Uncle Steve.

"Look who came to see us," Willow said.

Uncle Steve stood up from his chair, his eyes flitting back and forth between the floor and Adam. He had grown silver-haired, too thin, the kind of thinness without muscle, his sun-bronzed skin loose and leathery. Man, had he aged, Adam thought; he was probably thinking the same thing about him. Slowly, Adam crossed the room. "Great to see you, Uncle Steve." They shook hands. "What brings you here?"

"I just thought it was time."

They both sat down at the table. Uncle Steve seemed nervous, twitchy in his movements, including an involuntary tic in his left eye—the antithesis of a chilled-out Californian.

"Where's Aunt Betsy?"

"Oh, she wasn't able to come. Amy had something going on."

Adam nodded. "How's Amy doing?"

"Great. But busy. Two little kids. They keep her hopping."

"I bet they do. How old are they now?"

"Gayle is nine, and Emma's turning seven next month."

An awkward silence filled the room. Adam couldn't think of a thing else to say.

Anne spoke up. "He brought something for you."

Adam followed the direction of her gaze. A large box from J.C. Penney stood on the table, taped up and labeled for shipment. "What's that?"

"Your things," Uncle Steve said. "After you left San Diego, Betsy boxed up the things in your room, mostly your baseball stuff, and stowed them in a storage locker. We were waiting to give them to you when you came back to visit, but ..." His voice trailed off. He took a sip of water from the glass in front of him.

"But better late than never?"

"Yes," Uncle Steve said. "Better late than never."

Adam didn't want to open it, not now anyway. He had just been through all that emotion with Cory, and he wasn't up for opening some long-lost package in front of an audience—watching, waiting for some kind of happy response from him, or maybe tears would be better, or who knows what kind of reaction they were expecting? The belongings inside that box were personal, items that had meant everything to him at a time in his life when he felt most helpless, and he sure as hell didn't want to lay eyes on them again with everyone staring.

Anne gave him a gentle nudge. Adam rose from his seat, slid the box over to where he stood.

"Here's the thing," Uncle Steve said. "Before you open it, I want to tell you I'm sorry."

Apologies, too? Adam couldn't do this. Not right here. Not yet.

"Hear me out, Adam," Uncle Steve continued. "This is as difficult for me to say as it is for you to hear. Inside that box, along with your things, there's another package that we never forwarded on to you. It was sent from a nursing home in Mobile, Alabama."

"Mobile, Alabama?" Adam murmured. "…You mean, from Aunt Theckla?"

"Yes, probably so." Uncle Steve tic'd and twitched a little more, gulped from his water glass until it was dry.

"Do you know what it is?" Adam asked.

Uncle Steve shook his head. "I have no idea. I only just discovered it when Betsy and I were getting your things ready to send to you. I was going to send it UPS, but I decided not to. I decided it best to bring it in person."

Adam was silent; he realized he was being a prick. It must have taken a huge chunk out of Uncle Steve to travel all this way just to bring him a box.

"It was a terrible oversight, not to send you the package from Mobile right after it came," Uncle Steve said. "And I'm sorry. I'm really sorry." He looked earnestly into Adam's eyes.

"Don't be sorry," Adam said, his voice softening. "It was good of you to bring it, Uncle Steve. Very thoughtful. And I'm glad you're here. I really am."

"Go ahead, honey." Anne handed him a steak knife to slit the packing tape. "Open it."

Adam reached over, cut the taped lid with the knife, reached inside the box. One by one, the items emerged. His globe, his collection of baseball cards, his cherished poster of Don Baylor in full California Angels uniform from the year he was an All-Star and won the American MVP Award. Adam's very first baseball, Uncle Freddie's ball. He curled his fingers around it wishing he could throw it across the kitchen, toss his troubles away … At the bottom of the box sat the other one, wrapped in brown paper and string and addressed to him in San Diego.

He cut the string, tore off the brown paper. Inside that box was a smaller one, an envelope taped on top, with his name on it, in Aunt Theckla's handwriting. He set the envelope aside and kept going, opening the package as quickly as possible, with all eyes glued on him.

Out came an old baseball cap. He held it up for the others to see before planting it on top of his head. A solid fit. "This is the cap Freddie used to wear," he said.

"Freddie?" Uncle Steve asked, as if Adam had never mentioned the name before.

"Aunt Theckla's husband," Adam replied.

The rest of them were nodding, smiling. They looked a little disappointed, maybe because Uncle Steve had flown across the country just to bring him a cap, or maybe it was because Adam had shed no tears over it. He'd never been much of a crier; his mother had cried enough for all of them. Besides, he was relieved that the public unveiling of the contents was over. He slipped Theckla's note into his pocket. He would read it later, when he was alone.

As he was moving Theckla's box aside, he felt its heaviness—there was something else in there, a hard object beneath the layer of tissue paper. "Wait a minute," he said. He pushed the paper away. "Holy mackerel."

"What?" Anne asked.

"I don't believe it!" he said. Theckla's note might offer an explanation. He retrieved it from his pocket, slit the envelope open with the steak knife, read it. Passing the note to Willow, he waited for her reaction.

"Oh, my God!" She gasped. "How could it be?"

"Go ahead," he said to her. "You can read it out loud."

Willow looked up at him with a dazed expression, cleared her throat a couple times before she began to read:

Dear Adam,

When your mama was saying her final goodbyes to me, she gave me this Bible. She told me it belonged to a young pastor who'd made quite an impression on her life. One look will tell you that it's a very special Bible, with some very special papers inside of it. This Bible has worked its miracles for me and for a lot of old Black folks, both in my old apartment, and the ones with me now, close to death here in this nursing home. I'm praying it does the same for you. I figured it was time to get it back to you, the way all important things come back, by and by. I've also tucked some photographs inside, your mother's favorites.

More than you can ever know, you've been a blessing in my life, in both Freddie's and mine. When you become that pitcher in the minor leagues, or the major leagues later on, look up in the stands and know that Freddie and I will be there, cheering you on.

All my love,
Aunt Theckla

Carefully, Adam lifted it out of the box, an old, black, beat-up Bible with half the cover torn off.

"So Mom never even put it inside Lily's coffin?" Willow asked.

"Apparently not." Adam shrugged.

"Unbelievable," Anne said.

"My God." Uncle Steve sounded equally flabbergasted. "I haven't seen that Bible since I was a kid. I had no idea it was in there. I wish I would've gotten it to you sooner, before you had to ... or maybe you didn't do it yet."

"You mean the disinterment?" Willow said. "Yes, we already did it."

Adam clutched the Bible. It certainly didn't look like an item that would cause so much upheaval, to so many for so long, though it did appear as if it had traveled a million journeys. And it had—from a fancy southern plantation to a slave hut built in the dirt; to Birmingham, Alabama; to Hyssop, Louisiana; to Weeping Willow; to a nursing home in Mobile; to a storage locker in San Diego; to right here in this kitchen, and soon, it would be on its way to New Orleans. After all that, Adam felt as if he were holding a piece of the Holy Grail.

†††

Later that night, as they arranged themselves on the oversized sofa, the Bible sat in a place of honor on top of the mantle. Adam suspected that Willow was chomping at the bit to get into it— to study the papers stuffed inside, the plethora of handwritten marginal notes that would take months, maybe years, to go through. But Uncle Steve was in town for just a few days, and it would have to wait.

Adam found himself settling into Uncle Steve's company. Maybe it was because Aunt Betsy wasn't with him, but he seemed a changed man from the one they had grown up with. Or was it the wine? Poor Willow and Rocket, sipping their colas, while the rest of them sat with warming cheeks and softening hearts.

After they'd gotten over the discovery of the missing Bible, Adam had squirreled away the set of Kodak pictures that Theckla had stuck inside. Since he'd forfeited the opportunity with the note, he wanted to savor them privately first, so he took them outside, to the pitcher's mound, and looked at them there.

He recalled the year they were taken; a historically significant year. They were taken in 1968, on the day Robert Kennedy had come to campaign in Langston, Indiana—where Adam and his mother were living at the time—during his brief, tragic bid for the presidency. They had gone to a street rally, with hundreds of others eager to see Kennedy and, maybe, be lucky enough to shake his hand.

His mother used to keep these photos in a shoebox beneath her bed. Every then and again, she would bring them out to the kitchen table, where she shuffled through them, her eyes dreamy as she relived that lost moment in time. Sometimes she would talk to Adam as she studied the photos, reminiscing about that rally in great detail. The endless sea of Blacks and Whites reaching out to touch Kennedy, their arms tangled together in hope and excitement, the sixties' music piped in on loud speakers, the old WWI and WWII vets waving little American flags on wooden sticks, the homemade signs, and, of course, Bobby Kennedy himself, sandy-haired and sunburned as he stood on the hood of a car, quoting Tennyson. He spoke about seeking a newer world.

Other times, when she looked at the photos, she didn't speak at all. Funny thing was, not one of the pictures had Kennedy in them. Still, Adam remembered that these photos were the be-all and end-all to his mother—in them, she saw her utopia, the sorrows of the world melting away for that instant, and she had managed to capture it on Kodak.

With help from the wine, Adam was ready to share them now.

He stood up from the sofa, passed the first photo to Willow, a shot of Leon standing amid the crowd, a young Leon with a full head of nearly black hair, a suave mustache dipping down each corner of his lips. On top of his shoulders, he was hoisting a giggling blonde toddler with a mop-top Beatle haircut. Tears in her eyes, Willow fell speechless. Eventually, she passed it on to Anne, who sat beside her on the left.

"How handsome Leon was!" Anne said. "Is this *you* on his shoulders, honey?"

"It's me, all right." Adam nodded.

Rocket jumped up from his seat and peeked over his mother's shoulder to get a look. "That little boy is you, Dad? How old were you?"

"I was four."

"Who took the picture?"

"My mother did. My mother took all five of these pictures. Here's the next one." He handed it to Rocket, who had reseated himself next to Willow. "This is Freddie," he announced to the group. Freddie Chavis was standing among the crowd, jubilant, pumping his fist into the air. He didn't quite look the way Adam remembered him; in his recollections, Freddie seldom smiled.

"Oh, my," Anne said. "I finally get to see the famous Freddie Chavis."

"The man who taught you how to pitch!" Rocket was ecstatic.

"The very one. And here's a picture of his wife, Theckla." In the photograph, she was beaming at her husband, her face lit up like a schoolgirl's.

"The both look so happy," Anne said.

"It was a happy day," Adam replied. "Everyone was happy. Everyone was excited. I don't really remember it too well, of course, but my mom kept it alive in my memory."

"Theckla seemed like such an old woman when I met her," Uncle Steve said. "But she's younger in this picture than I am now."

Adam gazed down at the next photograph. "I have no idea who this guy is, waving the little American flag." He stood up and handed it to Uncle Steve, who didn't recognize the man either. No one did, until it finally came around to Willow.

"It's Walt!" she cried. "Leon's dad!—this is my *grandfather!*"

Slinging her arm around Willow's shoulders, Anne leaned over to get a second look. "Finding these photos is like opening a time capsule, isn't it?"

Rocket glanced at the photo. "He looks nice, Aunt Willow."

"He *was* nice." She pulled something out of her pocket, a small, lacquered, oval-shaped icon of some sort. "See this?" She held it up to Rocket. "This belonged to him. His mother in Poland gave it to him right before he got on a ship for America when he was just a little boy. It's the Black Madonna of Częstochowa."

"Who's that?"

"The mother of Jesus."

"She was Black?"

"She is *here*, isn't she?"

"Is Jesus Black?"

"I guess we'll have to wait and see."

Rocket paused for a moment, deep in thought. "Didn't Walt's mother get on the ship with him?"

"No. She wanted to. But she wasn't able."

"Why not?"

Willow paused, as if collecting herself. "She was too poor, and her husband, Walt's father, was very sick. But she wanted their son to be free and have a better life in this country. Things weren't the same back then as they are now. There were no planes. No computer, no email, no Skype, or Twitter, or Facebook. When people all over the world left their home countries to come to America, they had to travel on big boats called steamers, and it was a long, difficult voyage, especially for poor people like Walt. Many times they never saw each other again, like Walt and his parents. His mother gave him this Madonna of Częstochowa right before he boarded, to let him know she would always be with him."

"But she wasn't."

"Not the mom he could see. But she was always with him, believe me."

"It must be really old. Can I hold it?"

"Sure." Willow tucked it into Rocket's palm.

Before Adam handed out the final photograph, he noticed the blurred image of his mother's left index-finger on the top of the photo as she had snapped it, and he was struck by the thought that they were viewing these iconic pictures—iconic for them, anyway—through her own eyes after all these years. "Here's a picture of Uncle Adam," he said, passing it to Uncle Steve.

"Oh yeah," Steve said. "That's him. My baby brother in James Bond sunglasses." He took a sip of wine. "What a dashing guy he was, huh?" He turned to Rocket. "You know, you remind me of him."

"I do?"

"Yeah, you do." Uncle Steve's eyes were fixed on the photo. "And just like you, he wanted nothing more than to become a doctor."

"He did?"

"He sure did."

"Did he become one?" Rocket sat down cross-legged in front of Uncle Steve, eager to hear more.

Uncle Steve bowed his head. "No, he didn't."

"Why not?"

"He got injured during the Vietnam war, that's why." He handed Rocket the photo. "He lost an arm. See?"

"Oh … that's a bummer. That must have been really hard for him."

"It was." Uncle Steve got down on the floor beside him. "But you know what? I bet he's busting with pride that you're picking up the torch right where he dropped it."

Rocket's eyes lit up. "I wish I could've known him!"

"I wish you could've known him too."

Adam sat down on the far end of the sofa, his mind drifting as they passed the pictures back and forth, over and over again, the way his mother used to shuffle through them. There was always another story to tell, another question to ask. It gave him a warm feeling to sit back and listen, to observe the continuity of life, to realize that each family member had been a piece of the pattern, a link in the chain. Even now.

Uncle Steve had come all this way to make amends, and Adam loved him for it. And it was okay that Rocket didn't like baseball. Genes got transposed and reordered in their own purpose, and Rocket had picked up a goodly share of Adam's, the first Adam, the youngest brother of his mother, the one he himself had been named after. And it made sense. Magnificent sense.

Adam had always felt as if the Ketchfield genes were a poison inside him, a poison he was terrified he'd pass along to his son, but look at him, just look at him. Adam grinned as Rocket persisted with question after question the way he did, the same way Willow was prone to do.

It was true, we carried those who came before us in our genes. But that didn't mean we were determined by them. We each had our own unique blueprint. Our own reason for being. We could cultivate the good seeds, learn from the bad. But it was our choice. Every minute we were alive, we had a choice.

And that included Cory.

Cory still had a choice. Cory still had a chance.

††† †††

They remained seated in the living room, laughing and reminiscing, when a call came in around ten that night on Willow's cell. It was Booker.

"I hate to phone so late," he said, "but I wanted to let you know that my doctor is releasing me tomorrow. Cyrus is here, and he wants to head straight back to New Orleans."

-THIRTY-TWO-

THE ENDS WE START FROM

WILLOW stayed up until four a.m., thumbing through the Bible and the inserted pages, knowing this would be her only chance before they were turned over to Booker later that morning. When Rocket woke up, she would give the inserts to him to scan on his computer so they'd have copies for themselves. She wished she could do the same for the entire Bible, but it just wasn't possible.

In the margins, Pastor Ray had highlighted verses or words on every single page and written numerous notes and annotations in the margins. In some places, he filled in the Hebrew or Aramaic translation of a certain word, making its intended meaning clearer. In other places, he made a note in the margins when God had touched his own life in some significant way. Willow was no Bible scholar, to be sure, but she could only imagine what a gold mine it would be for those who were.

Finally, she unfolded his magnum opus, The Book of Raymond, an augmented version of the sermon he gave in the park that Sunday morning when Lily first met him, a vivid testimony of his personal walk with God, his own discipleship; love the guiding force, the front and center of it all. It gave Willow goose bumps to read it, the sheer realization of how much love there is available in the universe, circulating, unending, yet how blind we are to it. Our best moments; our inspired moments; our most joyful moments whether they be peaceful or spectacular; the moments that break our hearts wide open; the music that moves us; the recurring, evolving themes of our lives; the awe-inspiring beauty we encounter in nature; the unique coding in our DNA—and the people, always the people, who share our journey. Of these treasures, we can never be robbed. Each of them comes from love, the unending love that circulates in and through and around us. And yet, despite all that love, we choose to focus on the monsters, large and small. Why do we do that?

Willow didn't consider herself a religious person. What did that mean, anyway? As Walt used to say, religion was man's way of putting God in a box, making him as small as we were. When the truth was, God was ever-present, everywhere, in everyone—in the atheist as much as the monk. As close, as pervasive, as our breath.

Sadness used to be Willow's most authentic place, but now it was joy. Not stoic, fakey "put on a smiling face" happiness. But joy. She had read some of Henri Nouwen, and she liked the things he had to say about joy. "Joyful persons see with open eyes the hard reality of human existence, and at the same time are not imprisoned by it," he wrote. Joy went deeper. Joy was independent of circumstances. When love replanted suffering in its rich, tilled soil—bit by bit, drop by drop, tear by tear—suffering transformed into joy.

†††

As Willow was getting dressed for the day later that morning, her cell phone rang. It was Sgt. Timothy Olson, the detective who had taken over the case, calling to introduce himself and fill her in on the latest details. It pained her to hear about Telles Salvo's arrest, how he didn't have any means of coming up with bail, how his life, and his wife's, were in ruin. When he was finished, her only question was, "Has Nick left town yet?"

"He left yesterday," Sgt. Olson said. "Finally! He's lucky Denver still gave him the job."

"What do you mean?"

"That knucklehead almost lost it!" He laughed. "His dream job, the one he'd been waiting forever for, because he insisted on staying here until your father's killer was caught. Denver Homicide made the job offer to him the day after your dad was murdered, and they were losing patience with him. We kept telling him, 'Just go,' but he wouldn't budge … But that's Nick for you."

Willow squeezed her eyes shut—the confirmation she'd been hoping for. No, she might not be in Nick's picture, or he in hers, but that was Nick for you. The man she thought she knew was exactly the man he was. The one embedded in her heart.

††††

Booker was sitting on the bed when Willow arrived, dressed in street clothes that clearly revealed to her how much thinner he'd gotten since the shooting. He was both surprised and delighted to find Adam had come along with her. As Adam bent to give him a hug, she sat down in her usual chair, the strap of a large purse dangling on her arm. Cyrus wasn't in the room. Booker told them he was getting some last-minute discharge orders straight with the nurses.

"So this is it?" she said.

"Nah, nah, it's not it." Booker shook his head. "It'll never be it. We're family, remember? Come down to New Orleans any time you want. You've always got a place to stay with me." He tapped his heart with his balled fist. "You've always got a place in here."

Adam gave her a look, a *C'mon, sis, give it to him* look.

"Okay," she said softly, rising from the chair and moving toward Booker. "We brought a going away gift for you." She opened the large handbag and pulled it out, resting the closed box on the tray beside the bed.

Booker paused a second before opening the lid. When he did, he stared in wild-eyed disbelief. "No! Oh, my God, no! It can't be, can it?" He looked up at her. "How?"

She told him the story of how. How it came to reappear in their lives, and Booker listened, incredulous. His fingers trembled as he touched the worn leather of the half-cover, as if making certain it was real. He lifted it from the box, raised it to his lips, kissed it. After resting it on the bedside tray, he took out some of the papers stuffed inside and unfolded them, slowly, carefully, like sacred scrolls. And then his face dropped into his hands, and he wept.

Cyrus rushed into the room. "What are you doing to him *now*?!"

"Stop it!" Booker said, through his tears. "Stop it right now, boy! Open up your eyes and look! Look what they brought to me! To us!" His hands still shaking, he held up the Bible.

"Is that ... *the one*? Uncle Ray's?"

Booker nodded. "This family and their father, they gave me a gift I can never repay. They gave me back the most consecrated part of our family history. They gave me back my brother."

Cyrus looked at Willow, then Adam. "I'm sorry ... Willow, is it? And—?"

"Adam. This is my brother, Adam."

He reached out to shake Adam's hand. "I'm sorry, Willow and

Adam. I know you paid a big price to do this for Pop. A very big price. And I want you to know I appreciate it. I really do."

Booker reached for his cane, struggled to get up from the bed, and after he did, he put his arms around Willow, holding her there against him in a father's hug, like *her* father's hug used to feel. She didn't want to let him go. He seemed to be feeling the same thing, yet for different reasons. For him, this was the end of a lifetime's search. For her, it was the end of Leon's final chapter, and when Booker let go of her, the last living piece of Leon would let go too.

Before they parted, Willow took out her phone and snapped several group photos. Cyrus did the same, so that she could be in some of the pictures too, and he sent them to her on the spot. She checked to make sure she'd received them, and there they were: *family*. Monroe had made them family. Monroe had woven Raymond Roberts' blood into their own. This long and winding journey had been the right one; it had been redemptive and healing. It had stretched across time, across the generations of two families; it had passed through the hell fires of murder and hatred.

And Love, with a capital L, had the final word.

THIRTY-THREE

HEALING

BEFORE Uncle Steve boarded his plane that Saturday morning, both Willow and Adam promised to come for a visit in San Diego. Afterwards, Willow moved back into Leon's house; *her* house. It was high time. Especially after Adam had made certain to paint out the blood stains on the back deck.

Walking back inside felt different. Every time she came into this house after a lapse of time, it seemed to change. She recalled the first time she had seen it while still in her twenties, a pitiful-looking place back then, for which she'd felt not an ounce of connection. It had never been much of a house, nothing special or charming about it, even after Leon's remodeling. But like a chameleon, it took on different personalities. No longer Leon's deathtrap, or the lonely, foreboding place she'd abandoned after Cory's call in the middle of the night, it now seemed a house of renewal, rebirth. A house that knew more than most houses came to know about its occupants because it had grown up and grown old along with them, absorbed their sorrows within its walls, harbored their secrets, and swathed them.

Willow still couldn't bring herself to enter her father's room. The best she could do was close the door, leave it for another day. But the rest of the house she could change up any way she chose. Booker's room was clear of any trace of him; a blank slate. Regardless, she decided to keep her bedroom in the attic.

Adam and Rocket arrived and spent the day with her, staying into the evening to help her get resettled, rearrange things, and convert Leon's man cave into her art studio. The sunlight was especially good in that room—who could paint in an old, dark basement? Anne had remained at home to finish up new curtains she was making for the space. Willow had brought back her easel and paints from Adam's house, and Adam and Rocket carried her blank canvasses up from the basement.

"Are you gonna keep the bird clock?" Rocket asked her.

"It's staying exactly where it is."

Like Willow, Rocket was enthralled by the attic—the old rolltop desk, the creepy lampshade, the brick chimney. He had never been up to the attic before—neither had Adam—but now they explored it with the same curiosity as she had done, the unfinished side too, with its mountain of junk. Together, they made a quick sweep for hidden treasures, and Rocket pulled out the statue of the Virgin Mary with the broken nose, Grandma Mary's statue. Come spring, Willow told him, she planned to set it out back, by the deck.

Later, they helped her frame the Kodak photos that Rocket had enlarged on the printer, along with dozens of other pictures from old family albums, and new ones too, including the images taken with Cyrus and Booker at the hospital. She took down her old painting that Leon had hung on the largest wall of the living room to clear a space for the new collection, her own little Wall of Fame like Walt had created at The Mazurka Inn. Lastly, she added a charcoal sketch she'd drawn of a great-grandmother she never knew, Walt's mother, standing alone on a pier, waving at a distant ship. Whether it was arriving or departing was up to the viewer.

They were all here now, the living and the dead.

†††

After Rocket and Adam went home, Willow stared at the photographs. While she was sketching that drawing of her great-grandmother, it got her to wondering, what if she had made a different choice than to put Walt on that steamer? What if Willow's mother had made a different choice, and Willow had never been born? Were their sacrifices really worth it?

She entered her new art studio, flooded with sunshine, the urge to create too strong to ignore. After opening several jars of oil paint, she mixed the colors on the palette and began painting unconsciously, the way she did, uncertain what image might begin to appear on the canvas. When she realized what it was she was creating, she kept on going. She blended the paints into various shades of graduated pinks and violets, adding dabs of lavenders, reds, blues, and whites, until she achieved the precise range of progressive hues. Unlike her earlier paintings, there was no obscuring moonlight. This time, Willow chose a bold, bright sun to reveal their spectrum of colors. Finally, she was getting it right.

She was painting the fireweeds, those beautiful, astonishing flowers that somehow found a way to grow over the most traumatized, devastated places—including her own.

†††

A month later, well into the heart of autumn, Willow was lying against the headboard in her attic room, rereading the Book of Raymond. All the purple tassels and the old braided rug were gone. She had updated the space to better suit her—a high-post bed with new sheets; a lamp with a Tiffany-style shade for the matching nightstand; an Oriental area rug; mesh-colored blinds in the window; and a new mattress, though they'd had a devil of a time getting it up there. She kept only Leon's bedspread, Clarissa's dresser, and the old rolltop desk.

Nightfall was the optimum time of day to do her best thinking, and what she was thinking was that there was work to be done here. Willow wasn't going to fight, and she wasn't going to flee. The town for which she was named continued to resent her, but there were sprouts of hope. Yesterday, Dolly Schmidt had reached out to her, inviting her over for coffeecake. Healing, like grief, took place in stages. Besides, she couldn't leave the weeping willows quite yet.

Willow was exactly where she needed to be, and this house, this malleable house, the exact place. Ezra Pound described it as a "periplum," a journey where a traveler ended up back where he or she started, only the end point looked different than it had before—just as this town looked different—still familiar in every aspect, yet she was able to *see* it again, and see it anew. As "The Four Quartets" put it, she *knew* the place for the first time.

Settling against the pillow, she contemplated this notion. Pastor Ray had told Lily that we were travelers here on this earth, in the midst of our journeys. Pilgrims in periplum. Like fools, we scrambled to find the purpose for our lives, some visceral, tangible value to justify our own existence, some significant contribution or accomplishment we could make—such as if she had evolved into a master artist like Vincent Van Gogh or Leonardo da Vinci. But would even that bring fulfillment?

She doubted it.

"We set sail with sealed orders," Pastor Ray had quoted Kierkegaard as saying, meaning, it wasn't meant for us to know our own purpose. Maybe our purpose was to trust that there was one simply *because* we exist, and leave it at that.

Our mothers and fathers put us on this perilous voyage—a voyage certain to break us into pieces—and they watched from afar as we set sail. Yet long after the steamer departs, love remains; their sacrifice worth it after all. Love is what we carry with us, and come what may, we arrive at our destination whole. Not just whole, better than whole; a broken and re-mended whole.

Could it be that there was only one meaning in every poem, in every song, in every work of art, in the beat of every heart? The same meaning, however it was written, painted, sung, or lived, whether simply or complexly, happily or sadly? One meaning, and one meaning alone: To bear witness to Love, in all faces and forms, as we make our way home.

†††

Later that night, Willow had a dream. The spring night was warm with a lovely breeze. She and Leon were on the front porch of his parents' home, he on the bench of the swing, Spike curled up at his right foot, Tommy Dorsey, his childhood dog, at his left, while she perched on a nearby chair. Walt stood by the side railing, puffing on a cigar.

A feeling of anticipation shimmered in the air.

One by one, they began arriving, carrying casseroles—her mother alighting beside Leon on the swing; Adam, Anne, and a chattering Rocket; Uncle Ricky plunking his bony body down on the top step; Pastor Ray and Lily, nestling Monroe; Uncle Adam with both arms; Theckla and Freddie Chavis in his baseball cap; Uncle Steve and his family; and Grandma Mary, bringing the largest (of course) casserole of all.

With each new arrival came another flurry of joy. Willow's heart leapt when Nick zoomed in on his Harley and strolled up to the porch. Booker and Cyrus arrived soon after, and dozens of faces she recognized from her past, as well as some she didn't, but were known by the others. Even Gus Sultanski, from Walt's old bar, showed up. Finally, came Cory, with a giant bag of potato chips.

Somehow the porch had become a port, a landing place, able to hold them all in its giant cupped palm. Songs played softly from somewhere. Neighbors called out their greetings. Sumptuous aromas wafted from the casseroles. There was a lot of laughter on that porch.

Or was it a porch?

In front of them, where there should have been grass; below them, where there should have been concrete; above them, where there should have been sky; beside them, where there should have been houses; swirled the astonishing mountains, plateaus, and valleys of the Orion Nebula, where thousands of stars were forming before their eyes.

Also by BARBARA J. DZIKOWSKI

Series #1 AND #2 of THE MOON TRILOGY